CW01033266

ISLAND CALLING

Also by Francesca Segal

FICTION

The Innocents

The Awkward Age

Welcome to Glorious Tuga

NON-FICTION

Mother Ship

Island Calling

FRANCESCA SEGAL

Chatto & Windus
LONDON

1 3 5 7 9 10 8 6 4 2

Chatto & Windus, an imprint of Vintage, is part of the
Penguin Random House group of companies

Vintage, Penguin Random House UK, One Embassy Gardens,
8 Viaduct Gardens, London SW11 7BW

penguin.co.uk/vintage
global.penguinrandomhouse.com

First published by Chatto & Windus in 2025

Copyright © Francesca Segal 2025

The moral right of the author has been asserted

Map © Fred Kroner, Whiskey 'n' Ink
Illustrations courtesy Shutterstock
Extract from 'The Poem of Queen Esther' by João Pinto Delgado, translated by
David R. Slavitt © Oxford Publishing Limited (Academic). Reproduced
with permission of the Licensor through PLSclear.

Penguin Random House values and supports copyright. Copyright fuels creativity, encourages diverse voices, promotes freedom of expression and supports a vibrant culture. Thank you for purchasing an authorised edition of this book and for respecting intellectual property laws by not reproducing, scanning or distributing any part of it by any means without permission. You are supporting authors and enabling Penguin Random House to continue to publish books for everyone. No part of this book may be used or reproduced in any manner for the purpose of training artificial intelligence technologies or systems. In accordance with Article 4(3) of the DSM Directive 2019/790, Penguin Random House expressly reserves this work from the text and data mining exception.

Printed and bound in Great Britain by Clays Ltd, Elcograf S.p.A.

The authorised representative in the EEA is Penguin Random House Ireland,
Morrison Chambers, 32 Nassau Street, Dublin D02 YH68

A CIP catalogue record for this book is available from the British Library

HB ISBN 9781784745400
TPB ISBN 9781784745417

Penguin Random House is committed to a sustainable future
for our business, our readers and our planet. This book is made
from Forest Stewardship Council® certified paper.

For Miranda

From deep in her soul, she hears an answering voice:
'Your life,' it says, 'is a part of your people's life.
You are not separate.'

João Pinto Delgado, *The Poem of Queen Esther*

Dramatis Personae

Charlotte Walker	Tuga's visiting vet
Levi Mendoza	bartender and handyman; Charlotte's landlord
Dan Zekri	recently appointed chief medical officer
Walter Lindo-Smith	Levi's brother-in-law and good friend
Maia Lindo-Smith	Levi's sister, married to Walter, currently working in England
Rebecca Lindo-Smith	Maia and Walter's seven-year-old daughter; Levi's niece
Annie Goss	twelve-year-old islander
Marianne Goss	Annie's mother, and the island's baker
Moz (Fermoza) Gabbai	teacher at the island school; Garrick Williams's sister
Saul Gabbai	Moz's husband; newly retired chief medical officer
Garrick Williams	island pastor; Moz's brother
Joan Williams	*Garrick's wife, died recently*
Katie Salmon	recently arrived physiotherapist
Betsey Coffee	runs Betsey's Cafe on Harbour Street
Elsie Smith	customs officer; mechanic; amateur reptile enthusiast

Sylvester	keeps the general store on Harbour Street
Taxi	cabbie and radio announcer
Grand Mary (Mary Philips)	Island Elder, the oldest (and by far the richest) Tugan
Martha Philips	a tortoise

Miscellaneous Islanders

Queenie Lindo-Smith	the clinic's cleaner
Calla and Winston	clinic nurses
Nancy Gabbai	Saul and Moz's daughter; part-time nurse and bartender
Vitali Mendoza	Levi's father, a carpenter
Anwuli and Isadora Davenport	an elderly couple who keep sheep
Nicola Davenport	islander
Chloe Ben-Ezra	Nicola's teenage daughter
Natalie and Oscar Lindo	run a small farm and share four young children
Cecil Lindo	eight-year-old son of Natalie and Oscar
Lusi Zekri	Dan's mother; Saul Gabbai's sister
Johannes Zekri	*Dan's father, who died in a boat accident*
Mac	keeps a store out of town
Rachel (Mac's Rachel)	island midwife and herbalist; Mac's wife
Zimbul Fairclough	recently appointed to Island Council
Oluchi Thomas	radio announcer and member of Island Council
Ocean Rodrigues	one of the fishermen
Sophie-Pearl Rodrigues	Ocean's wife

Miscellaneous, Off-Island

Alex dos Santos	twelve-year-old islander, now at boarding school in Kent
Caleb dos Santos	Alex's much older brother
Ruth dos Santos	Alex and Caleb's mother and Marianne's beloved foster mother; recently had successful surgery in London
Lucinda Compton-Neville	Charlotte's mother, a QC practising in London
Evangeline	Lucinda's PA
Captain Lars	competing in a charity scavenger hunt; captain of the visiting rust bucket

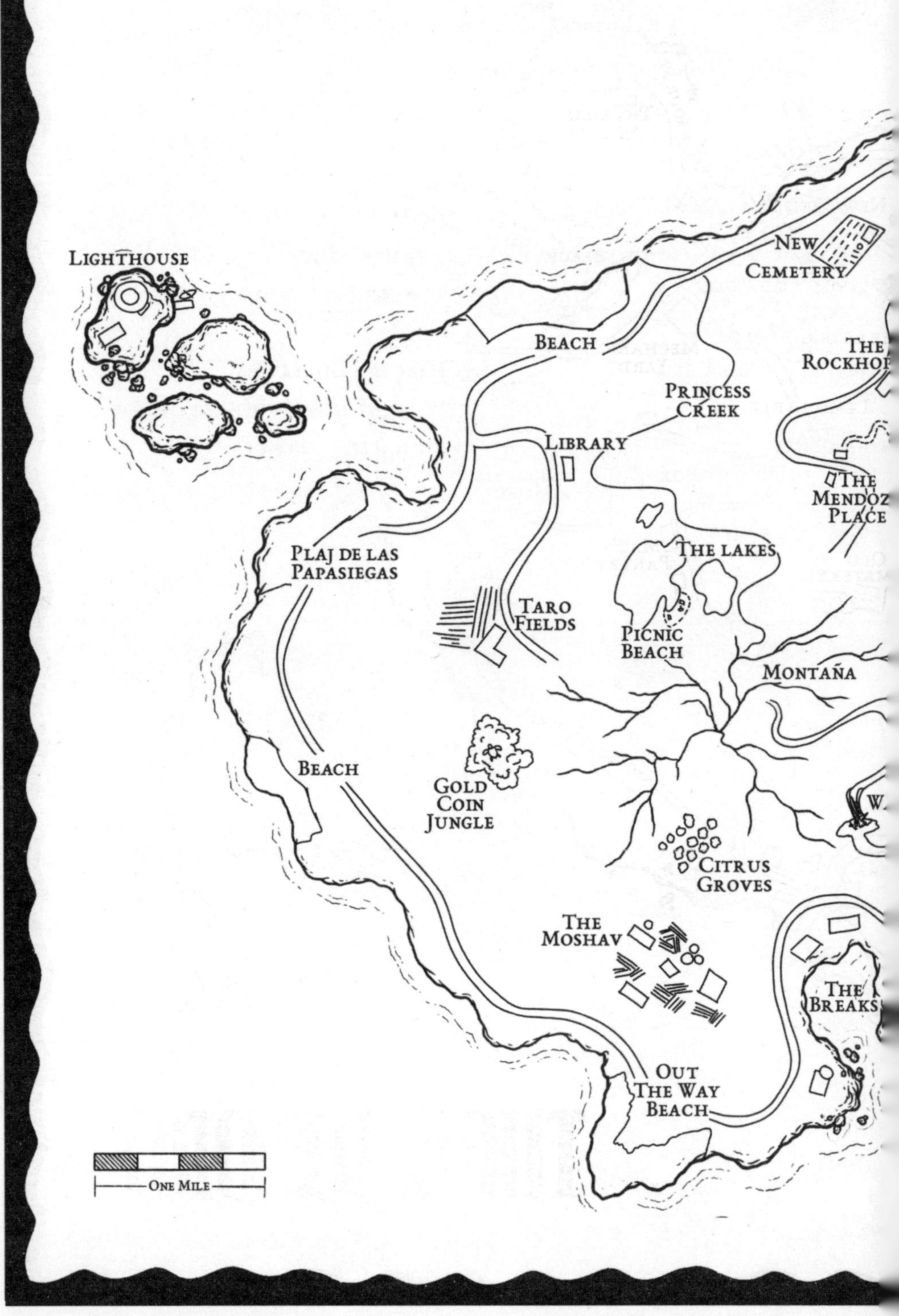

Lighthouse
New
Cemetery
Beach
Princess
Creek
Library
The
Rockho
The
Mendoz
Place
Plaj de las
Papasiegas
The lakes
Taro
Fields
Picnic
Beach
Montaña
Beach
Gold
Coin
Jungle
Citrus
Groves
The
Moshav
The
Breaks
Out
The Way
Beach
One Mile

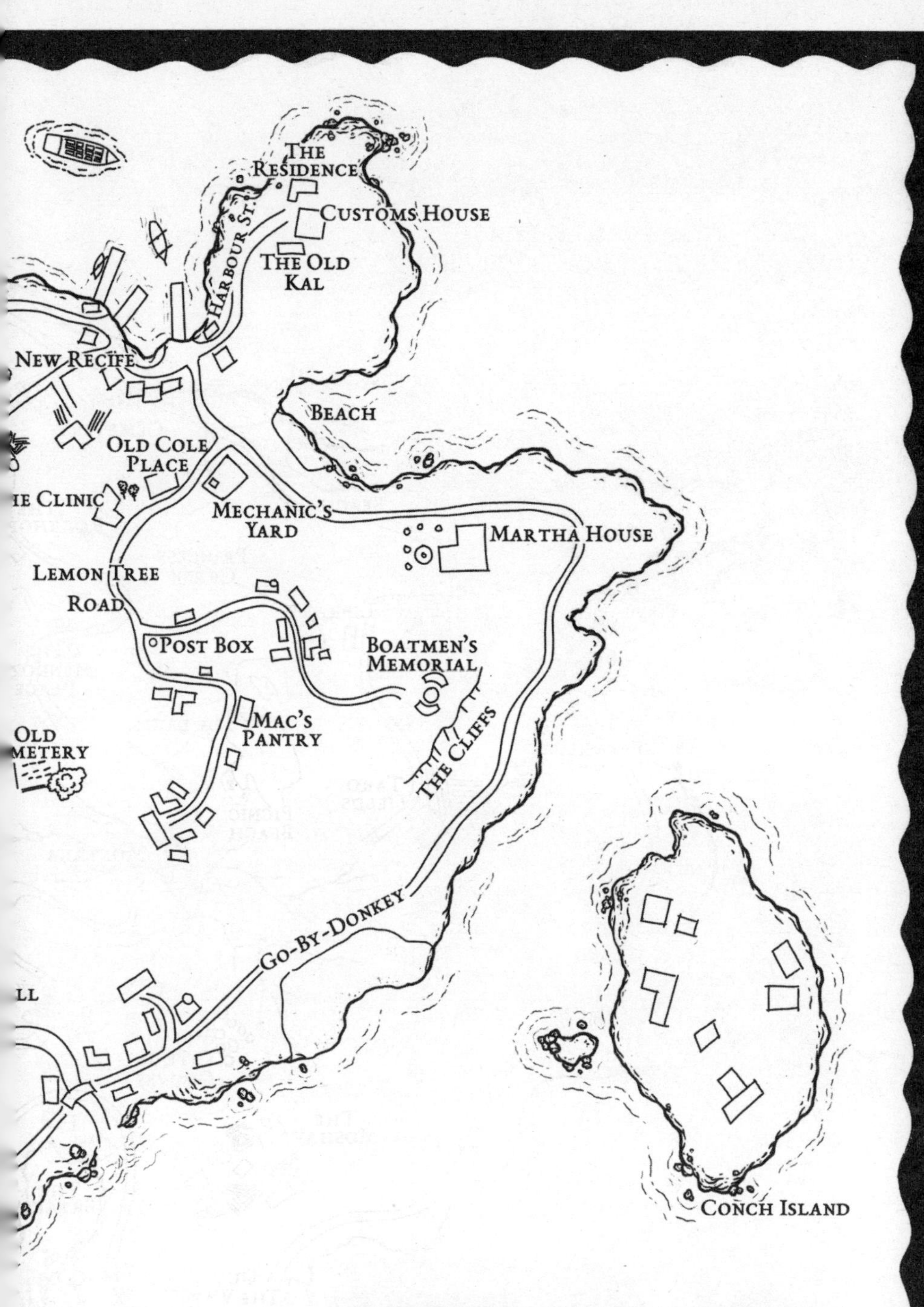
The Residence
Customs House
Harbour St.
The Old Kal
New Recife
Beach
Old Cole Place
Mechanic's Yard
Martha House
Lemon Tree Road
Post Box
Boatmen's Memorial
Mac's Pantry
The Cliffs
Go-By-Donkey
Conch Island

TUGA DE ORO

I

All across the island, mothers were nervous. The citrus groves were flowering and fruiting simultaneously despite the humidity of Island Close; far too fecund a metaphor beneath which to enact the night's revelries. It was Tu B'Av, a festival of courtship that fell on the August full moon, by whose clear white light confessions were unburdened, hearts were risked, familiar faces considered anew. There were bonfires, music and feasting, the day's snapper catch not frozen for modest export, but grilled for the pleasure of the island over smoking oil drums. The trees were hung with lanterns, the earth between them scattered with traditional Tugan blankets. Low canopies of twisted branches offered ample privacy beneath which to make mistakes. Last Tu B'Av, newly arrived Charlotte Walker had offered her excuses and stayed quietly in her little cottage, made anxious by the atmosphere of romantic possibility. She had imagined the evening a blur of moonlit citrus-smoke and tacit permission. This fantasy turned out to be accurate. But this year there was nowhere she'd rather be.

At the makeshift bar, Betsey was pouring small tots of a glossy liquid into a row of miniature jam jars, some of a number that seemed to find their way on to the island from the breakfast buffets of passing cruise ships and were repurposed everywhere from Betsey's Cafe to the medical clinic. Etrog liqueur was the rich grassy-gold of new olive oil, thick as syrup, a stronger limoncello made not from the fruits but from the heady, fragrant leaves. It was meant to be taken as a shot. Betsey pressed one into the hand of anyone passing.

'*Paz*, Dr Charlotte. You know, I was thinking if any beast causes you trouble tonight it will be that moshav donkey. Jennets always foal during a full moon, I find.'

'Thank you,' said Charlotte, wondering if she might discreetly tip the drink out behind a tree. Betsey caught her hesitation and clapped a hand to her forehead.

'Streuth, forgive me, I'm remembering now you've no head for it, I'll get you some fizzycan. That was a night, wasn't it? You'd not have wanted a foaling after that shindig, I reckon; you'd have been seeing double, and telling the farmer it was twins.'

Charlotte, embarrassed, agreed that the doctor's recent retirement party had not been her finest moment. She'd suffered a shock that particular evening, though she did not share this mitigation with Betsey, who served titbits of gossip at her Harbour Street cafe along with every hot drink, a well-meaning public service. If she could help it, Charlotte would never tell anyone. Indeed, if she could erase her own memory, she would. Meanwhile, she very much hoped that Betsey was wrong about the donkey. She was having a night off.

Betsey took back the jar and replaced it with a lemonade, and Charlotte followed her gratefully on to the topic of Dexter, Betsey's corgi, who'd been limping on his back right paw first thing this morning, but later had been haring after every crab on the beach, so it was probably no more than morning stiffness, didn't Charlotte agree? Charlotte listened, nodded, assuming what she hoped was a professional air. She was the only vet on the island and so, however often she got drunk and disorderly, no one could exactly take their business elsewhere. Still. For Charlotte, once had been too many.

At that moment she saw Levi Mendoza approaching through the dusk and bonfire smoke, his dark hair still wet from the lake, his teeth very white in the darkness as he caught sight of her and grinned. Never had she been so aware of her heart as a muscle than these last weeks with Levi; powerful, involuntary, and entirely responsive to the maddening, charismatic man now coming closer in the darkness. Levi worked on her like an enchantment. Uptight, self-conscious Charlotte had been freed from the constraints of being her lifelong, London self. She had let go of the theoretical, the defensive, the prudent. With Levi, a thought in her head became the words on her lips, and restraint, which had been her religion, had been entirely abandoned. She was unable to recognise herself, though she could see clearly enough that this new self was dangerous, unsustainable, and probably an improvement.

Now Levi's hands were around her waist, drawing her into the shadows, away from the low yellow light of the candles that flickered on the folding table of the bar.

'Exactly how long you planning to stay at this jamboree?'

He spoke close against her ear, and his fingers had begun to trace lightly up her inner thigh.

'We just got here. I thought I was meant to be dancing for you in a moonlit field while you wave a ribbon, or something.'

Levi laughed, her favourite sound.

'I ain't here to select a maiden from some antique courting display, Dolittle; I know who I'm going back with, and what I plan to do when I get there. If it's dancing you need we can dance at home.'

Her hand slipped up the back of his T-shirt with the ready pleasure of possession. For a moment he held her close and they swayed together, as if the music had been a ballad and not what it in fact was: 'I Get Around' by the Beach Boys, sung and played by Taxi, on the accordion. Then, over Levi's shoulder, Charlotte saw Dan Zekri looking in their direction, wearing an expression that might have been anything from disgust to envy – or perhaps she had imagined it and he hadn't even noticed them, and was simply scanning the groves for a friend. She looked away, burying her face in the warmth of Levi's neck. Finally she disengaged herself. This would not do; she would not last ten minutes at the festival if Levi pressed her to him much longer, or she would make a fool of herself entirely without the aid of any local liquor. She told Levi she was going to find Elsie, and then walked with purpose in the opposite direction from Dan. Just to be on the safe side.

Tugans dried citrus rinds for fire starters, and near the bonfires the darkening grove smelled sharp and sweet. Charlotte had searched earlier but had seen no sign of bats patrolling, for with a ready fruit supply elsewhere they turned their noses up at citrus, preferring to feed in the old jackfruit and mango trees further down in the humid valley. She had seen them rise an hour earlier, silently crossing the cloudless sky. Reptiles would always be her first love, but the Tugan bats were an unexpected source of delight. Crepuscular animals, now was their time.

High on the flank of the *montaña*, this was the driest point of a lush, wet, tropical island, and the etrog trees had taken unlikely hold. They were far from home, far from the dry sandy soil of the Mediterranean, but still, they were doing all right. Much like the earliest Tugan settlers, their pockets filled with seeds when they escaped first from persecution in Europe to Recife, and then from new persecution in Recife to the safety and self-determination and near-lunar isolation on the tiny, uninhabited island of Tuga de Oro. This was home now, and it was enough.

2

Charlotte had never seen gentle, earnest Elsie Smith in anything other than a rotating cycle of boiler suits and she found her strangely touching in a white cotton sundress, paired with the same dusty and faithful work boots of her many assorted day jobs. In place of her baseball cap Elsie wore a crown woven of fresh mintberry leaves, and had two more strung over her forearm, like rings at a hoopla. She looked vulnerable, somehow stripped of armour, and even taller than usual. The loose white frock showed the muscled shoulders with which Elsie usually hauled tractor tyres at the garage, or lifted tortoises for Charlotte, as well as revealing a previously unexposed stick-and-poke tattoo of a gecko on her left bicep. Elsie saw Charlotte's eyes rest upon this image.

'She's from long ago,' Elsie said fondly, stroking the blurry lizard with her fingertips. 'On Out the Way beach when we was thirteen, Maia did it. At school we read a book about prison, said prisoners used to do it with battery acid and a safety pin. Worked out grand.'

'She has a very friendly expression,' said Charlotte, with as much enthusiasm as she could muster while her medic's brain screamed, *Hepatitis! Septicaemia! Sulphuric acid poisoning!* Adult Elsie stood before her, perfectly healthy. Nonetheless, Charlotte made a mental note to tell the nurses that Dan should add tattoo safety to his public-health talks. She would have told Dan herself, if they were currently on speaking terms.

'Any chance you seen Little Doc? Or Walter?' Elsie asked now, as if she'd been following Charlotte's line of thought.

'Walter, no. Dan was that way, I saw him a minute ago. Everything all right?'

'Nothing happening tonight. Trouble on its way, though.' For a moment Elsie looked worried. 'And I'd have been here in the groves already if I'd not been hours rag-chewing with my pal ZD9ZS, and then I'd have missed the signal. Here, take one of these. You ain't in a frock,' she added, noticing.

For Tu B'Av the single people on the island wore white, and soon all the unmarried women would dance a ribbony maypole together, weaving closer and closer to their rivals, under and over, through and beside, describing ever smaller circles. When they could draw no tighter, the unmarried men came forward and took the fraying ribbon ends, and it was their job to reverse the dance, wider and wider, looser and wilder, freeing the pole from its satiny wrapping. However much braver she'd been feeling recently, Charlotte could not entirely abandon her fear of spectacle, and could not imagine herself maypoling. She looked down at the denim shorts and white T-shirt that earlier had seemed a passable compromise. Her trainers were also white, or had been, before she'd worn them through a year of Tugan jungles. The truth was that she had felt a touch of angst getting ready for Tu B'Av, a festival rarely attended by FFA (Folk From Away), for it took place in the middle of Island Close, when for five months the seas around the island were impassable. Tuga de Oro had no airport, and even the biggest naval vessel wouldn't pass within five hundred miles. Island Close was hurricane season.

In any case, she had no definition for what was happening between herself and Levi. Whether she was single or not was anyone's guess. But Elsie had been extending a mintberry crown for so long it was clear that she would hold it out fixedly until Charlotte accepted it.

'It can be a tortoise snack tomorrow,' said practical Elsie. 'I'll get on now. If you pass the doc, tell him I'm looking.'

Charlotte agreed that she would, although she had no intention of passing Dan. Instead, relieved to have been spared one of Elsie's disquisitions on the joys of ham radio, she set the circlet of leaves on her head and went in search of Levi, in the spirit of Tu B'Av. She would tell him that she was ready to go home.

Charlotte Walker had been on Tuga de Oro fourteen months, overstaying the year-long research fellowship that had first brought her to the island to study a relict population of rare gold coin tortoises. By now she should have been reinstalled in the orderly basement flat of her mother's vast north London townhouse, a sanctuary three floors below her own childhood bedroom, in which the kitchen table doubled as a desk, and her mother's housekeeper discreetly descended the stairs once a week to run the Hoover. She should be back to gainful employment as a herpetology postdoc in a bright, friendly lab at the Zoological Society of London, advancing her career, accumulating publications in all the right and relevant journals, moving steadily towards either a teaching post or a lab of her own, or both. She definitely should not still be working as an ad hoc farm vet for an eccentric collectivist community on the world's most isolated island, living in a miniature cottage with a palm-thatch roof, and sleeping with the man who'd built it.

But then, so much was unexpected, recently. She had not expected that the question of her own paternity would end in the discovery that her father was Garrick Williams, the island minister, who had not known of her existence and was unequivocally horrified upon learning of it. The orderly deck of her life had been tossed high in the air; until the muddle of cards landed she would remain in suspension, and all bets were off.

Charlotte had stayed on as the unofficial island vet, although Garrick had made it more than clear that he wanted nothing to do with her. It had not seemed right or even possible simply to go straight back home again to England, and these last weeks had gone on with an oddly settled normality. Farm visits and clinic days; jungle hikes and research. Certainly the continued rejection by a father she'd longed for was – not optimal. Emotional mess of any sort usually drove her, tortoise-like, into a tense, defended retreat, and she was aware she probably ought to feel worse than she did. Perhaps she had yet to experience its full impact, but it was as if she had stepped through a portal to another universe, and was in no rush to return to the real one. It was hard to feel sad while she lay in a drift of pink sea hibiscus on a sun-washed sugar-sand beach, watching a shirtless Levi grill fresh octopus. When he glanced up and grinned at her, she felt electric. She felt immortal. London represented reality and on Tuga, however briefly, she was having a welcome break from herself.

3

Elsie found Walter watching the band, holding the remains of a baked banana that his daughter Rebecca had just handed him.

'Two days out, they said, or three,' said Elsie quietly, not wanting to alarm the little girl, who stood close beside her father, one finger through his belt loop.

'Bad, is it? Patient can't make it back where he came from?'

'Heart attack, they're thinking, or heart something – life and death, captain says. Ain't a fancy yacht, it's another of them rust-bucket challengers.'

Walter pulled at the bill of his cap, adjusting it, thinking. Anyone who knew Walter knew what he would say. Still, Elsie waited in a respectful silence for him to say it.

'Well. We have to try, don't we.'

This was not a question but a statement. It was Walter's turn as head of the coastguard and as such he made all decisions about medical evacuations and compassionate landings, with advice from the chief medical officer. From the beginning, islanders had been dependent upon passing sea traffic for trade and travel; when the rare opportunity presented itself to repay the favour, Tugans would not hesitate. Last year a crew member on a cargo ship bound for Walvis Bay was stricken with appendicitis; even now, with satellites and advanced meteorology, there were occasional and sometimes devastating shipwrecks. Indeed, they had lost many of their own men when a fishing boat went down six years earlier, a tragedy that still rippled through many an island family. It had been Walter's boat, in fact, though by chance Walter had not been aboard. In Island Close no one should ever be near enough to put Tugan sailors in such danger, but from their current coordinates it would take this yacht weeks to reverse its course. You didn't need the CMO to tell you that a cardiac incident had to come ashore.

'I don't know their vessel but we'll not bring her in right to the kelp beds in case the weather turns. If they got an inflatable tender they ain't to send it, they'll kill themselves faster than any heart attack. I'll go out.'

Pressed against him where she'd been most of the evening, Walter's daughter Rebecca turned her face against his side, chocolate smearing from her cheek to his shirt. A fisherman's child, she knew the risks, just as she knew about the doomed boat six years ago, and that her father would have captained it, had he not put a nail through his foot the night before. In the South Atlantic, falling atmospheric pressure could whip up winds of eighty knots with little warning, and currents here were idiosyncratic, even at the best of times. One moment the water might be stirred and streaming, the next a hidden, angry tide could hurl up rearing crests, gouging holes in the sea. Her father placed a huge warm hand on her back, pulling her closer.

'All right, *mi vida*,' he said softly. 'It the right thing to do. I will be just fine.' And then to move the conversation safely on to dry land he said to Elsie, 'If we get the patient onshore and they make it, they will be here till Island Open.'

'Nine weeks or so, still. Not so bad, we've houses empty. What about Ruth dos Santos's?'

'Island Council will pay, bring in a little rent for Marianne.'

'Good, she deserve some luck,' said Elsie, with approval. 'Don't reckon she thought Annie'd take Alex going so hard.'

'Don't reckon she had much choice in the matter,' said Walter, who knew better than most the sacrifices a mother would make to secure a child's future. His own wife had been working off-island for more than a year. Since she'd been away Rebecca had grown two inches, and lost three teeth.

Elsie nodded. 'So we put them in Ruth's house till Island Open, and their vessel calls back. If we can get them onshore. And if they're not dead before they get here.' She set her final mintberry crown on Rebecca's head and stood back to admire her.

'I'll come see you first thing at the yard, tell Dan if you see him. Now it's marshmallow time,' said Walter, hoisting Rebecca high on to his shoulders with sudden decision, so that the girl laughed despite her solemn face. She leaned forward, and he could feel the sharp little point of her chin through the top of his cap. He took an ankle in each hand and nodded to Elsie, and then set off for one of the bonfires. Tomorrow plans would be made, though each knew they might not, in the end, be necessary. The heart-attack patient still had to survive two or maybe three more days at sea and, more to the point, a Tugan crew, led by Walter, would have to take the rigid inflatable out on the hostile, remorseless ocean.

'Ain't it ready?' A barefoot Annie Goss kicked at the foil-wrapped bananas that lay, a row of fat silver logs, in the embers at the edge of the bonfire. They were hotter than she'd expected and Miss Moz saw the shock of pain cross her face, though the girl made no sound, merely stepped back and quickly crossed her thin arms over her chest, defiant. Moz wielded her toasting fork at the other children.

'You all shift, you hear me? Get away.'

With the other hand she shooed Annie back too, and in doing so found a moment to squeeze her shoulder, and stroke the tangled blonde hair. That child could walk across hot coals and not flinch, Moz thought, with a pang. She had never known Annie lose face. She had a ferocity that Moz, in all her years of teaching, had rarely seen. Oh, but she was enchanting, this one; tender beneath her bravado; loyal and big-hearted. Miss Moz did not have favourites. But still, in class it was hard to keep a straight face when Annie Goss was clowning for Alex dos Santos. Or had been.

'Go play for five minutes,' she told the others. 'Watching won't cook them faster, I'll call for you.'

There were murmurs, and her small pupils melted into the darkness. They would not go far; each had earmarked her own particular banana.

Annie was rubbing the side of a filthy foot against the ankle of the other. Maybe she'd really burned herself, but Moz couldn't see. Under normal circumstances she'd have left it, knowing that nothing got past Marianne. But since Alex had been sent to boarding school in England, Annie had been staying out all hours, missing meals. Annie was grieving, and Miss Moz's heart went out to the girl. It was as if she no longer had ground beneath her feet. Lifelong, she had been hand in hand with Alex, for they had been raised together, tumbling like pups. At night they'd slept entwined since the cradle, breathing one another's warm breath. For Annie, home was where he was; the only life she knew was by his side, roaming the island till the first silent bat crossed the pale sky. But Alex had gone and now, six weeks past her twelfth birthday, anyone might see that Annie had lost the greater part of herself, left to a life lopsided by his absence. It had happened so suddenly that his disappearance came like a death. She had not spoken a single word in Marianne's presence since Alex's ship had sailed.

'Where's your mother?' Moz asked Annie now.

Annie shrugged, looking down.

'Baking, probably.'

'What do you mean, "probably"? If Marianne working you should be helping her. Show me that foot.'

'She don't need my help,' said Annie, sullen. She tucked one ankle behind the other. 'Foot's fine.'

Moz decided to leave it. With the toasting fork, she rolled one of the bananas on to the scrubby grass, picked it up with tongs, and dropped it on to a plate. With her nails Moz carefully opened the top of the hot foil and the scent rose of fresh vanilla, of coconut sugar and ripe banana and melting chocolate. Annie's eyes were round. For as long as she held Annie's treasure Moz knew she held a captive, so she spoke fast.

'On the contrary, *kerida*, she need you more now, not less. I know how you're hurting. Believe me, I can imagine. I see you. You not only lost your brother but all your plans, all your imaginings together. You missing the other half of your heart right now. But your mama sent Alex out of love, I promise you. She had one chance to set that boy free and she took it. She raised that boy. She must miss him too.'

'Sending people away ain't love.'

Moz was mashing at the inside of the banana skin with a fork, her words quick, her actions slow.

'People always saying this and I know it makes no sense now, but – one day you will understand. She'd die for you, your mama.' She handed the plate to Annie but held on to it, and for a moment they stood, woman and girl, the plate between them. Moz looked at Annie's angry bitten nails, fingers red from the strength of her grip.

'I hate her,' said Annie quietly.

4

Charlotte had been frowning in concentration at three bottles of men's dandruff shampoo on a shelf in Sylvester's general store, willing one of them to morph into 300ml of Shu Uemura, when Anwuli Davenport had tapped her on the shoulder, wanting to talk about her border collie. The dog was in obvious discomfort, scooting around the yard in a strange bottom shuffle, and so Charlotte had booked her in for this morning's clinic. She was now hunched over the vet's-room computer, anxious to revise the position of canine perianal glands. This was the island's quickest internet connection and, still, it was terrible.

There was a knock at the door and Elsie Smith entered in socked feet, holding her work boots in one hand. Elsie was back in her threadbare navy boiler suit, patched with swatches of stone-washed denim at both knees and elbows, and with 'Elsie Mechanic' hand-stitched across the lapel in lemon-yellow embroidery thread. Her fading green baseball cap bore the legend 'Kiss Me, I'm Irish', which, while it may have been true of the hat, was definitely not true of Elsie. Today she was a mechanic; on ship days Elsie was the island customs officer. At other times she was an enthusiastic radio ham and volunteer in the communications department, guiding passing ships on Tuga's VHF, and spent rare days off assisting Charlotte in the jungle. She was also, when needed, a member of the Tuga de Oro fire service. But the passion closest to Elsie's heart (after steam trains, clocks and electronics) was reptiles. In this, she and Charlotte had found an unlikely area of communion.

'*Paz*, Dr Vet Charlotte. Can I come in?'

'Of course. I'm free till my next patient. You can keep those on in here, I don't actually know how clean the floor is.'

'Yes, you waiting on Anwuli,' Elsie said helpfully, as if Charlotte might have forgotten. 'Ten minutes, I reckon; she stopped a time at Betsey's. Bringing you a something.'

As ever, Charlotte marvelled at the islanders' perpetual and apparently effortless awareness of one another's co-ordinates. And yet there were secrets enough, she knew, and then shook her head, to dislodge all intrusive thoughts of Garrick. She looked again at Elsie.

'Are you OK?'

Elsie shrugged. 'I don't know. Hilary ain't right. She's depressed. And she's been getting a bit, a bit *fatter*,' this last word whispered, as if the lizard might hear, and take offence. 'But she's been off her food, so I don't see how.'

'Trust your instincts. If you think something's wrong then we need to have a look.'

Elsie had taken a seat at Charlotte's desk and was relacing her boots. When she looked up she seemed on the verge of tears.

'She wouldn't even eat a booby egg this morning. Anyone who know her know that ain't right.'

'As soon as clinic's over I'll pop by and give Hilary a proper once-over,' Charlotte promised, and Elsie, grateful, gave a wan smile.

Hilary was an enormous, middle-aged red tegu lizard that Elsie had raised from a hatchling. As island customs officer she had confiscated a pair from some yachting tourists who had come ashore without a permit to export the animals from Argentina, and certainly without a permit to bring them on to Tuga for the month of their stay. The travellers had yielded the two baby lizards without too much complaint, already out of their depth with specialist animal husbandry, while at sea no less. One lizard had died within days, Elsie had told Charlotte, probably from shock, or poor care. The other had become Hilary. Elsie had decided that one lizard without a mate could no longer pose a threat to island biosecurity, and Charlotte had not the heart to remind her that it was disease management as much as invasive breeding that made import control so crucial. The animal should have been euthanised. Still, it was before her tenure, and far outside her remit. Hilary was now twelve years old, stately and demanding; as responsive as a puppy, but only when the mood took her. She was a beautiful animal – sleek, rotund, undoubtedly overfed, but Charlotte knew better than to interfere unless consulted. She would give Hilary a check-up this afternoon, and that might offer the opportunity to make gentle enquiries about the tegu's diet.

Elsie took her leave and at that moment came the scrabble of claws, and the office door was nosed open by a border collie, a blue merle, who escorted in a woman in her early eighties. Anwuli's close-cropped white hair was invisible beneath a huge woven sun hat, her denim dungarees rolled up, just below the knee, and at her waist she wore a bulging bumbag branded from a pharmaceutical conference that took place, the peeling print proclaimed, in Boston, 1986. Anwuli was smiling, and holding out to Charlotte a glass tumbler of coffee. She had covered not an inconsiderable distance of uneven ground with this hazard in her hand, and Charlotte leaped forward to relieve her, grateful Elsie had tipped her off and she had poured her own coffee down the sink moments earlier. With little money, islanders found their own ways to pay her.

'What total bliss, thank you,' she said, taking the glass. 'Such a treat.'

'From Betsey, she know it's your favourite. Ice melted on the way here, but still cold.'

Anwuli sat down in the swivel chair that Elsie had recently vacated. 'Isa sent you these, as well. Reckon you need pepping up for this job.' From a faded carpet bag she produced some unlabelled jars of jam – variegated amber, streaked tangerine, cloudy saffron – and lined them up on the desk. 'Pineapple, papaya, mango.'

At her feet the collie stood erect, head cocked, regarding Charlotte with one brown eye, one a pale ice blue. Charlotte cocked her own head in reply, and then reached to stroke a silky ear.

'It's fine, it's all part of the job. That's very generous of Isadora, thank you both.'

'We kept hoping she'd manage it herself, scooting her bum all over the yard. I used to be able to do it but my arthritis makes it tricky, and Isa can't see well enough, with her cataracts. We should have been put out to pasture long ago. Poor Cilla, stuck with us.'

'Cilla will feel much better once we've sorted her out. I'll give her a quick once-over, then we'll get started.'

Charlotte tied back her hair, and snapped on a pair of purple latex surgical gloves. The vet's room had run out of surgical masks, but she didn't want to waste time leaving her small domain within the clinic for the main doctors' office and contending with their idiosyncratic storage system, nor indeed their jealous guarding of medical supplies. Cilla the sheepdog worked hard for Anwuli and Isadora, not only herding their tiny flock but also opening and closing doors, picking up any household items that fell on the floor, and collecting the eggs from the small henhouse, placing them reverently in a raised basket on a low bench in the yard, saving work for her now-elderly owners. She was a treasured family member, and deserved to be comfortable.

Charlotte pushed a step over and Anwuli indicated the exam table. Cilla scrambled up the stairs and stood proudly, a dog in show. She had no lead, and had never worn a collar, but her discipline was absolute. The hair around her startling eyes was silver, her long nose was mottled black and grey; a muted cheetah. Charlotte bent to examine her. She was coming round to mammals, she conceded, allowing herself to be sniffed in return. If affection was a risk, it was also a reward.

'No wonder she's been dragging herself around the yard, she's been desperately trying to relieve the pressure. She's in great shape otherwise.'

The hall door opened and closed; there were voices outside the consulting room. Charlotte carried on, keen to get the job over with, for while she had practised on a model as a student, she had only done this a handful of times on a real animal. Soon she had Cilla in a muzzle, while the acquiescent animal bowed her head slightly at the indignity of it. One ice-blue eye, one toffee brown, fixed Charlotte with a woeful expression.

Anwuli held the collar of the muzzle and bent down to address the dog.

'Now, enough of this foolishness, *kerida*. It will be over in a moment and then you'll be a happy girl.' To Charlotte she said, 'It's not been a problem for years.'

'She's come into the house more, hasn't she.'

'Yes. Gone soft in her old age. But then, who hasn't.'

'I think maybe what's happening is that coming into the house has possibly changed her diet, and her bowel movements aren't hard enough any more to empty them effectively.' Charlotte was keeping up a light patter while squeezing lubricant, trying to transmit absolute confidence. 'She's not gone soft. Her poo's gone soft, basically.'

She lifted the wagging tail and inserted a finger. Cilla barely flinched. Charlotte stared into the middle distance, trying to imagine her own textbooks. She was fairly certain the anal sacs were located at four and eight on the clock face, in which case it was easier to do the right one first.

In the hallway there was a hubbub. Dan's voice, unexpectedly raised. Charlotte frowned in concentration. She found the right gland, hugely engorged, and began to increase the pressure between her thumb and forefinger. The first side yielded easily, a surprising quantity of watery black discharge like tar, stinking, Charlotte thought, like the fetid swamps of hell; pungent dog shit combined with the stench of rotting fish, saturating the thick wad of gauze. When she was satisfied the gland was empty she dropped this gauze into a stainless-steel bowl, picked up a second piece and rotated her wrist to feel for the left. This time the angle was considerably more awkward.

The volume of voices in the hallway increased. Dan Zekri, exercised about something. He was unexpectedly hot-tempered and of late he'd had a hard time; still, he'd be wiser to take some deep breaths and stop shouting in the middle of his workplace. Now a voice that sounded like Walter Lindo-Smith. A row was unfolding in the clinic waiting room.

'You've risked lives.' That was Walter.

'Wasted scant resources.' Dan.

And then Elsie's voice, a surprising addition, and chiming

in with uncharacteristic firmness. 'Illegal immigration is what it is.'

There was the gland – she had it. Firm, like a grape, and almost perfectly positioned between forefinger and thumb, despite the uncomfortable angle of her wrist. Then outside the commotion became louder again, and she heard another woman's voice, commanding, cut-glass, clear.

'What a needless fuss you're all making, I've told you why I'm here.' Unruffled, unapologetic, closing down further argument.

Charlotte's hand contracted as if in spasm and warm black pus, viscous and reeking, fountained from the dog's rectum and on to her arm, her shirt, her face. At that moment the door opened and, in a cloud of Dior and disapproval, her mother entered.

5

Somehow, by who knew what devilry, Lucinda Compton-Neville was on Tuga de Oro. It was as if the very moment itself had sprayed Charlotte with horror, a fear response, like squid ink. Her nostrils were filled not only with the reek of pus but pus itself. Charlotte stared at her mother with wild eyes, her cheeks dripping. Then she turned and vomited into the stainless-steel kidney bowl.

'Christ,' said Lucinda, lifting a tissue-fine pashmina of palest lilac to cover her nose and mouth. 'Darling, what a welcome.'

Charlotte, panic-stricken and casting around desperately, caught Dan's eye. He snatched up some paper towels and hurried forward, burying his nose in the crook of his elbow as he approached.

'*Guay de mi*, that's – I'm sorry, I wanted to run ahead and warn you—'

'Mummy? What's happening? How did you—'

'The SOS from the nearby yacht,' Dan told her, one hand steady on the small of her back as she frantically tried to clean herself. He stood beside her now, a reassuring presence, albeit one audibly breathing through his mouth. 'We were told there was a passenger with a life-threatening heart condition. It turns out the patient was your mother.'

'I am right here, young man,' said Lucinda, shooting Dan a look that made him visibly wither, 'and can perfectly well speak for myself.'

Charlotte wasn't keeping up.

'Are you OK?' She stopped wiping her face and stepped closer to her mother, who held up a hand in warning and stepped back. Anwuli released her grip on Cilla and the dog nosed Charlotte's arm, tenderly. Life for Cilla was once again rosy now that her discomfort had ended, even if everyone else's had only just begun.

'Do you have a life-threatening heart condition?' asked Charlotte hoarsely.

'Oh, *that*.' Lucinda waved the hand that held the pashmina, then returned it swiftly to nose and mouth. 'I do recall saying it was a matter of the heart, and perhaps I might have said that it was a question of life and death. Those little radios aren't the clearest out at sea, you know. If it was interpreted literally that's hardly my concern.'

'Walter took the boat out,' said Dan, coming back to life with the fortifying resurgence of his anger. 'Walter and Elsie risked their lives to get the stretcher out, the seas are deadly this time of year, and today was no exception. Why on earth did you need lifting on to a stretcher?'

'Shock. I'm much recovered,' said Lucinda airily. 'Though I must have a cup of tea and truly I can't stay in here much longer, this room absolutely reeks to high heaven. Charlotte, I cannot see how you can stand these extraordinary working conditions.'

'Impacted anal sacs,' Charlotte murmured, as if from the depths of an unspooling bad dream.

'Is it over?' asked Anwuli, speaking for the first time. Like all of them she had been looking at Charlotte's mother like something that had risen through the floorboards, but now she shook herself into action. 'Shall I take Cilla, Dr Vet, she all done, you reckon? Seems you busy now.'

'What? Oh, yes. She's all done. She might need a shampoo.'

'It might be you needs the shampoo,' said Dan, low into her ear, and despite the circumstances, Charlotte laughed. Lucinda raised her eyebrow at Dan, and his smile collapsed. Elsie alone betrayed no sign that anything was amiss; her professionalism was absolute. She now stepped forward, and addressed Charlotte.

'Dr Vet, this lady is saying she's your mother, and we need to know if that's the truth so Immigration know how to proceed.'

Dan was nodding along, muttering something that sounded like 'grounds for prosecution'. He tried to take Lucinda by the arm and she shook him off.

'Oh, you're all making an awful fuss. Of course I am her mother, and in any case, doesn't that make me the mother of a sort of, oh, islander-by-descent? Surely that grants me a temporary tourist pass, or whatever documentation you want to wave about until Lars calls back for us. Now listen, everybody needs to stand down, we'll be out of your hair in no time. I've come for my daughter. Why on God's green earth is everybody gawping?'

'No one is allowed to stay on the island who ain't got plans to leave it,' said Elsie stolidly.

Lucinda gave a mirthless laugh.

'Oh, we plan to leave it, don't you worry. In the meanwhile where is Charlotte's blasted father?'

Everyone's gaze now swivelled to Charlotte, once again desperately scrubbing at herself with the hem of her ruined T-shirt. She paused, and felt the blood rise to her face.

Charlotte had told everyone – as she herself had believed until only six weeks earlier – that she had no father, had never met him, had no idea of his identity. Of the recent Garrick revelation, she had told only Levi.

At that moment Garrick Williams himself appeared in the doorway, and they all turned. Dan, for one, felt relief. Here was the minister, and precisely the right person to arbitrate.

For forty years, Garrick's wife Joan had taken charge of the practicalities: managing the diary; managing the household; managing Garrick. Since her death five months earlier, he had not yet begun to manage himself. His iron-grey curls had grown too long, and now straggled from beneath a pink baseball cap. His heavy brows were lowered into a frown that was becoming, with him, a habitual expression. As usual these days he avoided looking at Charlotte, though the smell that emanated unmistakably from her corner of the room made him glance, fleetingly and with alarm, in her direction. To Dan he said, 'Moz told me I was to come, that there was an emergency. Am I needed? May I be of assistance?'

'Ah,' said Lucinda, triumphant. 'You see? There he is. Goodness, Garrick, you were wearing an awful hat just like that one in London thirty years ago. Anyway, here he is, as I was saying. Charlotte's father's here and he can sort this all out. Garrick, go on. Make yourself useful and vouch for me.'

As if in slow motion everyone turned to look again at Garrick Williams: long-married pastor; unimpeachable moral authority; declaimer of sermons; internalised judge of all their secret misdeeds. Before them his face was changing through an extraordinary spectrum of colours. Puce; ashen; florid tomato; deathly pale. His mouth opened, and then closed again. He shut his eyes as if to exclude the scene before him, and he raised a shaking hand to cover them, like a man playing hide and seek. In this position he remained, absolutely motionless, absolutely silent. While Dan and Elsie were staring at Garrick, Charlotte, overwhelmed by nausea, turned and vomited again quietly, into the sink.

6

When Charlotte came out of the shower her mother had made herself a cup of tea, and repaired the infinitesimal derangement of her blonde chignon. Only hours earlier Lucinda had been strapped to a rickety portable stretcher and lowered over the side of a yacht into a dinghy, in a howling storm. Yet somehow, despite her adventures on the high seas, she looked impeccable. Her only nod to the humidity had been to remove her blazer and pashmina, and these familiar London items now hung from the banisters, on Charlotte's single good hanger. It was unthinkable that her mother could be on Tuga de Oro and yet here she was, sipping Earl Grey from an elegant little cup and saucer that Charlotte, in more than a year in this tiny cottage, had not known was in the kitchen. Lucinda now made a great show of looking around, as if noticing the room for the first time.

'This is a sweet little mouse house. I thought you said your bed was in the kitchen? I can't see how it would fit.'

'It was. Levi – my landlord rebuilt it upstairs, finally.' So we'd have some privacy while we were in it, she did not add, turning quickly away. Lucinda had always had an uncanny ability to read her face. 'Are you hungry? Would you like anything else to eat?'

'I've been jounced across angry oceans longer than Odysseus, I can't think about food at this moment. I need precisely this cup of tea, and possibly a chiropractor.' Charlotte drew closer, towelling her hair, at which Lucinda raised her hand as if she were stopping traffic, wrinkling her nose. 'I'd say you're not entirely in the clear, smell-wise. What in God's name were you doing to that animal? Actually, don't tell me, it's best forgotten. We have more important things to talk about.'

Charlotte took a step back, sniffing at herself.

'I will wait for a less – *pungent* moment to make my case in full but if you would like the synopsis, it is that I've had just about enough of this now. You've made your point. You're very brave and impressive and independent but it's time to go home to London, and get on with real life.'

Charlotte waited, aware that more was coming. When Lucinda was in full flow there was nothing to do but wait, and allow the full tsunami to rise and smash and decimate, and eventually recede.

'Consider me an envoy from the land of the sane. And the air-conditioned. I've travelled for four and a half weeks by planes, trains and automobiles and, latterly, a reasonably terrifying open-sea voyage on a boat worth one thousand dollars, sharing a cabin the size of a matchbox with a man who wears a string vest. And if you would like to know why, it is because you wrote to say you'd identified Garrick and were therefore staying an additional six months "or longer".' Here her elegant, manicured fingers made ironic speech marks, her face inviting an imagined audience to join her in sheer disbelief, and Charlotte thought, for the millionth time, this is what she must be like in court – the torrent of words, the animation of her face, the conviction of her voice all uniting with the force of pure, electric theatre. No wonder she won so often. 'I could hear the metallic clang of mental derailment from across the seas. Your carriages had uncoupled and you were off the sanity tracks, and heading over the cliff. I can only assume this is some sort of breakdown, thinking there is anything for you in this godforsaken place, and I saw how it would be if I left things to take their course. You are ridiculously sentimental and far too easy to manipulate because you're a rescuer, you always have been, and that's all very well with stick insects and baby sparrows and God knows what else you tried to stuff into a shoebox, but it's quite another thing when it leaves you feeling as if you are actually *helping* some random island. Honestly, Charlotte, I consider it more than a little arrogant that you truly believe you're making the blindest bit of difference. I'm sure it's all very flattering to think that they can't possibly do without you, but I must point out they've done perfectly well without you until now. One ought not to patronise. In any case, you're barely a vet; surely they can aim a little higher.'

Charlotte flinched at these blows, which landed.

'And so six weeks ago I thought—'

'You decided to come six weeks ago?' Charlotte was so surprised she risked an interruption.

Lucinda idly picked up some of Charlotte's tracking notes and folded the page in half, to fan herself.

'Islanders can't be very enterprising. Of course the berths on that eccentric little shipping service are booked up till kingdom come. And you'd already made a big song and dance about how impossible it was to get on and off and that you were on some sort of waiting list, as if it was an organ transplant. Hopes and prayers, hopes and prayers for a berth. What rot. I simply did some research and found some heavenly Swedish-Canadian boys doing a charity scavenger hunt. They're sailing in their rust bucket from Namibia to Brazil via various places, and I offered a healthy donation to their cause, and that was that. I had to hang about in Walvis Bay for a bit but the Wi-Fi was perfectly serviceable, and then Lars arrived and swept me up and off we went. He has to drink a bottle of stout at the Volcano Club on Ascension, and then he'll be back again and he'll take us to Buenos Aires or Natal. I must say on one minor point I am rather cross with Lars, he did promise the luggage would be taken care of. Ten days without my laptop is obviously not possible, I shall have to buy another.'

'Ten – I don't think he can come back in ten days. They won't let him even anchor, and they certainly won't send a boat out again. It's hurricane season.'

She didn't address the absolute impossibility of shopping for new or indeed any computer equipment on Tuga. To contradict her mother went against a lifetime of instinct, self-preservation and basic training. But she was trying to assimilate this new reality that her mother was here, and would have to remain here against her will, and probably against everyone else's. Lucinda clattered her teacup into her saucer with displeasure. 'What on earth are you talking about? They sent a boat out this time.'

'That was medevac, they thought you were having a heart attack.'

'That hulking woman in the boiler suit said I was an illegal immigrant, surely they'll want me deported.' Lucinda looked pleased, certain she'd won this point.

That hulking woman, thought Charlotte, *risked her life for you. And Walter too.* She remembered Rebecca's frightened face and felt ashamed. No one who had stood before the Boatmen's Memorial could fail to understand the stakes. But all she said was, 'Yes, but they'll deport you on Tugan time, when it's Island Open. Not before.'

Lucinda wore an expression of mounting disapproval, and a compression of her lips that Charlotte had learned to fear. She knew instantly that she had transgressed. Charlotte might easily have been five, in trouble for setting her goldfish free in the bathtub for an afternoon's holiday. Once Lucinda was displeased she rarely stopped at the immediate incident, and instead would unfurl a list of earlier accumulated crimes, silently logged, sometimes for months.

'I'm tired. This humidity is unspeakable. And I must say I am deeply hurt by your negativity, and your lack of welcome as well, while we're on the subject. You needn't sound so overjoyed at the thought of my deportation. I do not think you can fathom the disruption of all this to my life. Your ingratitude in just running off the way you did, your selfishness in pursuing a course that is so clearly an insult to your education, your background – I have held my tongue till now but, really, you have disappointed me deeply. And now I have turned myself inside out to travel here, Charlotte, and the least you could do is be even moderately polite.'

Charlotte apologised, the only path through familiar treacherous thickets that had sprung up ahead. They were at the ends of the earth, and somehow it was all, instantly, the same.

'Take my bed,' she said, quickly, urgently. 'I'll sleep on the sofa.'

'Good of you,' said Lucinda acidly, and swept into the bathroom, stopping to snatch a clean towel from the middle of the chest of drawers and betraying as she did so that, while Charlotte had been wiping tacky globs of canine anal fluid from her eyelashes, Lucinda had combed every corner of the cottage.

As a child Charlotte had longed for nothing more than her mother's availability and now, decades too late, that ready availability had been delivered in greater quantities than anyone could stomach. Like Midas, Charlotte thought, with angst and a rising claustrophobia, unfolding the spare set of Levi's tie-dyed sheets to make up the sofa. This would be her bed now for who knew how long. Whatever Lucinda might presently believe, no one could get off the island until it opened. At that moment the power went out, and a series of ringing expletives issued from behind the bathroom door.

7

News of Garrick's alleged indiscretion had saturated Tuga de Oro. On the whole, the customers of Betsey's Cafe felt themselves a worldly lot and were inclined to believe the rumours, while the feeling in the moshav rec room was that it was all a vicious falsehood, and the slandering FFA woman with her wild claims and her fake heart attack should be thrown immediately into a jail that they would happily clear for the purpose. (There had not been a prisoner on Tuga de Oro for sixty-eight years, and the two former cells had been requisitioned by the Botika Moshav, for the storage of larger handicrafts.) The version transmitted to tiny Conch Island was that the vet Charlotte Walker had fallen pregnant by the grieving minister. Since that garbled news had crossed, the tide had come in, burying the sandbar, and leaving Conch alone with its misapprehension. Now it would not be set right until the morning.

Conversation at Betsey's had paused, briefly, for the cuckoo clock. A pine chalet around which wire roses twined, it had belonged to Betsey's parents and was mounted, in pride of place, on the wall opposite the coffee bar. Its painted daisies and swinging, pine-cone pendulum camouflaged effectively against a wallpaper of psychedelic tangerine and tea-coloured flowers, and it was something of a rite of passage for new visitors to bump their heads on one of its scalloped eaves. Today, the cuckoo's rasping calls interrupted the detonation of the greatest scandal of the decade. It was too soon for clarity of thought, or thought at all. All they had, in these first shocked moments, was feeling.

Betsey was in tears, dabbing at her eyes with the tea towel she kept tucked into the waistband of her apron. Dan Zekri would have told her this was a health and safety violation, but Dan Zekri was not here.

'I don't believe it. She's Garrick's *child.* There's no sense in it, I can't fathom. Thirty years ago Garrick was married to Joan!'

Anwuli reached across the dark laminate of the coffee bar and patted Betsey's hand.

'I'd not have believed it myself if not for his face. It was like he'd seen a ghost. And that grand woman, cool as a cucumber and dressed like I don't know what. Like some *ambassador.* Two days they been preparing the hospital for a heart attack at sea, and now it turns out ain't nothing wrong with her, save that she was Garrick Williams's *mistress.* She recognised him straight away. She knew his *hat.*'

Anwuli managed to make the word 'hat' sound like an obscenity. Beside her Isadora Davenport stirred coconut sugar crystals into her saloop with a clinking teaspoon, and shook her head.

The pastor cultivated the distinct and deliberate impression of being a man high above impulse, exempt from need, elevated by virtue of his spiritual superiority. Now it turned out Garrick was a pompous hypocrite. Sylvester, recalling all the times a Wednesday sermon had left him feeling chastised or guilty for some minor, private wrongdoing, felt taken for a fool.

'It make sense, thinking now,' he said slowly, 'why some

fancy academic vet end up here. We ain't had vets queuing up to move here before now, and it ain't like the tortoises haven't been here all along.'

'It makes me wonder –' here the shock crossed Anwuli's face as thoughts began to coalesce even while she spoke them '– did Garrick put Joan up to it, is what I'm wondering? Tricked her into choosing Charlotte? His wife the administrator of the fellowship that bring his secret daughter here. Bit too much of a coincidence.'

'It's terrible, poor Joan,' said Betsey, with feeling, and began to cry again. 'It's terrible,' she repeated softly, and nobody had anything to say to this, because it was. For this to happen to honest Joan, who had never concealed a thing in her life – it was too much.

Joan Williams had died quietly this last April, after an illness that had taken the island by surprise. She had been a woman of endless patience. Gentle, earnest, unassuming, beloved by all of Tuga de Oro. Married for four decades and without children of their own, supporting the community had been Joan and Garrick Williams's shared enterprise. But everyone knew that Joan's true calling was anticipating the needs of her busy and self-important husband. She had been devoted to Garrick, to whom she had ministered with a kind of obsessional abasement astonishing to her friends, and accepted by Garrick as his due. The older people remembered, hazily, that there had been some trouble in the baby-making department. Joan had been unwell several times, or there'd been a false start or two. Something of that sort. Clearly there had been no trouble in that department for Garrick.

'Can you imagine,' breathed Isadora, 'Joan spending all that time with the vet, bending over backwards to make her at home on the island, knitting her welcome blankets and whatnots and never knowing it was her husband's *love child*.'

'Ain't love that came into it, from what I saw,' said Anwuli darkly. 'Poor vet, as well, I felt right sorry for her. Can't choose your parents, after all.'

On a long shelf above the coffee machine Betsey had displayed various treasures. Her mother's old biscuit tin, the shape of an English thatched cottage complete with climbing red roses, stood beside a seashell picture frame that showed an old sepia photograph of a young couple side by side, on Out the Way beach. Pride of place at the centre of this shelf was a white Meakin porcelain teapot, hand-painted with wild orange poppies, left to Betsey by Joan in her will, among many small, thoughtful bequests. Betsey now gave a guilty glance towards this teapot, as if Joan herself might be listening, from within.

The world had shifted on its axis. Garrick Williams, island minister, had feet of clay. Feet of clay, and a tortoise-loving FFA love child, whose dimples – Garrick's dimples! – ought long ago to have announced her.

8

In the morning, Lucinda descended from the bedroom and swept silently past Charlotte into the bathroom, where she stayed a long time. Charlotte, who had passed a sleepless night on the sofa, made coffee for them both, and fretted. When Lucinda eventually emerged she was wearing Charlotte's best white T-shirt together with her beloved combat trousers, and was cloaked in the same impenetrable haughtiness with which she had last night taken her leave. Even amid other anxieties, Charlotte grieved the dispossession of these trousers. They were the only sensible workwear she had on the island, and an essential part of her uniform for humid jungle fieldwork. She'd ripped them on a coral cabbage, and Elsie had recently mended them by hand-embroidering a tortoise over the large tear.

'Coffee?' she asked. 'Toast? Mango?'

Lucinda fluttered her fingers minutely in the direction of the coffee pot and Charlotte hurried forward to pour. As she was offering the milk jug there came the sound of wheels on track, and Charlotte looked out of the open top of the kitchen's stable door to see Grand Mary's little red car beneath the spreading avocado tree, and Grand Mary glowering at her from within.

'I take care of her tortoise,' Charlotte explained to her

mother, who still had not spoken. 'I wrote to you about her – Martha, she's a hundred and fifty. The tortoise, I mean. Excuse me a minute, I'll just see if everything's all right.'

But Lucinda rose with her, picking up a cotton bag of Charlotte's, which clinked as she lifted it to her shoulder. She had come instantly to life.

'Might that be Mary Philips? She has come for me, in fact.'

In answer to Charlotte's look of obvious confusion she went on, 'I shall be staying at Martha House until Captain Lars returns in his rust bucket. It seemed sensible to make arrangements to stay somewhere passably comfortable. The former Administrator's Residence was the obvious choice of course, but apparently it has been allowed to fall into woeful dereliction.'

'But . . . how? You didn't go out yesterday.'

'Well, clearly I didn't leave it for yesterday. I read of Martha House when I knew I had to come here. I simply emailed Mary and she agreed to be my host for a brief visit.'

Outside, Mary had begun to press continuously on the car horn. Lucinda departed, taking with her Charlotte's sun hat and water bottle, and conceding with only the slightest nod of the head to meet Charlotte later, for dinner. She had followed Charlotte to the ends of the earth, only to remind her she could do perfectly well without her.

9

Levi had tactfully vanished. He hadn't come to the cottage last night, nor had he been up to his nearby workshop in the morning, and so Charlotte assumed that news of her visitor had reached him. She could not yet envisage the impending collision of Lucinda Compton-Neville QC with Levi Mendoza, but now that she was briefly at liberty she longed to see him.

When he wasn't in the Rockhopper or his shack on the Rockhopper's roof, Charlotte changed tack and decided to go to her room at the clinic so that she herself might be easily found. But turning from the incongruous cobbles of Harbour Street into one of the smaller lanes, she caught the sound of 'Thousands Are Sailing' playing on a tinny speaker. The Pogues were a sure sign that Levi was nearby.

Levi was up a narrow bamboo scaffold tower in the main hall of the Old Kal, scrubbing at a large patch of damp on the ceiling, and wearing a white vest and a pair of denim shorts so ancient that they had frayed almost to the pockets. She had become accustomed to, even fond of, his idiosyncratic wardrobe, despite her objective understanding that it was terrible. Although at present he was also wearing work gloves, and a snorkel mask.

'Explain?'

Levi grinned, his cheeks strangely contorted by the mask's pressure. 'Bleach solvent above my head. Health and safety.'

'Like painting the ceiling of the Sistine Chapel.'

'If you say so, Dolittle. Hold on.'

He removed gloves and goggles. Then he swung down and came forward to put his arms around her. Charlotte leaned her head against his chest and closed her eyes, exhaling fully for the first time in twenty-four hours. Already the sense of calamity was receding. It was as if she had been plugged instantly into the mains of Levi's own steady and steadying confidence.

'Something happen?'

'My mother happened.'

'Whole island know that. I meant, what happened to make her come?' Without taking his hands from Charlotte's waist he stretched backwards to look through the open doorway, towards the bright sunshine of the street. 'She with you now?'

'No, madly, she's gone to Martha House, of all places. Apparently she arranged it all with Grand Mary by email weeks ago. So Mary at least knew she was coming, which she might have mentioned but never mind. She's taken half my clothes, and all my skincare products.'

She was aiming for breeziness, but Levi didn't laugh. He was studying her face with an uncharacteristically serious expression.

'Someone sick? She needing help?'

'No one's sick. Or maybe she thinks that I am. She's here to "bring me to my senses" and take me home.'

Now Levi did laugh, and then stopped abruptly when he saw that Charlotte was in earnest.

'You ain't serious. Take you home?'

'I'm absolutely serious.'

'She risk Island Close for that?'

'She truly thinks I've gone mad, and she could only reason with me in person.'

'*Guay de mi*, that ain't at all what I was expecting you to say. Well. I'm glad she ain't ill, but we got phones, now, on Tuga. Who got money to travel here for a conversation?'

For a moment Charlotte wondered what Levi saw when he pictured her life in London. Having money on the island meant that you could patch your roof, mend your barn, buy in fertiliser, maybe keep an old car. Real money meant you were from elsewhere, FFA, and could afford thousands of pounds for a berth to visit the world's most remote inhabited island, merely for the sake of tourism. She did not think Levi could fathom the kind of money represented by a mortgage-free London townhouse in a Royal Park, a hefty inheritance, and the best part of forty years of commercial practice at the Bar.

'She just tell her boss she's taking months off and that's fine?'

'She doesn't have a boss, she's a barrister,' said Charlotte, as if this ought to have been obvious. 'She probably just told her clerk not to assign her anything.'

Levi withdrew from her and went back to work. He crouched over a tin of primer, levered off the lid with a putty knife and began to stir it with a long stick. 'Her clerk? What's that, like her servant? Butler?'

'It's not that funny, all barristers have them. It's how they get work,' said Charlotte irritably, wondering why the idea of her mother encountering Levi now made her want to take her chances and swim the seven thousand or so miles of frigid Atlantic back to England, away from both of them.

'*Guay de mi*,' said Levi again, but with less warmth. He

was mixing a little too hard. 'Forgive me, Dolittle. Funnily enough I ain't been to law school.'

'No shit.'

It took Charlotte a moment to realise what she'd said. She knelt down beside Levi and put her hand on his arm. 'I'm sorry. That sounded—'

'Just the way you meant it.'

He wiped the stick on a rag and dropped it with a clatter, carefully closing the tin again. Then he swung nimbly back up the low scaffold, and set the primer down in readiness by his feet, reaching for the goggles and gloves he had hung over a projecting bamboo pole. He picked up a spray bottle of bleach, and returned to scrubbing the ceiling. The goggles made it impossible to read his face.

'Levi—'

He did not turn but frowned, still scrubbing. She had hurt his feelings. Charlotte stood a while in indecision, wondering how to fix it, and also, inopportune but pressing, how best to ask him whether they might conceal from her mother whatever was between them, just for now. Not out of shame; rather a practical self-defence, to protect it from the punishing scrutiny of her mother's gaze. But this misunderstanding had not exactly prepared the ground to ask a favour.

When after several moments Levi did not relent, Charlotte gave up, and stepped back into the dazzle of morning sunshine. Sooner or later she would have to go to work.

10

'The *donkeys*!' was how it began at the Rockhopper, as an apprehensive Charlotte held open the screen door to admit her mother and her own humiliation. 'Why are they assembled outside the pub, of all places? Please tell me I'm not going to find donkey burger on the menu.'

Charlotte did not say: it is perfectly obvious, it's so people who haven't driven might ride home again at the end of the evening. She did not say: any donkeys still in the yard at closing time would be invited briefly inside, to drink with gusto from the drip trays. She had ceased answering Lucinda's anthropological questions when she realised that her mother did not actually listen to the answers. Instead the questions were a way of taking in everything she saw, assessing it, and spitting it out processed, stamped and diminished. Charlotte had long understood that anything she treasured should be guarded from her mother's attention.

All heads turned to follow them as Charlotte led the way through the Rockhopper. There were Anwuli and Isadora, sharing a ceviche with their young neighbours; here sat Taxi and Sylvester finishing their pints, a tavla board open between them in an advanced state of play. If the fancy took them, they might soon amble over to the corner stage to pick up their instruments, and what on earth might

Taxi decide to play, now that Lucinda was present? 'Mean Streak'? 'Devil Woman'? So much for unobtrusive assimilation. So much for quiet good work. But then Anwuli blew a surreptitious kiss, and the solidarity made Charlotte stand just a little taller.

At the back of the room stood a single pub booth of dark mahogany, whose stained-glass panels would offer at least a modicum of privacy. Charlotte slid into one side, grateful for even this temporary shield, and her mother sat down across from her, oblivious to the curiosity they were attracting. Instead she gazed upwards at the old fishing nets strung from the ceiling, on which were suspended any number of objects – partially functioning coloured fairy lights; electric storm lanterns; a string of lipstick-pink illuminated hearts wrapped around a piece of pale driftwood; jars of long-dried mintberry left over from Saul Gabbai's recent party to mark his retirement as chief medical officer. Over each of the windows were chinking strings of snail shells, collected by the smaller children for a school project. Charlotte watched her mother taking in each element. As ever, there would be details obvious to Lucinda that Charlotte had never noticed, for her mother's devastating perspicacity would always illuminate the flaws.

'What a festival for the senses. Is there some sort of, *theme night*?'

'No. May I get you a drink?'

'What's safe, darling? Best to steer clear of all these toddies, I imagine. G&T? Maybe you should have a little quinine. I must say you're rather wild-eyed, now that I look at you. Might you be malarial?'

'No malaria here, luckily,' said Charlotte brightly, snapping open a menu she knew by heart and retreating behind it. Lucinda nodded a courtly greeting towards each table, as if she was their visiting MP, recently elected by a landslide. She held her own menu at elegant arm's length, and frowned.

'"Booby egg". Now I understand why you suggested eating at home.'

Charlotte half-rose with hopes of escape, but her mother gestured to her to sit. They were there now, and the theatre of it well suited Lucinda, who never shied from an audience.

'Are raw vegetables safe? How's the water?'

'Yes. Clean. The food is pretty spectacular on the island, actually.'

'Everything's relative, but I shall risk a crab salad. So. I hope you're satisfied now you've met your father,' said Lucinda, setting down the menu and driving the point of her lance instantly and remorselessly through Charlotte's most tender spot. 'There's your big mystery. I must say, I feel somewhat vindicated by all this. Do you see now what an irrelevance he is? I presume this grand quest to find your father has not resulted in an open-armed welcome to the paternal bosom?'

'But if you'd told me—'

'Absolutely not. No. You are not to try and blame me for any part of this. It was a nothing. It was less than a nothing, to call it so much as a fling is an overstatement. You must picture him thirty years ago, of course. I must say time has not been kind to him. But he was rather handsome, sort of dimpled and swarthy and muscular, from farm work he said, of all things. A minister who did farm work! Very exotic.'

'I don't think that word is really acceptable these days,' Charlotte offered, tentatively, and was rewarded by a stare so icy that she physically retreated until her head pressed hard against the mahogany booth behind her.

'If you'd like me to tell you anything at all, then I shall thank you not to police the vocabulary with which I do it.'

Lucinda began to cast around the room, hand raised, looking for a waiter. 'Also, this was thirty years ago, and the fact is that at the time that is what I thought. Do stop paralysing an old story with contorted liberal anachronisms.'

'Sorry. I want to hear.'

'And he was terribly serious and pompous, representing some miniature sort of island no one had ever heard of. It was a bit of an adventure. We had a ferocious debate about the restoration of British citizenship, which of course then passed with the British Overseas Territories Act. At the time that act gave me the horrors, even though I was of course theoretically in favour, because I kept thinking he would show up any day, brandishing his shiny new passport. Who could imagine anyone staying here if they didn't have to? But it never happened, thankfully. The entire whatever-it-was was scarcely forty-eight hours, beginning to end. He was such a prig while we were rowing, so utterly self-important, and then was unexpectedly attentive in the bedroom—'

'Oh, *no*, please—'

'All much better fun than one would expect, and so it happened once or twice more that weekend. He was absolutely mad for me, as I recall, it was as if he hadn't seen a woman in a decade. Then he got terribly guilty and upset, which was rather hypocritical considering his enthusiasm until that point. So I said hadn't he to be getting along and he agreed and he left and that was that. Truly, I didn't give the man another thought – I mean, I quite literally did not think of him again for even a nanosecond from the moment he hopped out of my bed. Your bed, in fact, as I moved it down to the basement flat when I bought that fabulous Hypnos memory foam ten years ago.'

Charlotte resolved, upon her return to London, to invest in a new mattress.

'And then a month or so later I was in a deposition and felt a touch green and wondered if I was up the duff.'

'Shh, *please*!'

'In any case, with the exception of your own bouts of unusual priggishness you turned out a carbon copy of me, bar the dimples. He is an absolute irrelevance, do you now see? Call him a pilot light, if you will, but I cooked the rest of you. And I raised the rest of you, in case you hadn't noticed, and I truly thought I'd taught you better than to set store by such utter rubbish as, what – "knowing where you come from"? You've made it worse, now, I do hope you can see that. While anything was possible then anything was possible, and I think it was quite generous of me to leave you a whole childhood with your castles in the air, and a fantasy parent better than the one doing the tedious work of taking care of you every day. I can only imagine the petty and unimpressive specifics feel worse.'

As happened so often, her mother had cut close to a painful truth. It was true that lifelong her father's identity had been a mystery, and while she'd ached for the lack of him, his ghost had nonetheless shimmered with a touch of hopeful glamour. He could have been anyone, anywhere, and each possibility offered a route to a clearer identity of her own. He was a movie star. He was Scandinavian royalty. He was David Attenborough. The reality was a curmudgeonly married minister, cornered, panicked, rejecting. It was not only unexceptional. It was sordid, and sad.

Having won her point Lucinda appeared, fractionally, to relent. 'I did warn you. He never knew you existed and I saw his face today, Charlotte, and it is quite clear he'd like to go back as fast as possible to not knowing. He doesn't want you within a hundred miles.'

'No. I know.'

'Has he made any sort of overture?'

Out of the corner of her eye Charlotte saw Levi returning to his post behind the bar.

'Hmm? No. I'll get our drinks, one minute.'

11

Levi grinned when he saw Charlotte approaching the bar, and she felt a warm flood of relief. She might be losing her mind, but she had not lost Levi. Calm, clear-eyed Levi, who knew that she had been thoughtless because she was under strain. And she hadn't even had to explain about her mother; he understood. He gave a barely detectable wink.

'Dolittle.'

'Mendoza.'

'*Ke haber.* What can I help you with, this fine evening?'

'One G&T. And one fake G&T, please. Just the T.'

'You can't tell your mama you don't want one? She don't know you a messy drinker?'

'Oh, please, I can't explain. I could tell her, but . . . '

She trailed off. It was déclassée to be teetotal, one of the many facets of Charlotte's disappointing social failure. Lucinda would have preferred a daughter drunk and topless in the fountain of an Oxford quad to one shy and sober and alone in the Royal Veterinary College library, but the nuances of all this were hard to compress into brief whispers. Charlotte returned to the table, and a moment later Levi arrived with a tray.

'Ah, yes. About time. Might you turn up the air conditioning in this corner? It's like dining in a Bikram studio.'

Levi set down their drinks and tucked the tray beneath his arm. Then he removed a pencil from behind his ear, producing a notepad with a flourish. This was all performance. Charlotte had never known him write down an order before.

'Only air conditioning on the island in the clinic,' he said cheerfully, pencil poised. 'Serious illness, heart attacks, that sort of thing. Bad luck, to find yourself air-conditioned on Tuga.'

Charlotte gave him an imploring look after this heart-attack reference, which he ignored. Lucinda appeared oblivious. She had already left her deception far behind, cast off with her pashmina.

'But your establishment has a functioning refrigerator.'

'Last I checked.'

'Two crab salads, in that case, and a vat of iced water.'

Levi nodded. On his way back to the bar he made a great show of taking the single large fan that was cooling the entire Rockhopper and redirecting it exclusively towards Charlotte and Lucinda, at whom its tinsel ribbons rippled and pointed. Charlotte slumped lower into her seat.

'The humidity! At least my bedroom is somewhat ventilated.'

'How *is* it at Martha House? How exactly did you arrange it, again?'

'I've already told you, I just emailed Mary and made a business proposition to her. She's a businesswoman.'

'Is she?' Charlotte asked. 'No one really knows what she is, she's always just so . . . ' she was going to say *mean*, but thought this sounded infantile '. . . enigmatic,' she finished, lamely.

'Hardly. She's simply an old lady with a large house, it is barely worth discussing. Now, I am going to find the loo. Wish me *bon courage* for the adventure.'

When Lucinda had gone Charlotte dashed back to the bar. 'I'm sorry. She didn't even say thank you for the drinks.'

'Maybe she'd be nicer if she knew we passing time?' asked Levi, but it was without reproach. 'You ain't lining up to introduce me, I see.'

'She definitely would not be nicer, I can assure you. No lies, I promise. Just a brief – omission.'

'That's lawyer talk, if ever I heard it.' Levi stroked her cheek. 'Maybe you the one should have gone to law school.'

'Oh, please forgive me – truly, I have no idea what I was even talking about. I miss you. Can I come over later?'

'Next hop I will ask her to have a caper with me. You know, show her I know my manners.'

But before she could absolutely ascertain he was joking, Charlotte felt a gentle tap on her arm and turned to find Nicola Davenport standing behind her.

Charlotte knew Nicola only in passing, a woman in her fifties whom she saw in the clinic whenever Nicola came for physiotherapy, in recovery from a recently broken leg. Nicola's fifteen-year-old daughter Chloe was the island's next hope for a local doctor, and sometimes came after school to watch Dan if he was running labs. Most had faith Chloe would do it. As a much smaller child she'd needed two baby teeth pulled out and had, under Saul Gabbai's careful supervision, pulled them out herself.

'*Paz*, Dr Vet, I'm sorry, I see you busy.' Nicola made an awkward spherical motion with her hands in the direction of their booth, as if Lucinda was something Charlotte was in the process of sculpting. 'I'd not come over, only I've a calf scouring.'

'Of course. Shall I come now?' She had no idea where Nicola and Chloe lived, and wondered, hopefully, if it was very far away. Preferably all the way over on Conch.

'Oh, no, tomorrow just fine. She up and about, spry little thing, suckling and all. Just a touch.'

'Are you sure? Have you got calf and dam apart from the others, now?'

Nicola chuckled. 'Ain't no others. We've only Ribbon, and now the new calf come Chloe has called her Lacie. I'll not disturb your dinner any longer. Chloe keeping a close watch, she'd come out for me if Lacie took a turn.'

Lucinda was returning. Charlotte promised Nicola Davenport that she would stop in the following morning on her way to the clinic, and hurried back to her mother.

'There is some kind of – ditty – on the wall. "In this land of sun and fun,"' Lucinda began, as sonorous as if she was reciting grace over meals.

'"We never flush for number one,"' Charlotte finished. 'I know. Catchy. There's a lot of fresh water on Tuga but people still feel it's right to be careful.'

'Very public-spirited. I must say I have always despised such euphemisms as number one. On the other hand I can't immediately think of an easy rhyme for "urinate".'

'Terminate?' Charlotte offered.

'Yes. Surrogate.'

'Exterminate.'

'Oh, that's excellent.'

'Decerebrate.'

'Decerebrate!'

They went on. Face to face over a dinner table, there would soon be no hiding from the QC's professional cross-examination. Why was Charlotte really here? What was she doing with her life? When would she cease and desist with this self-indulgence and re-engage with her reality? But, for now, this was a flash of the best Lucinda, a shared inside joke rare but disarming, intoxicating even, especially when

Charlotte did not become its object. She felt a sudden, unexpected lightness, like a good, deep breath.

Levi delivered the crab salads, setting down their plates with a flourish.

'This is Levi Mendoza,' said Charlotte, quickly, in a brief spasm of bravery.

'Your – landlord?'

'That's me.' Levi offered his hand. '*Ke haber.* Pleasure to meet any mother of Charlotte's.'

Lucinda gave him a sharp look, trying to determine whether he was joking, or stupid. With uncharacteristic generosity she went with the former. 'Yes, well. Unluckily for her I'm the only mother she has, despite a new interest in collecting parents. A recent acquisition has not been a success.'

'That so.' Levi picked up their empty glasses. 'Well, on Tuga de Oro we honour our parents, successful or not. You ladies enjoy your dinner. Holler if there's anything at all you need.'

Lucinda glanced at Charlotte who was staring down at the table, her gaze anywhere but upon Levi's compelling, beautiful face. Lucinda narrowed her eyes.

'I feel fairly confident our needs are best met elsewhere,' she said, crisply. 'Thank you for the crabs.'

12

Walter had had another bad night. Rebecca had appeared yet again in the small hours, a ghostly figure in a faded Minnie Mouse nightgown and clutching her wooden mermaid, two ragged teddies, and a walnut shell that contained a tiny piglet, made for her by her grandfather over on Conch. And it would be fine, Walter supposed, suppressing a yawn, for Rebecca was mostly silent, wanting only to curl beside him surrounded by her toys, her face buried in her mother's unoccupied pillow. But invariably his own sleep for the night would be over. She did not quite snore, but breathed heavily. However far he rolled away, teetering at the opposite edge of the mattress, eventually a hot little arm flung out and startled him just as he began to drift off, or she would rotate until a sharp foot kicked his ribs, his shoulder, his solar plexus. At around three in the morning he had retreated to the concrete floor, one arm aloft so that he might hold her hand, though his shoulder prickled with pins and needles. Walter was tired.

Now he was with Levi servicing the RIB, the rigid inflatable boat used by the coastguard. They were changing the filters, and fitting new pressure release valves to the tubes, which would guard against sudden fluctuations in temperature. Levi did not see the need for these valves, Walter knew. They'd lasted fine without them until now, adjusting the pressure manually, but after a single tentative question, Levi had kept this opinion to himself. The boat accident six years ago had not been Walter's fault, as Maia and Levi found endless ways of reminding him. Not his fault, Walter conceded on his good days. But it had been his boat. It was this sense of culpability that meant Levi would never deny Walter expensive pressure release valves for the emergency-response RIB.

For now, Levi was scrubbing at the tubes with degreaser and a yellow cloth. The two men had always worked well together. Others slacked off when paired with Walter, knowing he would shoulder the lion's share without complaint, but not Levi. Walter started on the other side and for a time both were silent, each at his task.

'Rebecca and I going across to Conch low tide this Saturday,' Walter said, after a while.

'I'll come,' offered Levi. Then he added, lightly, 'Might bring the vet.'

'That would make your niece happy, she a big fan.'

Levi grinned. 'Rebecca got sound taste.'

'And the vet's a fan of you, *badj*, by the looks of things. She met your folks before now?'

'Not yet. They'll get on fine, I reckon. She having a rough ride now, though, *guay de mi*. I know she feeling bad you went out on the rough water after her mama. What a story.'

'All done, now,' said Walter, simply. He was not a man to look backwards. 'Charlotte tell you any more?'

Levi shook his head. 'I ain't been over there. I know she ain't never told her anything about her father being – who he is.' He sat back on his haunches. 'Dolittle not long found out herself. And now her mama here like a hurricane and the whole island knowing everything, all of a sudden. She dealing with more than her fair share right now.'

'Weekend on Conch be a good time away from all that.'

'You reckon I should invite 'em both? The mother too?'

'Perhaps I ain't met her under the right circumstances,' said Walter slowly, 'but I'm not thinking that fancy FFA will love Conch. Probably she like plumbing.'

Levi frowned for a moment.

'But I'd say it only matter how the vet feel about Conch, or plumbing. Or anything else. It ain't the mama you passing time with.'

Levi made an indistinct noise. Walter yawned deeply.

'You falling asleep right here.'

'Ah, I'm all right, just need to knuckle down. Radio?'

Levi turned on the portable set, in time for them both to catch Taxi announcing that tomorrow was the deadline for submitting a consent form for School Worming Day, brought forward for reasons no one need dwell upon, and ain't no one pointing fingers. All the children would be de-wormed tomorrow lunchtime regardless, with or without submission of the form, but it was nice to do a thing properly. Parents who'd lost their form, or indeed wanted a worming tablet for themselves, were to call in at the clinic. Taxi closed this bulletin with 'I Got the Itch' by Lord Nelson, prompting Walter to wonder if in fact it had been worms had woken Rebecca the previous night. Stock-keeping and child-rearing had a decent amount in common, except the pigs had the good grace to stay out of his bedroom.

13

Betsey had brought a tray out to them while they worked, forest-green melamine printed with bounding English hares. Upon this she had laid two scalloped china plates of grilled-fish sandwiches and papaya chutney, and two glass bottles of fresh mango juice. Walter and Levi were perched on the hot black tube of the RIB with this laden tray balancing between them. It took a moment to identify the woman who was approaching them, picking her way fastidiously across the yard, dressed in Charlotte Walker's embroidered cargo trousers and an enormous, palm-front hat. Walter raised a hand.

'*Paz.*'

'Yes, *paz*, exactly, hello. Lucinda Compton-Neville.' She showed no sign of recognising the man who'd manoeuvred her on to the island in this exact RIB. Her eyes slid over Walter, and fastened upon Levi.

'You're the landlord.'

'Levi.'

'Levi. That's right.' Lucinda adjusted the startling hat, an action that required her to raise her arms up high and wide, like an evangelical preacher. 'I'm glad I've run into you. It's an opportunity to say thank you for your hospitality to my daughter. She's been so contented in that little nest of yours, and it's been such fun for her to take a holiday from real life while she works through . . . well. It's done her the world of good, to have a bit of fun.' She lowered her hands. 'I just hope it won't be too tricky for you to find another tenant when Charlotte leaves.'

Walter looked at Levi to see how this was received, but Levi was shielding his eyes from the sun's glare, his expression unreadable. Levi was not only his brother-in-law, but his dearest friend. Not a natural conversationalist, Walter nonetheless felt it incumbent upon himself to pose the obvious question.

'Why, when she leaving?'

'Oh . . .' Lucinda waved airily. 'Well, this Island Close seems a tedious business, but we're hoping for ten days, maybe a fortnight.'

Walter glanced back at Levi. It was obvious to both men that such a departure was impossible. But that wasn't the point.

'That ain't likely,' said Walter.

'Well. I pride myself on being enterprising.'

Lucinda's reply was directed entirely to Levi.

'But perhaps it's clearest simply to establish that Charlotte will be leaving at the soonest possible juncture.'

'It's my house,' said Levi, meeting her gaze. 'So I guess I'll just move back into it.'

Lucinda clapped her hands, as if a difficult problem had been resolved entirely to her satisfaction.

'Oh well, that will be perfect for you then, won't it? Best for everyone. You'll move back to your cottage where you're meant to be, and Charlotte will be back in London, where she's meant to be. Getting on with her life. That is what's best for her, after all.'

Levi stood up and drained one of the bottles of mango juice, and then set the bottle back on the tray, and placed the tray carefully on the ground. He picked up his rag and some UV polish and began cleaning again, strong, steady strokes across the tubes of the little craft. After some moments he glanced up to see that Charlotte's mother was still standing before them, arms crossed, apparently waiting. Their eyes locked, and Lucinda raised the faintest eyebrow.

'Understood,' said Levi, evenly. Then he returned to his work, and did not lift his head again.

14

In the afternoon Charlotte went in search of Levi. He still had not come within a hundred yards of his workshop, discretion and sensitivity for which Charlotte felt both grateful and guilty. At present she could not imagine a world in which she might confess to her mother her feelings for Levi – not least, she told herself, because she was not yet clear what those feelings actually were. All she did know was that Lucinda had declared she would pass the day in the cool and privacy of the Martha House library and that, assured of her absence, Charlotte longed to see Levi. This did not require examination or interpretation. It just – was. She felt an almost bodily need to have him near.

'Levi and Walter down the boatyard,' Betsey told her, putting three sticky slices of ginger cake on a china plate and handing it to Charlotte over the counter. All Betsey's paper bags had been soaked by a leak in the storeroom ceiling. For now, bone-china plates went out across the island and eventually made their way back, or were chased down by Annie Goss on her bike, employed by Betsey as a small but ferocious ad hoc debt collector. Betsey had ordered more bags, to be delivered by the shipping agent, but the Island Open boat was the most overburdened and chaotic of all the six supply ships and anything might come, or not come, or come in an unexpected form. One year Betsey had fallen in love with a Welsh dresser in a catalogue, which she had hoped would look beautiful beside the cuckoo clock. *Solid rustic oak*, read the copy beneath. *Classic carpentry joints. Made to last.* It was affordable, and the picture showed china of the sort Betsey collected displayed within it, and behind it flocked wallpaper not entirely unlike her own. In readiness, she had Walter Lindo-Smith in to level the cafe floor. It had taken twenty-six months to arrive, not an unprecedented delay, and when it did come, Elsie delivered it to Betsey on her palm in a funereal silence, a perfect miniature replica Welsh dresser, made for a doll's house. Betsey wasn't holding her breath for sandwich bags.

'Tell Levi I'm needing my tray back tonight, mind,' she said now, and Charlotte promised to return it herself, together with the plate. Then she set off on foot for the boatyard.

It was dry and hot, but it had rained heavily in the night. The track had softened into red mud that squelched and sucked at her boots, thickening in the sunshine into glue; the ruts and deep potholes were filled with opaque puddles the colour of terracotta. On one side of the road grew tall cinnamon trees, their bright glossy green splashed here and there with streaks of young leaves, poppy-red. There had been high winds, and the cinnamons had littered the track with their hard, dark berries, compressed by Charlotte's footsteps into the mud.

On the other side was a steep slope down to the ocean. Last night it had been roiling, dull and grey; this morning it was a plain of winking sapphire. For a moment Charlotte stopped and simply looked. There it was; the boundlessness, and the near-galactic extremity of their isolation.

When she reached the boatyard she found only Walter,

who accepted his cake and said that Levi had finished for the day, and he wasn't sure where he'd gone, only that it had been on the motorbike. Never a man of many words, Walter seemed particularly unforthcoming. Charlotte wondered how he was coping, in what seemed an open-ended period without his wife. As she turned to go Walter seemed to change his mind about something.

'Exercising on the beach,' he called, and then went back to loading his truck.

There was only one donkey grazing near the boatyard and it resisted Charlotte's attempts to call it over. The animal was not even fooled when she held out a morsel of ginger cake, and pride forbade her from going back to ask Walter for help. It was a great inconvenience that FFA were not permitted to drive. She set off again on foot, staying in the shade of dense bananas and the huge clustering taro, their frilled leaves the rich vegetable purple of red cabbage, and as tall as she was.

When she got to the beach she found Levi's belongings in a heap beneath a palm that grew at a 45-degree angle towards the water, over the pale sand. Here were his clothes, and a mismatched pair of plastic flip-flops, one black, the other striped in the emerald, lemon and deep blue of the Brazilian flag. The islanders kept a tall, open shed near Go-by-Donkey in which they displayed everything that washed up on the beaches: nine parts junk heap, one part treasure trove. Each of these flip-flops had been delivered by the ocean, one left, one right, both Levi's size and equally serviceable, six months apart. There was a lack of materialism to him, a tender care for the planet, that Charlotte found deeply moving.

She put down the plate and then sat down and began to unlace her boots, mud-caked, and now encrusted with fine white sand, like granulated sugar on a doughnut. She took a deep and grateful swig from the water bottle Levi had left behind, watching with pleasure as a lover-girl gecko ascended the coconut trunk. The tracks of diurnal crabs were visible across the flats and runnels near the ocean, and she felt simple happiness, and the return of a calm that had evaporated the moment she first heard Lucinda's voice ring out across the clinic. She could sit here and watch the noddies hover and dip, pattering their feet as they skimmed the surface. She and Levi could be alone here. Finally, they could talk.

He came out of the sea naked, like Nerites. The water ran in streams down his broad chest. He was a revelation each time she saw him, over and over, and she scrambled to her feet and went to him, laughing in delight, her arms outstretched to reach up and around his neck. But the approaching sea god did not smile. Instead he caught her wrists, stopping her before she touched him. Then he let go abruptly and began to walk past, up the beach, bending for a small towel. She stood and watched his back in confusion.

'Levi? What's wrong?'

He stepped into his shorts, and tugged a vest over his head. Then he turned to face her.

'Ain't nothing wrong.'

'But—'

'Ain't nothing wrong that wasn't wrong before, maybe I should say. I just seen how things are.'

'I don't under— How are things?'

'Things are . . . not your concern. You leaving. You leaving just as soon as you can get out of here.'

Charlotte felt her stomach fall, a sudden roller-coaster descent.

'You know better than anyone that we can't possibly get off Tuga for ages.'

She tried to sound casual, but her heart was pounding.

'I know how Island Close works. What I don't know is what you plan on doing come Island Open.'

'Oh, but Island Open is so far off—'

'You leaving when the island opens.'

Levi drew himself up and crossed his arms, like a bouncer. Though not a question, he waited for an answer. Charlotte squirmed.

'Not necessarily,' she said, eventually. 'Not straight away. It's not like, a desperate rush.'

'You were going to tell me, or just ghost it?'

'Levi, I . . . ' She began to feel panicked and, in her panic, defensive. 'But, you knew I was leaving at some point . . . I mean, that's been a foregone— It's hardly somewhere I could stay forever.'

Levi slung the towel over his shoulders and shook his head.

'Wow, girl. You all about how you nothing like your mama but funny thing, you sounding just like her, right now.'

'All I mean is that this isn't where I'm from, it's not where my actual life is.'

'No.' Levi bent for his bag, and swung it easily over his head so the strap crossed his body, readying himself to leave. 'But it's where my *actual life* is. So if you excuse me, I think I will get on with it.'

'There's every chance I might be here for months, though – I've got heart-worm vaccinations, and there's someone at Durham who wants to commission an entomology survey, and who knows when the next researcher could get out to do that, or if I'll even get funding for another vet placement, so really I should help him before—'

'Just stop. Stop all your new projects here, stop messing. Go back to that real life of yours.'

'Now you sound like my mother,' said Charlotte, straining for a joke.

'You should mind your mama. Fact is she know you, even if you don't know you.'

His face was closed, an expression she had never seen before. He was open as the clear, vast Tugan sky. Open and honest. Light, generous Levi, shut down. By his bike he halted.

'Trouble is, you think you insulting me, pointing out that I ain't been to law school, or I ain't got some fancy job, CEO of whatever, brain surgeon. But not everyone weigh up a person on their degrees. Not everyone's studying happen at school. I hear you talk to Zekri about Annie Goss, I know you think it's a tragedy I ain't had *access*, I ain't had *chances*. I ain't been to law school, it's true. You stating plain fact. And I tell you, ain't no power on this earth could get me there.'

Charlotte hung her head. She wanted to reach out to Levi, to touch him, to feel his strong arms enfold her, understanding only now how quickly and entirely he had become the source of her comfort just as much as pleasure. But another tiny voice whispered that this simplified everything. And now Lucinda might never need know.

Levi threw his leg over the motorbike.

'You hurting over family stuff, and I'm sorry for you. And it seems like you ain't sure on the things that make you happy, and I'm sorry for that too. But let me tell you something, just so we clear, and you can quit your pitying me right this moment.

'I love my life. I'm happy *just as I am*, you mind me? I got my workshop, the bar, I got the ocean. This island got a history that means something, if you'd trouble to learn it.

It ain't just – some place. Our ancestors came from a lot of different lives and what they had in common was running from persecution, and in a lot of cases persecution from the colonising forces that your Europe ain't even begun to reckon with, if you asking me. This island saved them, and then they chose different. We got real values here we live by, is what I'm saying. I'm proud of every word of our constitution, I'm proud of the way we live, the way we take care of one another, and it ain't some accident, we committed here to our founding values.'

They had never talked about any of this, Charlotte realised, and of course that was because she had never asked. But Levi wasn't finished.

'You know what contentment's like? I doubt you felt it. I had a life I liked before you came, and for me it will be just the same when you go back to whatever it is you chasing. Your mama's approval, maybe, though seems like that ain't made you happy so far. But ain't no way you can make me feel bad about myself by pointing out our differences, you get me?'

Charlotte nodded miserably. Her throat burned. The sand was hot beneath her feet, and she was aware of the sun, high and remorseless now, stinging the back of her arms, and the parting of her hair. She said nothing and could see no other way, for all that Levi spoke was truth. It was true that she had never planned to stay forever on Tuga de Oro. Still, it was also true that she had broken something beautiful.

15

There was only one place Charlotte could think of to go, plunging deep into the refuge of what she had come to regard as her jungle. It called to her. It always had, since her first exploratory visit and perhaps even before she ever set foot on Tuga, wrapping its surging tendrils around her heart; filling her imagination with its humidity and sweet flowers. It was immersion and erasure both. In the jungle she sweated and swore, hiked and climbed and scrambled until her muscles ached and her head pounded. She was a different person, and sometimes barely a person at all, instead a living thing among living things. It was cawing, scraping, clicking, screaming, and the ooze of mud, of sap. It was the opposite of control, which had otherwise been Charlotte's abiding principle. It was rot and decay; fertility and urgent growth. Given the chance, the jungle mud would suck her soft form into itself in mere days, and she honoured and respected its voraciousness. She did not matter here. But conservation mattered. Delicate island ecosystems mattered. Watching her gold coin tortoises, she knew that whatever Lucinda might believe, the work had value. And she, only she – only she *in the world* – was doing it.

To see the tortoises now, all she had to do was sit still, in her place. There were not many, but they liked their old familiar haunts. Two hundred and seventy-eight tagged, and six weeks since she had seen any without the rose-pink or lake-blue epoxy resin markings. Few enough that some, old friends, seemed now to recognise her. So far this Island Close had been a little drier than average, but soon the true rains would make the jungle interior impassable and so in recent weeks Charlotte had come as often as she could, aware that each visit might be her last. And it was barely three miles from grandeur and solitude and perspective to their opposites: Betsey's Cafe, companionship, and an iced lemonade. It had been her happy place.

Base camp had expanded, so that she now had a netted hammock, and a cool box that went beyond the essentials, items transported visit by visit. Elsie had made her a rough table and stools from a fallen korason, and she had limitless drinking water from the creek which was clean, or certainly clean enough. Even with a rope she could not climb the palms, but she had learned to split a coconut with a machete for its meat. Together Charlotte and Elsie had painted markers on the trees at eye level so that a trail now led her east through the korasons to the flank of the *montaña*; and due west towards a beach that faced the blazing sunsets. She and Levi had camped here for a few days, the western reaches of the jungle, nosing Walter's ancient Land Rover as deep into the forest as it could go. Charlotte had heated creek water for tea over a tiny camping stove, while Levi had assembled a tent on the roof of the Defender – a construction of his own, he told her cheerily: an old barn door with post holes drilled at its edges cantilevering crazily off to one side, a thick foam mattress laid on top, and above it a teepee frame of bamboo poles that he had wrapped around with layers of mosquito netting. 'Now I know how I'm going to die,' she'd said to Levi, refusing to leave the side supported by the solid roof of the car, and he had laughed and rolled to the far side of the cantilever taking Charlotte with him, and had shown her, long into the night, just how much faith he held in the soundness and strength of his own craftsmanship. They had fallen asleep to the calls of the geckos and woken with the sun, huge moths silhouetted on their nets as if they'd been embroidered overnight in smoke-grey thread. As the sun rose they began to hear the friendly hiss and grunt of nearby gold coins, pursuing romantic assignations of their own.

Now, their tyre tracks had gone. Tuga de Oro would carry on as if she'd never been, and when she left she would slide off the island and leave no trace. Probably that was as it should be. Certainly as a conservationist it was a principle she upheld. The rain would wash her chalk paint from the tree trunks, the paths she cleared over and over would disappear beneath new, burgeoning growth. The table and chairs would rot. It would become impossible to imagine, standing in the litter and drizzle of Camden Town, that there was ever a time when she had been a community vet on a tropical island so small that she could retain the name of every animal she treated; when she had felt that each day's work improved the lives of known, specific families; when she had lain in the arms of a man she had trusted, and had believed hc understood her.

It had felt good to believe herself needed, but that illusion was gone. She had tried to make a life, and instead she had made a mess.

Was it geographical distance that had created the illusion of her independence? If it took running away to find autonomy, that seemed more childish than anything else. Ought she not, by now, to be able to withstand her mother's presence, while also knowing her own mind? The execution of it remained impossible. Nothing could feel right or safe or even tolerable for very long, while Lucinda sat in disapproval.

Charlotte knew she ought now to care less. But she had been formed both longing for her mother's attention and fearing it, for in the rare and intense moments in which Lucinda turned her forensic study upon Charlotte she was always found wanting. Why didn't she have more friends at school? Why hadn't she read any of the books Lucinda had bought for her?

Lucinda's idea of an only child in a big house had been one who passed the days like Jane Eyre – squirrelled in a nook behind the swagged curtains, greedily consuming all the fiction that would one day shape her into a great mind. Like a Brontë character, she had indeed been raised in a house with an actual library, and it was Lucinda's expectation that Charlotte would make her way obediently through it while she worked, a child scholar, companionable and mute. But Charlotte didn't want to read her mother's old *David Copperfield*. She didn't want to sit in silence in a chair, her plaits neat and her head bowed. She wanted to be meeting dogs in the park, or mucking out the horses in the stables. She wanted to be watching her tank of tree frogs, or cultivating the crickets they ate. She wanted to be in the garden working on her pond project, digging in a blue plastic washing-up bowl and populating it with the right algae to lure the longed-for newts. The mosquito larvae and rat-tailed maggots that did colonise it were fascinating – the perfect launch for her newly created ecosystem – though it had been a mistake when she spoke of these at breakfast. Lucinda had murmured that 'larvae' and 'maggots' were among her least favourite words in the English language, and had not understood that soon amphibians would detect the new body of water and control these populations. The washing-up-bowl pond was disposed of, and the gardener popped a hydrangea into the hole. Charlotte had cried, and her kindly nanny had taken her to the zoo once again, to cheer her up in Joan Beauchamp Procter's old reptile house.

The jungle was not silent like a library but loud, filled with the noises of the busy, indifferent tropics, and in the clamour Charlotte laid her head on Elsie's table and wept. She wept for the father of whom she had dreamed, before he coalesced into a specific, quotidian disappointment. She had longed for him her whole life, but he had never existed, and that realisation was a new bereavement. She wept for her beloved, vulnerable tortoises, even while she envied them their armour. She wept for Levi.

She did not hear Elsie until she was almost beside her. Loyal, earnest Elsie Smith, who somehow always knew where Charlotte might be found.

'Dr Vet,' Elsie said softly, crouching down beside her with the professional calm and comportment of a paramedic attending an accident, 'I am sorry to disturb you. I hope you OK. But you need to come now-now, I got the bike here. I loosed your donkey, so don't worry about her. That calf of Nicola Davenport's ain't doing good.'

16

When Saul came in, Moz was sieving her chicken soup with what could only be described as violent intent. He kissed his wife's flushed cheek and, though it sang out to him, restrained himself from reaching into the sieve for a soft petal of onion. Fingers in her cooking got him into trouble at the best of times and, from her demeanour, these were not the best of times. He stayed silent, merely rolled up his shirtsleeves and lifted a colander of vegetables from the sink so he could wash his hands. No longer chief medical officer, still he found it hard to renounce this weekday habit of collared shirts, though Moz had startled him the day after his retirement party by announcing her own retirement from ironing. The laundry was his job now, as was driving to the moshav for the milk, and taking full superintendence of and responsibility for their temperamental generator. As a result he had begun to devise various hanging devices that would minimise wrinkles as the laundry dried in the sun. Where had all this ingenuity been when it was she who did the work, Moz wanted to know.

'You hear,' Moz began, picking up a conversation that had been going on several hours earlier, in many ways part of a larger conversation that had been running between them for almost fifty years, 'what that woman done now?'

She began to stab at the chicken carcass with a wooden spoon, pressing its juices free. Saul did not need to ask which woman, nor did he say, *If you're about to tell me that she asked Betsey for an egg-white omelette, and when Betsey asked her what she was meant to do with three good egg yolks had said, 'Tip them down the waste disposal, for goodness' sake'* – the whole island knew about that already. But Moz surprised him, as she often did.

'Borrowed a laptop from Grand Mary. You knew Grand Mary had a laptop? Just sitting there?'

Saul shook his head. He had long ago accepted there was a great deal he didn't know about Grand Mary.

'Mary, who never been known to part with a single penny in her whole miserable life, who wanted Levi Mendoza arrested for taking a pomelo. She got six trees, how many pomelos can one old lady eat? A laptop! When Sylvester put up that poster fundraising for one new school computer, Grand Mary goes out her way to tell me she had chalk and slate when she was a girl and it did just fine. Can that even be true? She's only twenty years older than us, and I remember at school Johannes had one of those naked-lady pens. You can't go from chalk and slate to naked-lady biros in twenty years, can you?'

'Oh, I was so jealous of that pen. Johannes got her from a sailor. He charged us if we wanted a turn tipping her upside down.'

'More fool you for paying him. Anyway, now all afternoon that woman taking up the whole booth at the Rockhopper for herself, and frowning at Taxi if his tavla games got a little rowdy. She asked Nancy for the Wi-Fi password –' here Moz did break into a smile '– and Nancy said, all wide-eyed, "What's a Wi-Fi?" and kept asking her stupid questions, like she was born yesterday. Honestly, Charlotte's mother's the one born yesterday. What she think the Rockhopper would do with Wi-Fi? Satellite gives the whole island sixty-four kilobits per second on a good day.'

'She'll find out soon enough,' said Saul, peaceably. He retreated to the kitchen table to attend to the fresh dill that lay there, beside a pair of kitchen scissors. Mac's Rachel had recently started planting European herbs among the etrogs, with some success.

Moz turned round and glared at him over her glasses, which had steamed.

'Garrick need to man up, come home, and deal with all this,' she said decisively, and as if she hadn't said this twice an hour since her brother had absconded.

In the absence of Garrick to furnish his side of the story, they were left only with speculation and outrage. That woman Lucinda would tell anyone anything, it seemed, treating the entire island as a sort of theme park populated not with actual people but costumed resort staff, or perhaps actors at a museum that had re-created a historic village in its grounds. But however burning her own curiosity, Moz deemed it treachery of the highest order to speak to her.

'Did you have any idea?' Saul asked now. 'Did you ever have even a suspicion, at the time? I barely remember when he went, except Johannes coming back with that stupid displaced compound femoral fracture and a limp for the rest of his life.'

'Are you asking if I *knew* my brother was a philandering hypocrite?'

Saul paused his snipping. 'Of course. Sorry. Stupid question. But, Mozzie, truly, I didn't know either, you must believe me. I don't think anyone knew. I don't think –' here he paused, for expressing even vague compassion towards Garrick was a risk '– I'm not totally sure that Garrick can believe it.'

Moz blew air through her lips but said nothing, merely frowned as the drips of soup slowed, and then stopped. Saul took her silence as permission to continue.

'I think whatever happened with that woman was so far from his real life that he just . . . packed it away. I think he's had a terrible shock. Not just the exposure but also the shock of seeing himself as he knows we must all see him. The hypocrisy! A terrible shock. For us too.'

'You can say that again. All the years – I truly don't know.' Moz pushed a strand of hair from her eyes with the back of her wrist. Once flaming red, it was now a soft, pale grey, though with the years she herself had only grown in strength, Saul thought. She would always have the power and courage of Boudicca.

'We won't know till we hear from him, and I for one ain't going anywhere near the Breaks. *Guay de mi*, he can pull his socks up and walk back like a man.'

'He's been out there alone a time. Are we worried?' Saul asked carefully.

Moz lifted the pot of clear broth from the hob to the table with strong arms. Then she returned with the large bowl of pale chicken and softened vegetables and began to strip meat from bone with practised fingers.

'We are not. He shown far too much interest in preserving his own skin till now to do himself any harm. Let him fend a while. It's about time he take care of himself, do some cooking and cleaning for once, start to clear up his own messes. Did you get bread?'

'Marianne dropping it by. You said you wanted to check on her so I asked for delivery.'

'*Mi vida*, thank you, that was thoughtful. Annie still putting her through hell. Every time I see either of them they're just a picture of misery.'

Saul handed Moz the board of chopped dill, which she sprinkled with satisfaction into the soup. A moment later there was a knock on the half-open door and Marianne Goss appeared, holding up a *pan de siete cielos* in a string bag. This was a festival centrepiece, a special-occasion bread of intricate, layered braiding, and a little ladder ascending up one side of the loaf. Moz had not known Marianne to make it for years, and certainly there was no need for such extravagance this evening. Marianne was not a picture of misery. Instead she looked radiant, smiling as Moz had rarely seen her.

'Your ears burning, we just said your name this moment. *Kerida*, you look like someone dipped you in sunshine. Tell us!'

'I been speaking to Ruth, in England.' Marianne was almost breathless and, usually taciturn, an unaccustomed flow of words came tumbling out. 'Oh, Miss Moz, it is so wonderful, just hearing her voice like that. She was telling me what she's been doing, how she's feeling, all about Alex at school, and her living in Slough, meals she's cooked, and walking alone to do her shopping. Out! Carrying shopping! She's Ruth again, she's *back*.'

Moz opened her arms and, without hesitation, Marianne flew into them. As a rule Marianne was not tactile, and had not been even as a child, Moz remembered, but this new joy had altered everything. The two held one another and rocked. If anyone deserved this new beginning it was Marianne Goss, and Ruth dos Santos. As they pulled apart, Moz dabbed at her eyes with the corner of her cotton apron and looked to Marianne to continue.

'I knew the doctors thought it had gone well, you know, because Dan been emailing with the surgeon who said the actual operation was a success. But then she had those few very hard weeks just after, in hospital, and I couldn't speak to her and her recovery was so slow, and feeling awful while they changed her medication – tapering, they called it – but Dan said it must have felt like cold turkey, with what little they have let her have. And the truth is I never really thought she could get better. Never. Once we got her on the boat I thought, well, there's a chance. But it's been so long, all the kids' lives she's been unwell. It seemed impossible, I didn't actually believe anyone could help her.'

Moz pulled out a chair for Marianne to sit, but Marianne had too much energy to stay still and merely stepped forward, resting her hands on the back of it, drumming her fingers lightly. 'She went today for more pictures taken of her insides, a scan, but she don't need it really, she says, she knows she's better. Nothing hurting, nothing . . . everything fixed now. Her body just needs to get used to being without all that medicine, and she's so brave, she's doing it, now those first hard weeks are behind her – the shakes and headaches and all – she says she knows she can. She got no pain, that's the thing, that surgery was like magic. She's eating, she told me so many things she's tried. Whitebait! You ever heard of that? She's putting meat on her bones!'

Watching her with pleasure, Moz thought: *the girl is alight with love. Ruth has been her true mother, the second mother she lost, and now Ruth has come back to her.*

'She'll come home to Tuga her old self, I reckon,' Marianne went on. She picked up the huge egg-washed loaf and slipped the net bag off it, laying the bread carefully at the centre of their kitchen table and smiling down. 'And Annie will see her and she'll understand why Ruth and Alex had to go. Don't you think? Ruth whole again, and so Annie will see, and understand, finally.'

'You had no choice but to send Alex,' said Moz firmly. She had said this before, but it bore repeating. 'It would have been wickedness to waste that school place, and you weren't to know Ruth would get better after the operation, either, as you said. You couldn't keep Alex here just for Annie and she'll see that soon enough. You did a generous thing sending him, *kerida*.' Moz patted her hand. 'Oh, this is a good day. A good, good day.'

Here she allowed herself a quick glance at Saul. He too was beaming at Marianne, but his eyes swam with tears that she understood were joy and sorrow mingled.

Ruth dos Santos had been Saul's patient for decades, but this transformative surgery had not been at his instigation, rather at physiotherapist Katie Salmon's. Ruth, after a decade lost to agoraphobia and addiction, had now been entirely liberated by one simple off-island NHS referral – Saul would take the implications of it hard, Moz knew, and she could not lift it from his shoulders, though she suffered for him. It was his, and he must bear it.

He had been one man, overstretched, overtired. But the truth was that Saul had slipped. The truth was that he hadn't grasped the extent of the long-term physical damage exacted by Ruth's giving birth to Alex. Fiercely private, Ruth and Marianne had kept him at arm's length from their little household, managing Ruth's post-partum incontinence and the resulting opiate dependence without letting him approach too close, and a pattern had established over the years that he had neither examined, nor disrupted. Ruth said only that she had crippling back pain and he had allowed her to convince him, and had asked no further questions, or not the right ones. Shame had kept Ruth silent, but Saul should have paid closer attention. Several nights recently Moz had woken to discover the bed beside her empty and had risen to find Saul sitting on the kitchen step, looking out over the dark garden, smoking an expensive imported cigarette, the packet stale by many years, and for which he would have harangued a patient unendurably. (No one was allowed to court lung damage on an island without an oncology department. Although there sat the entire oncology department, smoking.) It was Ruth dos Santos that Moz sensed beside him on those nights, a silent reproach. It was a failure that shadowed his retirement, and shadowed all those many, many years of good. But Ruth was better, and Moz hoped he might start to forgive himself.

'Come eat with us, *kerida*,' Saul said now, speaking for the first time since Marianne had burst in upon them. 'We have an appropriate bread for celebrations, I see.'

'I couldn't help it, I made one for me and Annie too. Oh, Dr Gabbai, and she's coming back Island Open.' Marianne actually clapped her hands in delight. 'Ruth will be back for Santa Esterica! Thank you, but I will go home to my angry child.'

She smiled ruefully, and took her leave. Even Annie could not dent her pleasure today. If her own mothering was proving a challenge, for the first time in a long time, she herself had been fortified by a mother's love.

When Marianne had gone, Moz came to stand quietly behind her husband, placing a warm hand on each shoulder.

'Well, *mi vida*,' she said softly. 'That is some good news.'

He reached up and placed his hands over hers.

'I should have sent her years ago.'

'You didn't know.'

He tipped his head back to look at her, and she bent to kiss his forehead.

'I should have known.'

'Maybe so,' said Moz, after a moment, straightening. 'But you did what you could in good faith. And what matters is, she's better. And that family who've been through all they've been through can do some healing. Now –' she picked up the dropped thread of their earlier conversation '– what about my plan to get that FFA harlot teaching grammar?'

'Garrick won't like that one bit. That woman in the school, meeting everyone. Being conspicuous.'

'Well, I'd say Garrick's days of proclaiming right and wrong are over,' said Moz firmly. The broth-softened carrots and tender meat were safely in the fridge, base components of tomorrow's coconut curry. For now she brought a fresh ramekin of butter to the table and sat, not across, but close beside him. Marianne's loaf was still hot from the oven, and steam escaped when Saul broke apart the elaborately decorated crust. He felt the comfort of his wife's solid presence.

'I should have known to send her,' he said again.

'Let's talk after supper,' said Moz softly. 'I promise, I won't go letting you off the hook. Hair shirts later, if you like. But pull up the drawbridge now.'

The drawbridge was old code between them. It was time to set aside anything that lay outside and to retreat, just for a moment, into the fortified castle of their marriage. He had always loved her broad shoulders, but on them he sometimes saw the weight of the entire island, their Atlas. She too needed care, however impossible she might find it to admit. He reached to take his wife's hand. Later he would be her sounding board as she fretted about Annie Goss, and he would do his best not to burden her further with his own, persistent guilt.

But for now, just for now, no shop talk. No outside sorrows. The two of them, two old lovers, eating chicken soup.

17

Working conditions on Tuga de Oro had never been perfect. The vet's room still held an odd jumble of antique branding irons and forceps; one shelf was nothing but cases and cases of autoclave indicator tape – why so much? – while still missing a ready supply of the most basic essentials like Agriject needles, and arm-length gloves. A third of the orders that Charlotte had placed never came. When she needed medication she often had to take it from the doctors' pharmacy, and each time estimate how much of the drug Dan's patients might need in a worst-case scenario. With the island closed, everyone in the clinic was conservative with stock, but for Charlotte in particular it was only ethical to proceed with a treatment if she felt certain it would not imperil humans.

But navigating all these challenges felt positively straightforward compared to this new set-up, her mother permanently installed at her computer like the world's least helpful office secretary, typing with excessive force, sighing a lot, composing emails to her own PA and clerks in London, and managing simultaneously to denigrate whatever Charlotte happened to be doing despite a manifest lack of qualification or interest. An elegant, scathing homunculus sitting in judgement, and in an increasingly eccentric series of outfits, composed with hand-embroidered or crocheted items bought, on credit, in the gift shop. It had been a mistake to admit that the clinic computers had the island's fastest internet connection (although everything was relative).

'I'm not having luck with cruise liners,' Lucinda said, drumming her long fingernails on the desk, as if in the past she had commanded Atlantic sea traffic with far greater success. Today she was wearing her own shirt tucked into a pair of very light white cotton drawstring trousers, which Charlotte was fairly sure were usually worn by the fishermen as underwear. 'I think my next port of call, as it were, is to get Evangeline to look into the naval schedules.'

'What?' said Charlotte, distracted. She had a patient, a big old German shepherd named Cookie, who needed a number of stitches removed from a recent surgery. Luckily the owners had dropped him off at the garden gate, so she had no need to explain the installation of Lucinda.

Cookie regarded Charlotte woefully from within the humiliation of his post-surgical Elizabethan cone. It had been, the dog's expression told her, a trying time.

'Four more,' she told him. 'Navel gazing?' she asked Lucinda eventually, pinching another suture knot with tweezers and lifting it slightly so she could work the sharp tip of surgical scissors into the tiny gap. 'Three more.'

'Nav*al*. Pertaining to the navy. If another helpful idiot tells me about the danger of the sea this season I shall scream, but it's my belief that an aircraft carrier would not need to approach too closely in order to dispatch a helicopter. There is *Up Yard* –' to depreciate her increasing familiarity with the island Lucinda had developed a habit of enunciating all Tugan place names as if they had the words 'so called' silently appended to them '– on which I believe one might safely land a Wildcat, for example.'

'No cats allowed on Tuga, I'm afraid,' said Charlotte, pleased with her own joke. Lucinda frowned. 'It's a good thought,' Charlotte added quickly, conciliatory. It was true. She found this – entirely fantastical – idea to be compelling, and gave herself over to it for a moment. A Wildcat descending in a whirl of propellers and she might climb aboard, safely enclosed in sound and metal, and simply – lift off. She would escape from the sordid embarrassment of Garrick. She could escape from Levi Mendoza. She would be swept away from the grave, tired eyes of Nicola Davenport, whose beautiful calf Charlotte felt fairly sure she had killed by failing to remember its existence until it was dangerously ill, irrevocably dehydrated, weakened beyond salvation.

Lacie had died within hours of her visit. Nicola had still pressed a jar of mango jam into Charlotte's resistant hands as a thank you for her belated, useless attendance. Teenage Chloe had stood behind her mother in their sparse kitchen, red-eyed and silent, her lower lip trembling. And Nicola had taken her daughter's hand and said firmly, as if on behalf of both of them, that there was nothing anyone could have done, that sometimes these things happened. Charlotte sensed that Chloe knew this rang hollow. Lacie had died of delay and veterinary negligence, and this family who had so little now had less. She experienced something like vertigo, whenever she thought of it. In a helicopter she would rise high above the scene of all her recent most egregious crimes, foremost of which, she felt, had been the crime of engaging too intimately with human animals. It never went well.

'The thing is, even the massive naval ships don't pass within a hundred miles of here in hurricane season. I don't think Lars can be a very experienced sailor if he agreed to do it in a little yacht.'

'He got me here in one piece, didn't he? God. Well, assuming there is even a shred of truth to your entirely unsupportive pessimism, what is the next best option?'

'Trade someone for a berth on the Island Open ship. Or Lars comes back. At Island Open.'

Lucinda slammed down her palm on the desk, and Cookie let out a volley of deep barks.

'Ugh, control that beast. I have had just about enough of your negativity. Rather than endless naysaying, how about thanking me for putting time and ingenuity into escaping this hellhole?'

Charlotte bent to settle Cookie, allowing the dog to cover her face with licks while Lucinda's back was turned. She couldn't help but feel a twinge of sympathy with her mother, or indeed any new FFA, encountering for the first time the absolute limitations of isolated island life. Lucinda Compton-Neville QC had managed to find the only conceivable means of getting onshore in Island Close. But however audacious (albeit appalling), it was not a trick that would work a second time. With all her privilege, financial wherewithal, connections and absolute self-belief, eventually she would come to understand that freedom of movement was now impossible. She was here until the island opened, eight weeks away.

'Submarine? There might even be one already lurking about within a few miles, how would anyone know? Imagine the bliss of it, we could just – submerge and be gone, and your hefting po-faced customs officer would be left waving her stamp pad at an empty ocean. What's her name? Elspeth?'

Charlotte's initial laughter at the thought of a submarine ceased in a sudden contraction of panic. She had neglected a scouring calf, and it had died. And now, between the drama with Lucinda and the drama with Levi, she had entirely forgotten to check on Elsie's lizard.

18

Elsie lived in a shack she'd built herself, far out, on the track that ran up to the Boatmen's Memorial. It had pallet-wood walls, beautifully painted, and a corrugated-metal roof which one day, Elsie had told Charlotte, she would upgrade to corrugated plastic, to increase Hilary's indoor-light exposure. It waited only for the right piece of plastic to come free. Charlotte had been struck over and over by the modesty of Tugan dwellings but she found Elsie's particularly poignant, a single room not much bigger than the bed itself. The loo was in a separate shed, on the far side of a neat dirt yard. A table and three mismatched chairs were outside at the front, and round the back was an outdoor tap with a rubber shower attachment, screened by sugar cane.

The shack door stood open and Charlotte could hear a voice inside, soft and low, speaking in a tone of tender intimacy.

'Just a bite, *kerida*. Come on, one bite for Elsie.'

Charlotte knocked and Elsie looked up, startled. She was holding a slice of banana on her palm before a huge, sleek lizard with elaborately swagged jowls. Hilary was the size of a Jack Russell, with a long, tapering tail that reached almost the length of the single bed on which she lay. She had recently shed her skin, and was the rich dark red of a boiled lobster.

Charlotte knelt and began gently to examine the listless animal. A healthy adult red tegu could reach twenty-two kilos; Charlotte estimated Hilary was heavier, due to Elsie's relentless overfeeding, and now this – a grossly enlarged abdomen. There was one obvious possibility, and Charlotte didn't like it.

'My guess,' she said slowly, trying to dredge her memory for college lectures, and then realised that the word 'guess' was not very reassuring and started again, 'my first instinct, I should say, is that she's egg-bound. It is quite a common problem in captive female lizards. At one stage of ovulation or another the process can get a bit stuck, and we need to help them along. First things first: I'd like to bring her in for an X-ray, so I'll go back now and get it ready.' She remembered seeing Elsie riding with Hilary held upright against her chest like an oversized baby in a sling, the lizard peering over Elsie's shoulder, and surveying the road as they left it behind. 'I'll find Taxi to come for you, so she doesn't have to go on the bike.'

Elsie gave a quick, stoical nod.

Readying the X-ray in fact meant checking the coast was clear, so that Dan Zekri would not discover that she was sneaking a reptile the size of a suitcase into the precious human X-ray suite. He had so far permitted veterinary access when it was absolutely unavoidable, understanding that the welfare of a farm animal like a working dog was essential to the welfare of the family who owned it. But a pet lizard with no practical use, possibly illegal and almost certainly infected with a veritable catalogue of viruses, did not seem likely to evoke his generosity of spirit. His brief tenure as chief medical officer had thus far been heavy weather. He would not want to risk a salmonella outbreak, particularly not one that actually originated within the clinic. Which was ridiculous,

Charlotte thought, immediately indignant before they'd even had the conversation, because she herself would take responsibility for disinfecting it afterwards and she'd almost certainly leave the room more sanitary than she found it. The clinic's long-standing cleaner, Queenie Lindo-Smith, was not exactly fastidious.

Half an hour later, the familiar diesel judder of a hackney cab announced that Taxi was outside the clinic, delivering Elsie and the patient.

'I drove nice and slow,' Taxi told Charlotte. He took off his cap and stood in the doorway looking appropriately sombre, and official. 'No one wants jostling about, do they, if they've a bellyful of swellings.'

Still, despite Taxi's care, the journey seemed to have cost Hilary what little energy remained. Elsie carried her in strong arms and laid her tenderly on the examination table where she remained, ominously still, without need of restraint.

'There are two types of egg-binding,' Charlotte explained. 'If it is post-ovulatory, this animal has run out of calcium and energy just at the final hurdle, but it's nearly there, and we can just give it a boost with a nice big calcium injection. Or even better, calcium with a touch of oxytocin, if Dan's got a bit to spare, and she'll pass these eggs by herself after that. That's what we're hoping for. Can you hold her like this? Yes, just like that. I'll get you the lead apron.'

Elsie's big hands were shaking.

'What's the other one?'

The other one, Charlotte didn't like to say, would be a nightmare for any inexperienced vet, let alone on Tuga de Oro.

'Pre-ovulatory follicular stasis. She can't pass those. I'd

need to take them out for her, quite urgently. But let's hope we don't have to cross that bridge.'

Elsie placed a protective hand on either side of the lizard's swollen belly.

'But if we do?'

'If we do, the idea would be to remove all the follicles and the ovaries with them, and that would hopefully guard against the same problem recurring again in the future. Not always, as interestingly if you aren't careful to excise absolutely everything then lizard ovaries can actually regenerate—' *Oh, shut up, Charlotte,* she said to herself suddenly, seeing the panic rise on Elsie's face.

'But without her ovaries? She'd never . . .'

Had Elsie hoped for another customs seizure? A handsome, glossy red male, jowls like a bulldog, with a friendly disposition and a good sense of humour? Watching Elsie struggle with something unarticulated, Charlotte wondered. But while the island would overlook a single animal, not even the customs officer could accumulate imported and potentially invasive species.

'They're not native,' she said gently. 'You could never have bred her.'

Elsie squared her shoulders and lifted her chin, and gave a quick, stiff nod, but huge silent tears still rolled down her cheeks. Hilary would not live forever. One day Elsie would again be alone.

19

It was pre-ovulatory follicular stasis: urgent; complex; life-threatening. Charlotte would have to operate. There was bleak comfort in the reality that without intervention, the animal would certainly die. Operating – even ineptly, Charlotte told herself – at least offered Hilary a chance.

There was a sharp knock, and Katie Salmon popped her head in.

'I heard you'd a lizard problem. Need an assistant?'

This was to Charlotte. Then Katie saw Elsie's face, and without waiting for invitation she pushed in and took Elsie's hand.

'We've not really spoken. I'm Katie, I know you're Elsie Smith and you keep everything running around here. Oh, you poor thing, you feel rotten. She's in good hands with Dr Walker.' Katie put a small arm around Elsie's broad shoulders. 'How long is it going to take? Why don't we go to the Rockhopper for a saloop?'

'Everything with reptiles is slow,' Charlotte told her. 'Hours and hours. Most of the day.' Then she had a sudden flash of inspiration, seeing tiny muscled Katie beside big muscled Elsie. 'What about a hike? Or a swim?'

'Oh, I'm desperate to climb Thursday's Peak,' said Katie

instantly, and Charlotte shot her a grateful look. 'And people keep telling me FFA aren't allowed without a Tugan.'

Elsie brightened, fractionally. 'I could take you up Thursday's Peak. It's proper risky climbing there.'

'Fabulous,' said Charlotte, and hustled them out of the door, closing it firmly. Elsie would be taken care of, indefatigably. Meanwhile Charlotte had lost her only chance of a surgical assistant.

Alone together, Charlotte and the lizard regarded one another.

'I will do my best not to kill you,' Charlotte promised, and imagined a sceptical expression crossing Hilary's baleful face. She drew up a cocktail of ketamine, medetomidine and butorphanol, and now realised she would have appreciated both Katie and Elsie's strength to restrain a powerful animal during an intramuscular injection that would probably not be greatly enjoyed. But here she was. She sterilised a patch of Hilary's thigh, and then clamped her hand over the thick neck. With the other hand she awkwardly stabbed the needle into the scales, relieved to discover Hilary so lethargic that she barely reacted. The tegu slumped, unconscious, now a dead weight. Charlotte flipped her with difficulty and regarded the soft pale underbelly, the four legs thrown apart in the unpromising pancake pose of roadkill. Then she opened the enormous mouth and warily fed a stiff tube down into the trachea, and taped it into place. She began to pack the warm sandbags around the limp body, covering the extended limbs with more towels, tucking Hilary in as if a bedtime story were to follow. Then she sterilised the belly, taped a tissue drape in place, and the panic truly began to rise. This was it.

20

There was a knock on the door.

'No,' shouted Charlotte, scrambling to her feet. She had been cross-legged on the floor, staring dolefully at the inert body of the lizard, now supposedly in recovery. The surgery was long over, Hilary had not stirred, and the room was so hot that Charlotte had stripped off to bra and shorts. 'Who is it?'

'Dan. Everything all right?'

Charlotte rose and went to unlock the door, tugging a T-shirt over her head. Dan strode in with confidence, saw the exam table and reared back.

'*Guay de mi*, what on earth is that?'

'Hilary. She didn't bleed to death which is actually a triumph but still, I'm fairly sure I've killed her. Come in. Join me, in my pit of doom.'

Dan stayed where he was.

'Well, at least shut the door, don't let the heat out. Don't worry, she's highly unlikely to do you any damage in this state.'

'Why *is* it so hot in here?'

'Hilary's metabolism. She'll never wake up if I don't get the medication circulating properly, and my sandbags have cooled.' She peered morosely at her patient. 'Her heart's still going all right, but she's not exactly peppy, is she.'

Dan closed the door behind him and inched closer, rolling up his sleeves. His eyes remained fixed on the operating table.

'I can't let her come round up there, she'll be all discombobulated and she'll fall off, but she's bloody heavy and I don't want to tear her stitches, flopping her about. I didn't think that part through.' Charlotte returned to her position, slumped on the floor with her back to the wall. She regarded the tegu with disgust. 'She'll feel rubbish when she comes round, and they can wake up aggressive. Don't look so worried, it'll be hours. Unless I've killed it and it's dead.'

Dan inspected the lifeless lizard.

'It doesn't look on top form,' he admitted, 'but herpetology's outside my remit.'

He sat down beside Charlotte.

'And to be honest, I am not exactly knocking it out of the park with the humans, at the moment.'

'Give them time. They just need to get used to you being in charge.'

'They think I'm a cad and a reprobate.'

'Well. You did move Katie all the way here and then chuck her. And you did punch someone at your own appointment ceremony.'

'Those were highly unusual circumstances,' Dan said, defensive, but a flush began to creep up his neck.

'What about me?' Charlotte demanded. 'I killed a calf by quite literally forgetting about it, and now I've almost certainly murdered the love of Elsie's life.'

'I'd have helped you, I could have been your anaesthetist.'

'Do you mean that?'

'No,' Dan said cheerfully. 'But I can say it now that it's over and I don't have to touch that dragon.'

'You're going to have to, I need you to help me get her down. Please? Before she wakes and falls.'

'Tail end only,' Dan said eventually. 'Only for you would I find myself doing something like this.'

They stood up, and together they laid the unconscious animal on a clean sheet on the floor. Dan washed his hands in Hibiscrub for an excessively long time. Then, having overcome his initial queasiness, he began to peer over the incision.

'Tell me about these stitches?'

'You have to go under the scales, lift them up like that. Like a seam on a crocodile handbag. Hence that funny mountain range, now. Isn't she beautiful?'

'Charlotte, she's hideous.'

'Don't say that! She can hear you. I hope.'

'Well, your work looks great, at least.' He glanced at the ancient vaporiser. 'And medics aren't often called upon to DIY an entire ventilator from a –' he looked closer '– a Fanta lid.'

'Want to see something?' Charlotte held out a stainless-steel dish in which lay the lizard's ovary: bright orange glossy follicles, like a dish of gargantuan baked beans. 'Look at all these.'

'*Streuth*. Well, she'll feel better with those out.'

'If she's not dead.'

'If she's not dead.'

'And yet, do you know, sitting on the –' Charlotte looked around '– admittedly not very clean floor of a consulting room that is probably fifty-seven thousand degrees centigrade and waiting for the ketamine to run out of an Argentinian tegu is still more peaceful than being out there, with my mother at large. Also, the general fiasco of my personal life.'

'Ah. Not going well with Mendoza?' said Dan evenly.

Charlotte shook her head and to her dismay felt a lump form in her throat. She busied herself with the instrument tray. If Dan was feeling sorry for her, perhaps it was the right moment to risk a small confession.

'I have to tell you something,' she said softly, and he looked up, his expression altered. She rushed on before she lost her nerve. 'I put Hilary in the X-ray machine.'

For a moment Dan looked wrong-footed, as if he had expected her to say something entirely different. Then he threw back his head and laughed, and the slight tension, which had shimmered into being in the silence between them, dispersed. Behind them came a faint scraping noise, and Charlotte spun around. The lizard was not dead. The lizard was waking up.

21

Saul drove the long way round to the Breaks, stopping at Papasiegas to pick for Moz a branch of the wild red lychees she claimed were sweeter than the paler, larger fruits she cultivated in her own back garden. On this circuitous route he passed not a soul, apart from the one person whose arrival had led to this calamity – the vet, Dr Charlotte Walker, presumably on her way to visit her tortoises in the jungle interior.

Charlotte was on a stationary donkey, peering up into the canopy with a pair of binoculars, and wearing a distinctive floral bucket hat that Saul recognised as belonging to Levi Mendoza, which she snatched off at the sound of his approaching car. Now she called out a *paz* and raised her hand, holding the crumpled hat.

As their eyes met she smiled at Saul and for a fleeing moment there they were, Garrick's dimples, and the lines of Garrick's features lightly traced within her own. The resemblance shocked Saul over and over, for the girl had been here a year and no one had ever noticed. But then, why would they? Father and daughter. Their relationship remained unfathomable.

Saul decided to abandon the clinic Land Rover just past Out the Way beach and to walk the rest of the way along the coast. He had the idea that the sound of an engine might scare his brother-in-law into further retreat and the truth was, he still had no idea what he would say once he arrived. Garrick had compounded the greatest island scandal in decades by going, in the universal tradition of disgraced public figures, into hiding – the difference being that on Tuga, everyone still knew precisely where he was. Maintaining the illusion of his solitude was itself a collaborative act.

The Breaks were Tuga de Oro's collective holiday huts, a row of simple pallet-wood shacks arranged in a semicircle above the beach of the lagoon, the rough boards printed at irregular intervals with BUCKNALL & PORTEOUS INTERNATIONAL, a name as close to deity as possible on a declaredly secular island, for Bucknall & Porteous was the Tugan shipping agent, responsible for all arriving and departing cargo. There were other clusters of holiday homes on the western beaches, but Garrick, Joan, Moz and Saul had always liked these Breaks the most, for the looming *montaña* was invisible behind them, it was close enough to hike to the waterfall, and from the thick shell pathway one looked out over turquoise water so still and clear that one could track the shadowed stingrays as they glided, close to shore.

The shacks themselves were not weatherproof, and in them one could not leave much more than some enamel cookware and a stack of drinking glasses. Instead, at the far end of the row, now entirely hidden behind tall fronded sugar canes, the community had long ago constructed a corrugated-metal shed, and here each family stored their particular holiday possessions on labelled shelves. Moz and Joan kept shared tins of spices and coffee, Garrick and Saul some whisky, and a tiffin tin of tagua-seed dominoes. The Breaks was where families came to vacation, to get away from it all. They were three miles, as the crow flies, from the hustle and bustle of Town.

Someone had been staying in the smallest hut at the end, for there were ashes heaped in the fire pit, and on a washing line strung between two date palms were hung the components of one complete outfit: a man's white shirt, white socks, navy blue trousers, and a respectably large pair of green underpants. A great many garnet-coloured hibiscus flowers had been laid out to dry in the sun across a plastic table, while more soaked in a small, dented aluminium saucepan at the fire's edge.

The stingrays were not in evidence, and instead Garrick was visible in the middle of the lagoon, apparently naked, and in a very dirty pink baseball cap from which wet, iron-grey curls straggled, and a beard that was burgeoning into eccentricity. He had a fresh banana-leaf basket on his back (poorly woven, Saul could see even at this distance) and held aloft a long hand-whittled spear. Saul watched him for a time, arrested in indecision, but Garrick did not move or appear to know that anyone observed him, and eventually Saul sat down in a white plastic picnic chair in order to unlace his boots. Then he took off his own clothes and hung them over the washing line, and waded out into the lagoon, calling out as he drew close, 'Nice spear, *badjanak*.'

Garrick glanced at the object in his hand as if only just seeing it. Saul looked down through the clear water, noticing, beside his own entirely naked form, Garrick had in fact fashioned himself some sort of loincloth out of a lavender-sprigged bedsheet.

'Hope there's nothing here that bites. Done well?'

Garrick tilted his basket to display a single blue-grey trowelfish.

'Bony.'

'Perfectly serviceable.'

'Or you could just come home for a chicken curry. Moz got five kilos of basmati from the last boat.'

'I am in moral exile,' said Garrick pompously. 'I'm not coming back for basmati, or anything else.'

'Nobody's exiled you. You self-exiled. Everybody had—' Here Saul searched for something to say that would not be inflammatory, already regretting his use of the word 'everybody'. 'We had a shock. You've got to allow us a shock, *haver*. It's shocking.'

'Is that what you've come to say?'

'No. I've not come to judge, I've come to listen. We all just want to know how you are.'

Garrick had remained as still as marble while Saul spoke these words, his eyes cast down through the water, their four sturdy ankles and bare feet visible. Garrick did not reply, but a flicker beneath the surface and then a stirring of the sand became the sure presence of a gliding ray. Garrick's arm came down, the spear driven straight beside him like a king's sceptre as he makes a decree. When the spear came up it lifted with it the small stingray, wings flapping in protest, pale white belly and gasping mouth exposed. Garrick extended his catch to Saul who drew it off with two hands, and stuffed the fish into the open basket. Garrick then turned and began to wade back towards the shore.

'Well, that's better,' Saul said, with some satisfaction on Garrick's behalf. 'That's a better dinner.'

Garrick made no answer and Saul began to feel irritated by his own conciliatory tone, by how far he had travelled and was still travelling, hurrying after Garrick, who appeared now to have styled himself some sort of rustic holy man, thereby elevating his sin to the realms of the spiritual instead of what it was, common or garden adultery on a business trip. Outside the Breaks Saul dried himself with his own shirt and restored his underwear and shorts, to regain some authority.

Garrick set down his basket and bent over the table, checking his hibiscus flowers. They were apparently dried to his satisfaction and he swept them into an enamel pie dish, clearing the table to gut the fish.

'You say you don't come to judge. You should.'

Garrick was cutting out the ray's liver, checking it for health. It was a beautiful pink, and so he laid it in a bowl and began to remove the wings. Where had all this competence been, these last decades? Saul couldn't remember Garrick cooking a meal in living memory. All of a sudden he was Robinson Crusoe.

'I dishonoured my marriage vows. And when Joan wanted more than anything to be a mother, I fathered a child by somebody else. I've made a mockery of my position on the island as any sort of moral authority. My rectitude is of vital importance to my flock.'

'But – hold on.' It was surprising, Saul felt, how quickly his own compassion had shrivelled in the face of this self-flagellation. *You've managed just fine being a bloody hypocrite till you were found out*, Saul thought, in Moz's voice. Aloud he went on, 'You didn't know about Charlotte's birth, but you knew you'd gone to bed with her mother in London. And it hasn't stopped you, until now, being a *moral authority*.' He added, more conciliatory, 'And in fact it hasn't stopped you helping so many others, all these years. I suppose what I'm saying is, you are an intellectual leader and you work hard for your congregation, and this will require great humility.'

'No,' said Garrick. There were red lights in his beard, together with the grey. 'Do you know, I have achieved the impossible. I am actually glad Joan is dead.'

Saul lowered his head. Compassion returned, and pity with it. Garrick had done something unforgivable, it was true. But there could be no doubt he was paying for it.

'I have brought shame upon myself, shame upon her, shame upon the community, and had she been alive I cannot—' He stopped himself. 'I'll have to leave the island. I've been in touch with the Center for Humanistic Spirituality in Chicago. I'll need a berth, and as soon as I can book one I'll go.'

'Look at you, man. You wouldn't last five minutes in Chicago! Chicago is – is, wind! Crime! Pizza!'

Here Saul petered out, knowing nothing more of Chicago than these three nouns. Garrick said nothing.

'So they've offered you a job, have they? The Center for Humanistic Spirituality in Chicago.'

'No, as a matter of fact. They replied immediately to say they had no vacancies, and in fact no availability to meet. But in the absence of any other options I felt it best to apply again in person.'

'Are you going to tell me what actually happened?'

'I betrayed my wife. I spent two nights with a stranger, and I was a stranger too, to myself. That was what it was. Two nights – I went back. Not one, Saul, two. I sinned.'

'For forty years you've preached against the very concept of sin. I'm not defending you, by the way. In any case how could I, when till now you haven't trusted me with anything but bare facts? But the reality is that – by a whisker, I grant you, Joan did not know. She died without any idea of this. The suffering is yours now. Joan is not suffering, you are.'

Garrick was silent a long time. Saul waited.

Eventually, Garrick said, 'Do you remember when Joan went to London all those years ago? It was a few years after . . . after all this. Her beloved aunt had died, and then

I had this idea – that she might have been to see a doctor. That someone in London might have fixed whatever had been going so wrong for her. Put an end to all those – false starts.'

'Miscarriages,' said Saul, who preferred direct language wherever possible, though Tugan medical practice frequently required extensive delicacy and euphemism. There had been six miscarriages, as he remembered it. Maybe seven. The last two the hardest in every sense: late, extended, dangerous.

'I thought perhaps you had put her in touch with someone there.' Garrick looked at Saul directly, for the first time, and Saul saw that the whites of his eyes were bloodshot. *Insomnia?* Saul wondered, reflexively diagnosing. *Allergic reaction? Crying?* 'Because she came back – she came back to me, in a sense, after that trip. So I guessed that was what happened, that someone had fixed something and it was finally safe for us to have a baby. And the irony of course was that she never again got pregnant, but at least we were . . . ' He frowned, pulling at his new beard.

Saul found he very much did not wish to discuss Joan's trip to London with Garrick. Instead he gestured at the flowers, the pan by the remains of the fire, the dish of dried petals like a potpourri. Long-ago Scout camps tugged at his memory.

'*Guay de mi*, that's not—'

'Ink, yes.'

'There's a biro on the Davenports' shelf, *haver*. Making ink is a hair shirt too far.'

'I am not a thief,' said Garrick, haughty. 'I'm drafting an open letter to the congregation. I brought a notebook with me but in my haste I found I'd forgotten a pen.' He opened a large black lined notebook, showing to Saul the red-ink quill scratchings of a lunatic. Saul found a pen of his own clipped to his shirt pocket, still hanging on the line. He gave this to Garrick, and placed a hand on his shoulder.

'Better make it a sermon. Come on, *badjanak*, it's time. Tomorrow is the Island Council public meeting, and you are head of Island Council. It's the right time, everyone will be there, and you need to face the music with dignity, get it over and done with. You can't stay here forever. Mac and Mac's Rachel have invited all their lot down here for their anniversary next weekend anyway. Write what you need to say, and then stand up and say it. Our ultimate authority is human conscience, Garrick – those are your words, and you're always on about it; that is the humanistic essence, isn't it? You've carried something heavy all these years. Set it down now, and make it as right as you can with the living. I'll stay with you while you write, and we'll go back together in the morning, you can read it aloud at the meeting. Then the worst will be over. Come on.'

Garrick made a noise in the back of his throat.

'Also, we'll need full representation in order to vote tomorrow. The current vet is pitching for permanent funding to hire a replacement veterinarian, after her own departure.'

Years of medical practice had honed his deadpan delivery. Still, that last sentence had been a challenge.

'The current vet,' Garrick repeated. 'You need me to vote on the plans of *the current vet*.'

'We do. Go on. I'll build the fire back, let's get that fish cooking.' Saul unzipped his backpack and took out two Tupperware boxes. 'Moz sent these, as well.'

'What's that?' asked Garrick, with some suspicion.

Saul disappeared into the shed, in search of chilli flakes.

'Chicken curry,' he called back, 'and a bit of coconut rice.'

22

It was Dan's first meeting as a member of Island Council, and a rare opportunity to be statesmanlike in public and thereby to redeem himself before Tuga's redoubtable matrons. He read through the agenda yet again, determined to acquit himself with calm and reassuring authority. There were four and a half other members of council: Garrick Williams, as Island Minister; Vitali Mendoza representing Conch Island; young Zimbul Fairclough, newly appointed on behalf of the moshav; and finally Oluchi Thomas, for the fishing interests. The half was a seat left permanently empty for Ruth dos Santos, who had not been well enough to occupy it for more than a decade but (rumour had it) would soon be returning, full-force.

Council met in private once a fortnight, but these bigger public meetings came only once a season. They were held in the large ballroom of Customs House, the councillors seated in a semicircle on a low stage, beneath a photograph of King George VI, taken on a visit to the island in 1947. It showed him standing somewhat stiffly beside an already fully grown Martha, long the beloved charge of Grand Mary's grandmother. Martha had been painted for the occasion, somewhat regrettably, and the image showed her huge domed shell dark-striped with a Union Jack, a decision mercifully muted by the sepia.

Looking out, Dan saw standing room only, and not much of it. Whole families had assembled on the benches at the back and against the panelled walls, and at the front a group of teenagers sat in a close ring on the floor, a bag of fresh walnuts spilling open between them. In the back row the Spencer sisters were knitting with tiny quick needles: beautiful fine-wool scarves to sell in the post office gift shop, winter wear for which the islanders themselves could find no possible use in their endless tropical sunshine. Further forward, Anwuli and Isadora were embroidering opposite sides of a tablecloth, their hoops close together, heads bent. Walter Lindo-Smith stood against a side wall, whittling what looked to be a mermaid. Mac and Mac's Rachel were sitting further back than they would have liked, but Katie advised that chairs with firm support were best for Mac's stiff hip, precluding the benches at the front. There was Katie, in fact; cross-legged on a heavy table against the wall, neat and nimble as a leprechaun, beneath an oil painting of a young Princess Alice in a pair of blue Tugan conch-pearl earrings. The island had gifted the earrings to the princess; Queen Victoria had gifted the painting to the island. The crowd rustled with the news that Saul had coaxed the pastor home the previous night. Possibly they'd come out in force to vote on the proposed expenses, but more likely Tugans had come to clap eyes on their philandering minister.

Garrick visiting their sick, or joining the others to help unload cargo or process the crab catch: that was one minister. Garrick hectoring from the pulpit each Wednesday was another, and it was this minister with whom they now took issue. He had implored Tugans to examine their consciences; he had preached at them every Wednesday evening about their ethical development, about humility, about social and indeed planetary responsibilities, and about many other worthy but fatiguing concepts that had, week after week, kept them longer from their suppers than felt seemly. He had made them feel small for their petty deceits and failings, from up there on what had appeared an excessively high horse. It remained to be seen if they would forgive his own, far grander mistake, as they might forgive themselves.

Betsey leaned forward across Taxi to address Sylvester, picking up a conversation begun weeks earlier, and continued on their brief walk here.

'I says, where you've an islander you've a secret. The minister's no different.'

'There's secrets and secrets,' said Sylvester stoutly. 'Only secrets you ever kept is recipes, and that sort of secret I can live with.'

'What about banana pancakes, after?' Taxi asked, hopeful. 'I ain't keen on all this thinking on an empty stomach. All this waiting and worrying ain't no good for my ulcer, I'm telling you.'

'I'll not make pancakes in the middle of the night. Not when I've cleaned,' Betsey grumbled, though both men knew that she would. 'Ooh. Look what the cat dragged in.' She nodded to the front where Grand Mary sat glowering, off to one side from the rest, walking stick across her lap like a musket. 'Speaking of secrets. And speaking of cats, if you know what I mean.'

They did, for rumours of Mary's secret menagerie had long swirled, despite the fact that no one had ever seen the six (or was it sixteen? or sixty?) illegal cats she was suspected of keeping, locked up in Martha House.

As Island Elder, Grand Mary had the right to give the final speech at all debates, although she rarely came. When she did she caused disruption, making endless disapproving noises, ignoring protocol, rustling sweet papers. The island children coveted these wrapped sweets; imported and expensive. What did an old lady want with Quality Street? They never seemed to run out, and rumour had it she had never been seen to eat a gold one. How many tins of Toffee Pennies had she accumulated, hoarded away in Martha House, together with her seething mass of feline captives?

'We're in for it now, she don't come without speaking.'

'And she ain't never spoken without finding something nasty to say.'

'I wonder what's got her goat: Garrick, or the vet money.'

Taxi raised his flat cap to scratch his head and then set it back, adjusting it with both hands. 'Vet money's got one or two goats, I hear.' He descended into a fit of coughing and Sylvester slapped him amiably on the back. When Taxi recovered he added, 'There's folk want that cash for sending a couple of our own youngsters to agricultural college.'

Betsey was indignant. 'What folk? Anyone lucky enough to have a goat ought to want a real vet.'

Sylvester frowned. He had lost the thread, and was not to be long diverted from the subject of the minister by any goat, aphoristic or actual.

Betsey crossed her arms and sat back, allowing Taxi to take over the conversation again. She was displeased with the widespread intransigence, for she'd travelled some distance in her thinking, since the painful first shock of disappointment. They had all depended upon the minister to be better, that was what she had come to realise. Better than all of them, certainly better than she was. Wasn't that his job? But the truth was that he was just a man, and there ought to be a different relief in shared human fallibility.

'No, but on what you said before,' said Taxi, who did not, it seemed, wish to speculate on Garrick's employment future, 'I hear that Grand Mary come about people picking the dybbuk marigolds. She want a key put on the old cemetery. A site of historical importance, she says.'

Before Betsey could reply, the door swung open and Garrick Williams entered, accompanied by Saul, who slipped his arm through Garrick's as if about to walk him down the aisle. Absolute silence fell.

Garrick was dressed in a stiff black suit and a white shirt, less like a wedding than a funeral. The hermit's beard was gone and his grey curls sprang in all directions, clean and damp. He clutched a notebook to his chest, like an evangelist with a Bible. He made no eye contact as he and Saul made their way to the front.

Saul looked startled to see Dan sitting in the council seats, but then gave a barely perceptible nod of the head, and shook Dan's hand.

'Forgot what was going on for a moment,' he said, slightly too loudly, as behind him Garrick took a chair and began thumbing through his notebook, frowning. 'Of course, you're CMO now, so you take my place. Quite right, quite right. Just came up to wish you the best, good luck and all that.'

In her seat in the crowd Moz squirmed. She had not foreseen this embarrassment. She and Nancy had saved Saul a chair, which she now patted. Her beloved old stag must be helped to make way for the young buck with unfailing public grace.

After Saul had rejoined the audience, a new silence fell. Each councillor was seated, looking expectantly at Garrick. Dan fought to suppress a strange nervous laughter that threatened to rise; beside him, Vitali Mendoza was running a callused hand along the edge of the table with great concentration, as if checking the soundness of the wood. The youngest councillor, Zimbul Fairclough, had only recently been elected, taking over from her mother who said she had quite enough voting on the moshav without adding more committees into her week, what with the livestock committee and the entertainment committee and the tractor committee. No, someone else could ride across the island to listen to spats about cauliflower seedlings and repainting the postbox, and now that someone was shy Zimbul, who could not believe – literally could not believe – that the disgraced minister was here, and seemed actually about to speak. Zimbul was twenty-four. She twirled the end of a long red plait, and looked at the floor. Then Garrick rose, and even the click of knitting needles ceased. Garrick cleared his throat, once, twice.

'Forgive me a moment. Before this meeting is called to order, I have one or two things of a personal nature to say.'

Saul and Moz sat grimly, hand in hand, as if attending a sentencing. Saul fixed his eyes on his brother-in-law. An honest apology would save him. This would save them all.

'I am aware of having recently become a – a diversion. A distraction, if you will. It had been my intention, my commitment, lifelong, to do what is best for Tuga de Oro and her people.'

The fingers that gripped the black notebook were shaking, and Saul felt suddenly anxious that Garrick might buckle and collapse before them.

'As such it is right for me to step aside today and allow the meeting to proceed unimpeded. To prevent further delay, I hope, for this assembly, that you will all permit Dr Saul Gabbai to stand as head of Island Council in my stead so that proceedings might, ah, proceed. In light of matters various and the subjects laid out on tonight's agenda, I respectfully withdraw my participation.'

And with that, as Saul sat open-mouthed, Garrick made his way to the side exit, his footsteps unsteady, but his gaze fixed and determined. No apology! No explanation! Almost everyone turned to look at Charlotte, who was presumably the embodiment of 'matters various'. They had been cheated, and they did not like it.

23

Moz stabbed a sharp finger into Saul's ribs and he sprang into action. It took some time before he was able to silence the crowd, not helped by the fact that his first point of business was to summon Charlotte Walker before them all to speak. Nonetheless, he could see no way forward except through.

'*Paz*. I call to order this Tuga de Oro Island Council public forum. Councillors are present, we excuse Ruth dos Santos on the grounds of absence, and we now proceed without further—' He was going to say 'distraction', but an impulse stopped him from endorsing Garrick's language with repetition. He knew they felt let down. Cheated of spectacle, which was perhaps beneath them; but it was also true that they had been cheated of their moral guide. And now, after so very many words over the years, he had withheld his words from them. Someone must say *something*.

'Listen. *Guay de mi*, I will add only one remark and then we'll move on. As a community, we know our own values,' Saul said, realising with irony that he was probably about to plagiarise a patchwork of Garrick's own sermons. 'I am not asking you to forgive and forget every mistake. And I understand feeling let down by— So I'm just saying, let's extend our compassion in all directions, not only where it's easy to do. And now I hereby invite our speaker Dr Charlotte Walker to join us, and present her, ah, findings.'

Since Garrick had first entered, Charlotte had been standing rigid in mortification. The meeting had taken on the blurred quality of a nightmare, or a classic anxiety dream in which she had come to deliver a speech naked. She looked out and caught Moz's eye and Moz gave a firm nod, a transmission of her own professional gravity.

Saul went on, 'By now I think you'll all have read the report submitted last Tuesday, outlining in detail Dr Walker's proposal to allot funding to recruit and employ a permanent veterinary surgeon on Tuga de Oro, to commence as soon as is feasible after her own departure. I know we have all been immensely grateful to Dr Walker for her care of our stock till now. We were fortunate that the island's chief anonymous donor put in place the Martha Philips Veterinary Research Fellowship, a programme sadly concluded since its administrator –' here he seemed briefly to lose his way, because any mention of Joan in this context seemed impossible '– and we have benefited from Dr Walker's expertise as a tireless volunteer and advocate. But it has been as a volunteer, and all that work has been at no cost to the island. That luck won't strike us twice. I'll say no more, and hand over to Dr Walker.'

Saul gavc Charlotte's elbow a quick squeeze as they passed, and returned to what was now his seat, in the centre of the room, between Dan and Vitali.

'What a privilege,' Charlotte began, but her voice came out rasping and near-silent. She'd begun to wish she'd stolen a beta blocker from the pharmacy. She cleared her throat. 'Isn't it appropriate that the elephant in the room is also the vet?'

This drew an explosion of laughter, dispersing a degree

of tension. Charlotte took a breath, and began her speech again.

'What a privilege it's been to work among you for these last fourteen months. In that time you have allowed me into your homes and farms, and I have seen up close the great interdependence between Tugans and their domestic and working animals. I believe there is a true need here, and that the improvement in productivity of the farms under active veterinary care would justify what I do know is a substantial cost. It would also ensure additional and much-needed biosecurity for the island to protect you all for the future, if your next vet is given a role in imports and ship inspections, working together with the medics, and of course the customs department.'

Here she nodded towards Elsie, who sat loyally in the front row.

'It is essential to hold a vigilant front line against alien species invasions, animal epidemics, and most importantly to guard against and watch for future zoonotic transmission: that is, when a disease makes the jump from an animal to human population.'

She had neared the end of her brief pitch, and no longer felt she might faint.

'On this last point alone, given the extremity of the isolation here it is particularly vital to safeguard the capacity of the health service. It is my suggestion therefore, as laid out in my report, that funds be apportioned towards a full-time permanent vet, in the hopes that a simultaneous application to the Foreign, Commonweath and Development Office would ultimately lead to funding from the British government.'

This last reference was a risk, when full Tugan independence remained a passionate and divisive local issue. But

Charlotte had gambled that it was still more appealing than a substantial, open-ended drain on local resources.

'I will personally oversee recruitment to ensure as smooth a handover as possible, even though in reality it is likely to be disjointed. We're unlikely to get anyone here for two or three years, looking at the availability of berths, but I wanted to initiate the process while I am still on the island. Thank you.'

She looked out at a sea of faces: familiar, supportive. Betsey. Moz. Anwuli Davenport, nodding along. Taxi gave her a smile, displaying his few, alarming teeth, the colour of long-steeped tea, and the ever-buoyant Katie Salmon offered a double thumbs-up. Charlotte folded her notes and dropped gratefully into a chair beside Elsie, awash with cortisol. From the council seats onstage, a slim, wiry man with a grey beard and wide dark eyes gave her a gentle, encouraging smile, and she realised, with a jolt, that this was almost certainly Levi's father. Was his mother also somewhere in the room? Was Levi?

Saul had led her to believe this vote was a formality, and that no one else was likely to speak. But there came the scraping of a chair and a tall man with long grey dreads and a smattering of freckles across his cheeks stood up. The tattoos covering his sinewy arms identified him as one of the fishermen, not an islander she knew, for her work better acquainted her with the farmers. She thought she saw a slight anxiety pass across Saul's face.

'All due respect,' said the man, always an ominous phrase with which to begin, 'I reckon many here remembering a similar funding vote a few years ago about the physiotherapist. Essential it was, that she come out. And it was pushed through by *some* –' here Dan's mother, Lusi Zekri, shot him a defiant stare and sat up straighter '– some who had motivations that weren't all to do with physiotherapy, is all I'm saying.'

From across the room Dan met Katie's questioning glance and gave a minute shrug – as much as he could offer with all eyes upon him. Neither had been on the island when the vote for Katie's funding had gone through, though he now remembered his mother telling him it had been 'considered from all angles', which probably meant there'd been a stand-up row. But since then, surely, Katie had proved herself unquestioningly an asset. He had presumed her universally beloved. Not universally it seemed, for Ocean Rodrigues lifted his chin and crossed his arms and went on, warming to a theme, 'We needing nets, we needing timber, we needing more freezer capacity, more diesel storage, and we ain't complaining, we got enough, and we get by. But all these new *public offices* –' the last words spoken as if in the harbour waited a ship of a hundred civil servants keen to disembark with clipboards '– what next? Little Doc fall in love with a dentist and next we paying for her to come, too?'

'I hope so,' Betsey called out sharply. 'A month every five years is woeful.' Beside her Taxi shuffled and pressed his lips over his own few, bronze teeth. Calla too looked offended. As the clinic's senior nurse, she had taken several correspondence courses in dentistry, and felt she had not done too badly, under the circumstances. Prevention was their best weapon. All the children were taught flossing at school now, they all knew to brush at home at lunchtime, and how many places could say that?

Ocean turned to Betsey.

'And a hairdresser? That come from public funds?'

'I think we are veering off course,' Dan called out. He stole another glance at Katie who was now staring determinedly at the sparkly purple laces of her hiking boots, and noticed Elsie Smith also trying to catch her eye. He dared not look at his mother. His father had long ago had an affair with Ocean's wife, Sophie-Pearl, the black-haired woman who now sat staring resolutely at her own fingernails, nodding beside Ocean in what was presumably a state of permanent, penitent agreement. No Rodrigues was likely to champion anything supported by a Zekri. Most islanders assembled would know the history; Dan had no idea if that made it all better, or worse. But ulterior motive or not, Ocean had opened a door. On the dais beside Dan, Zimbul Fairclough stirred and cleared her throat.

'All I think we saying,' she said, in a surprisingly clear, ringing voice, 'is of course it's been nice having a vet, for a time.' This was her first public speech in office, and she seemed to gather confidence almost visibly, with every word. 'But we ain't started with a pot of public money and said, right, what shall we do with this? It's all been the wrong way round. Dr Walker come here for her tortoises and we got used to her, and so now we're suddenly saying, let's carry on. And all Ocean's saying is, what would be the best use of that money starting from scratch? If we hadn't all got used to having a vet? Maybe it would have been a dentist, or upgrading the clinic. Or fixing up last year's hurricane repairs, or the school still needing computer equipment. I don't know, we're just saying, it ain't come about straightforward, is all. And I can't see that having a vet made much difference to Nicola Davenport's new calf, when it came to it. I'm thinking maybe we can do better.'

The meeting went on. Charlotte sat as her own utility was weighed and measured, compared with a new tractor, a guano harvest, an external pest controller, a swimming pool. She hoped the tall fisherman would never call her to tend to an animal, nor the young, red-headed councillor with the plaits who thought she could do better, both of whom she now felt obliged to loathe. Bringing up the calf was a low blow, not least because she felt sure that its death had indeed been the result of her own dereliction. She felt unexpectedly sorry for Katie Salmon: so earnest, so committed, so much of her identity invested in her work on the island, thrown as collateral damage under this needless bus.

When the debate eventually staggered to its conclusion the sky was pansy-black velvet pricked with sequin stars, and Tuga de Oro voted to allow Dr Charlotte Walker to recruit and hire a permanent, full-time vet. It had taken so long that Grand Mary, who had obviously come with something unhelpful to contribute on an entirely different subject, had given up and stumped off home. There was a silver lining, Betsey told Charlotte. But by then Charlotte had no interest in silver linings. She was irritable and exasperated, and barely cared what became of the clinic. She was tempted to stand up and announce that the whole exercise was probably moot, for who in their right mind would want to upend their lives to come here and contend with all this?

24

Determined to get a jump on the day, Dan came in early, despite another broken night spent ricocheting between, on this occasion, an eleven p.m. migraine to the west and then, just when he had fallen into luxuriant deep sleep, what turned out to be ferocious but not exactly life-threatening acid reflux at three a.m. down in Lemon Tree Valley. Both patients reported quite cheerfully that they'd been symptomatic since early morning, which meant that each might just as easily have called him out during regular office hours. Or even – but this was too much to hope – made an actual appointment.

He had expected to be first in, but when he arrived he found the lights on and Katie sitting at his desk. She was typing ferociously at the computer keyboard, and crying.

'Are you OK?' Dan asked, aware it was a stupid question; unable, nonetheless, to phrase it better. Katie rarely cried, certainly not in public places. He feared that he himself had somehow caused her tears, simultaneously chastising himself for the arrogance of assuming so. Working with his ex-fiancée had got no less complicated.

'Oh yes,' said Katie in a bright, high voice, and then let out a little sob, which turned into an odd giggle. 'Absolutely great. Just working on a Pilates poster and can't get these – is it Wingdings? Webdings? Who knows! Probably we just say emojis for everything now!'

Dan approached with caution, as if he had come in to find a skittish wild animal on his desk.

'Can I help?'

'Oh, no! Well, ha! I don't know.' She was still bashing at the old stiff keys, slightly too hard. 'It would have been nice to know my whole job here was a favour to you, you know?' On she went, *Ols Kal*, *Old Ksl*, eventually managing *Old Kal*, but then got the time wrong and pounded furiously on the delete key.

'You can't listen to Ocean, he's got chips on his shoulder that have nothing to do with you.'

He couldn't bring himself to tell her what those chips actually were – that twenty years earlier Ocean had come home from sea to find that Sophie-Pearl was not at home with their four children, but had instead been seen skinny-dipping at the Breaks with Dan's own father, Johannes. Instead he said weakly, 'That simply isn't true. You are essential here.'

'Isn't it? Am I? Not to you, clearly. And you weren't in that meeting either, when they voted.'

'That's true but – think about all you've done since you came, it's just not relevant any more.'

'Well. That's nice of you to say. But the fact remains that the money for my job was granted because I was engaged to you and they wanted you to move home to Tuga, and I was supposed to be the sweetener. And as if that weren't enough of a humiliation, now we're not even engaged.'

Dan busied himself raising the window blinds, but once this was done realised that he had to reply.

'Even if that was partly true, since then you've proved yourself a million times over. Honestly, there would be uproar if you tried to leave.' With more conviction he went on, 'Think about Ruth dos Santos. She's healing, she's continent, she's sober – going to NA meetings in Slough, by the way. Out, by herself, on the actual bus, in Slough. Can you even connect that as the same patient? You've literally saved her life.'

Katie sniffed, and wiped her face with the handkerchief he extended.

'Well, I'm glad about Ruth.'

Aware he was looming over where she sat, Dan knelt beside the computer.

'Katie, you are essential here. Much, much more important to Tuga de Oro than any vet could ever be. You must believe me.'

Then behind him he heard another, familiar voice, and felt the bottom of his stomach fall away.

'Nice to know,' said Charlotte breezily, and when he spun around he saw that she had retreated into her office and firmly closed the door. He turned back to Katie with more to say, but she seemed instantly to have calmed down. Cheered up, even, for suddenly she looked quite herself again. She nodded at the poster on her screen, satisfied, and clicked: print.

25

The first patient of the morning was Natalie, who had been in Dan's class at school and had been, since early childhood, his cousin Nancy Gabbai's best friend. She also happened to be the first girl Dan had ever kissed, on Old Year's Night when he was twelve, and their teenage years had been punctuated by some light-hearted and very pleasant dalliances, the last of which had been only weeks before he'd left Tuga de Oro for medical school. This was a fact best forgotten when she now presented herself as a patient. During his years in England Natalie had married a neighbour, Oscar Lindo, and they now lived with their four children, eight sheep and two pigs on a modest smallholding, south of Town. Whenever Dan passed her these days she was smiling and harried, several red-headed children hanging about her person: on her shoulders; in a piggyback; running far ahead of her. Today she had brought two – a baby strapped to her, and a three-year-old with an arm looped around one of her legs, sucking on a pancake. Natalie did not sit but instead hoisted the child into the patient's chair and stood in front of the desk, swaying to keep the baby asleep. Dan took his seat and looked up at her.

'*Ke haber.* How can I help?' he asked, warm, businesslike. He still had not quite managed to balance the informality with people he'd known lifelong with what he hoped would be the absolute sanctity and honour of the consulting room. Usually he settled on going straight to the point, just in case they were embarrassed and wanted to get their questions over with. There was time for small talk afterwards, when he was jotting down his notes.

'Pretty sure I'm pregnant,' Natalie told him, in a voice that suggested this had not at all been the plan. Jacob, in the chair, reached up towards her, and she took a sticky hand in her own, still swaying.

'I see.' Dan flicked backwards in her notes to check when she'd most recently given birth. 'Do you know the date of your last period?'

She gave a hollow laugh.

'I've not had one in years, have I. I'm still nursing this being.' She indicated the baby strapped to her with swathes of purple jersey cotton, turning to show Dan a face fast asleep, mouth open, soft cheek squashed into a comedic distortion. 'We hoped that might be enough, the feeding. But I've a gobful of spit when I wake up in the mornings and that's a sure sign, with me.'

As if she knew herself to be the subject of the discussion the baby startled awake, and began rooting. Natalie leaned forward and unwrapped her sling, hoisting the grizzling child on to her hip. Dan stroked a tiny bare foot.

'Good morning, little Maisie. She is –' he glanced down '– nine months tomorrow.' It did not seem the moment to mention that breastfeeding did not confer adequate contraception, whatever its rumoured properties. 'If you nip to the loo there's cardboard trays on the left. You can leave a urine sample for me there, and we'll see what's what.'

'All right,' said Natalie, businesslike herself, and handed Dan the baby. She left the room abruptly and both children began instantly to howl. Dan jiggled baby Maisie and rummaged in his desk for a monkey puppet which he began to bob from side to side in front of Jacob, who roared louder, in terror.

'Oh, hush up,' said Natalie equably, returning. Both children silenced at the sight of her. She retrieved the baby and Dan left, saying he'd be back in a moment with her results. As he took the sample into the tiny kitchen laboratory of the clinic he heard her singing 'Durme, Durme'. He had not heard it since his own mother had sung it to him, and smiled to himself, until he saw the changing colour on the hCG dipstick.

She was pregnant. She had known, but still, she wept. The baby was restive, and Natalie wrapped her, squirming, back into the sling, jigging and shifting until she could plug the howling mouth with a nipple. All the while she was in tears herself. Beside her Jacob whined that he wanted to go home, now. Raised on a farm, he was no fool. Even at three he knew that the word 'pregnant' was bad news when used to describe his mother. Dan danced his monkey puppet, thinking of the women who had peopled his morning: Katie, crying and working; Natalie, crying and simultaneously sorting out the constant shifting needs of her already numerous children, with no time to pause for anything of her own, not even to acknowledge a feeling. Meanwhile he tried with all his professional might to forget the startling fact that he had once been on familiar terms with that – now mercifully invisible – nipple.

'I think, given that we're not sure of timings, the best thing is to scan you, and then we'll know where you are.' He had made progress with Jacob, who reached out a wary hand to shake paws with the monkey. 'Do you want to wait for Oscar?'

Natalie sniffed. He could not pass her a handkerchief because Katie still had his, and he made a mental note to order disposable tissues for the office, indulgence though they were.

'He's done it four times,' she said, attempting a wry smile. 'Best get on now and know where we are with months.'

Queenie Lindo-Smith was sitting in the waiting room with her feet up on the mop bucket, knitting, and chatting with the assembled patients. Dan called her into his office to stay with the children while he took Natalie down the hall for a scan. And he was glad, once he'd begun, that they were without distraction. Poor Natalie. Poor Oscar. He took image after image, changing perspectives.

'You very quiet,' said Natalie, raising her head. Her voice had a new edge of fear to it. 'What's wrong? My baby OK?'

Dan had set the probe back in its holster and was using the trackball mouse to take measurements on a still image.

'Nothing wrong,' he said quickly. 'All well.'

He had no idea what to tell her. But it turned out she didn't need telling anything further, because her eyes fixed upon the dark screen of the ultrasound, and she was a woman who had done this many times before. She took a sharp breath.

'That's never my scan?'

Dan turned on his stool to face her, and said that yes, in fact, it was.

'I can see with my own eyes – "Baby C", you've typed. There ain't three in there?'

'Yes. Three healthy heartbeats,' said Dan, trying to keep his voice a professional calm. 'Three heartbeats, and I'd estimate you're about eight weeks. Do you want to hear them?'

Natalie covered her face with both hands and began to sob. One hand instinctively flew to her belly but it was sticky with gel, and Dan quickly handed her a wad of blue paper towel. He did not turn up the volume. Natalie wiped her hands, wiped her stomach, and sat up. Then she covered her mouth and stared in shock at the screen.

'Three more babies,' she whispered. '*Three.*'

Dan pictured their cottage: its two rooms, their children with less space than the sheep. As it was, the three oldest children shared the only bedroom while Natalie and Oscar and the baby slept in the living room, on a mattress that during the day was piled with cushions, to serve as the sofa. A working dog, their collie was supposed to sleep outside, but the children often snuck her in too. Theirs was a happy household, but a full one.

He remembered Natalie with her head thrown back, laughing carefree on the beach. He remembered family holidays together at the Breaks, nights when he and Natalie and his cousin Nancy would sit up late, tossing dried cinnamon berries on the bonfire like tiny firecrackers, and after a while Nancy would make herself scarce, and in the light of the dying fire Natalie would raise an eyebrow at him, and that would be all it took. He remembered her younger still, pulling faces in health class while a poker-faced Miss Moz rolled a condom down a stubby green banana, shushing their mortified giggles. He remembered, in short, that this was his old, old friend.

'Natty, listen,' he said softly. 'I'm going to send someone for Oscar in a minute, but before I do you need to know, you still have every option.'

She reached out and gripped his hand. 'I don't need to keep them, you're saying.'

'It's still early. You and Oscar can talk, and I'm here if there's anything you want to ask. About any choice.'

Now was not the time for a more practical conversation about possible outcomes if she did continue with the pregnancy, although his mind was already busy, calculating how soon he could get her off the island, referred to a teaching hospital with Level Three neonatal care. He would wait. None of that might be necessary. He went to the door to survey the waiting room, where three twelve-year-old girls were assembled, booked in before school as part of his HPV vaccination programme. Quietly, he asked Gertie's mother for permission to borrow her as an emergency messenger to the Lindo farm, promising to call round and do her jab at home this evening. The girl set off at a sprint, delighted by her reprieve.

Soon a husband would be on his way, terrified by an urgent summons to the clinic. But the forthcoming relief that nobody was dying would serve, Dan thought, as a very good way of putting into perspective that he might well soon become a father of seven.

26

It had become an unspoken arrangement between Grand Mary and Charlotte that she would come every now and again to cast a quick eye over the elderly tortoise, letting herself into the garden whenever she was passing. Now, with her mother in residence at Martha House, it was she with whom Charlotte scheduled these visits. Today, Lucinda was sitting between the open French doors of the incongruous library, wondering aloud why anyone should require quite so many years of specialist training for a job that seemed mainly to involve crawling around a dirt yard.

'It's for a faecal flotation test,' Charlotte explained. As two other tortoises lived here, it could often take a very long time to ensure a sample definitely came from Martha. Today had been pleasingly efficient, though she was unhappy with the consistency. 'It's to monitor her parasitic burden. It's a good non-invasive health screen.'

'*Faecal flotation.* What lofty intellectual heights you academics do reach.'

'Do you know if Mary's been adding the calcium powder to her greens? Her diet needs supplementing.'

'Would it surprise you to know that I do not?'

'Well, there's less than last time in the tub, that's good.'

'I am going inside to supplement my own diet, I think,'

said Lucinda, and drifted back into the cool of the house, leaving Charlotte to pack away her sampling kit.

Martha was now wallowing in her shallow concrete pool beneath the old mulberry, together with Goldie and Dusty, her two much smaller companions. When Charlotte approached she lumbered over to the edge of the sun-warmed pool and raised her long, narrow head, inquisitive, serpentine, permitting a quick inspection of her eyes, nose and mouth. Her mucous membranes were moist and pink and Charlotte scratched the heavy wattle, pleased. With a feed scoop she trickled water from the pool over and over down the neck and great dusty shell, as she knew Martha liked. The dull golden discs on the mountain range of her dark scutes gleamed briefly bright, while wet. Lucinda returned, sipping a cold ginger beer.

'How often is Mary letting her have melon?' Charlotte asked, washing her hands at the outdoor tap, and hoping that her mother had returned in a more obliging spirit. But Lucinda refused to be drawn on the matter of how much fruit Grand Mary was feeding the animal – too much, Charlotte felt certain – and instead argued, obstructive, that in her dotage Martha ought to be allowed to eat what she damn well pleased.

'If a woman can't be freed from the tyranny of diet culture when she's a hundred and fifty then I truly fear for humanity,' Lucinda said airily, though where this line of freedom lay was unclear to Charlotte, who had rarely known her mother to eat pudding. Meanwhile, she was determined to ensure that the tortoise produced a firmer stool.

27

It was the moshav movie night. For a collective, the moshavniks took a remarkably authoritarian approach to the choice of film, for as owners of the only projector on the island they felt it their right to shape the course of this particular cultural channel. Any Tugan might submit a request, but the three long-standing members of the film committee did not believe in period drama, action, horror, documentary or animation, with exceptions made to the latter only on special occasions, for the children. Elsie's heartfelt petition for *Calamity Jane* was repeatedly ignored. Where the committee was concerned, no genre could rival the uplifting escapism of the romantic comedy, with an emphasis on the twenty-year period beginning with 1982's *Tootsie* and ending at *My Big Fat Greek Wedding*, released in 2002 and considered both a pinnacle and the closing of the romcom's heyday. Tonight, Harry would yet again be meeting Sally. Still, attendance remained strong, with all ticket-holders granted two drinks tokens to accompany a picnic dinner. In many ways, familiarity relieved the need to concentrate, leaving them more resources free for socialising. But each month Sylvester and Taxi took it hard. They coveted the huge screen, on which they had long wanted to see *The Godfather* trilogy.

The wall of one barn was kept matte black, an endless job,

for the weather ate acrylic from wood with relentless determination, and to maintain uniformity of any surface was a battle similar to the painting of the Golden Gate Bridge. In front of this was hung a rudimentary but effective white screen, and the rising slope of the field beneath was laid with Tugan picnic blankets, a ring of chairs placed around the perimeter for the elderly, and pregnant.

Natalie Lindo was among this latter category, feeling queasy and irritable in the warmth of the evening. Almost from the moment she had known of the triplets, her discomfort had seemed to multiply. She sat in a white plastic picnic chair and stared at Meg Ryan, coveting not simply Sally's brown leather belt and chunky cardigan, but the cool weather in which one might wear such items. She fanned herself and nursed the current baby who slumped heavy, suffocating, over an already visible bump.

Concerned for Natalie's own health during a demanding fifth pregnancy, Dan Zekri had suggested not only multivitamins and iron supplements but also weaning Maisie. But Dan wasn't the one dealing with the night-waking, and if he knew a better way to silence a teething baby when she threatened to wake her siblings then he could come over at three a.m. and try it himself. In general, Natalie felt let down by Dan Zekri in this, the second chapter of their knowing one another. CMO he might now be, but a man without children was a child himself, that was Natalie's view, and couldn't be expected to understand that as a mother of four, she couldn't simply swan off to Southampton for an unspecified period of time. For this was his plan, to manage what he kept insisting on calling a 'high-risk multiple pregnancy'. From the moment she'd told him of her decision, he had wanted her to be a medical evacuation on the Island Open ship, hanging around England until the birth, which he said could easily come any time from twenty-five weeks and would be unlikely to 'be allowed' to go longer than thirty-four, though who needed to 'allow' her anything about her own pregnancy she couldn't rightly fathom, and her triplets would come into the world when they were good and ready. Natalie Lindo had had her four babies on Tuga, each without incident, and this last without even another soul, her early-morning labour so smooth and quick she'd not seen sense in waking Oscar. There was no reason why Tuga wouldn't do well enough for the next three.

Now she was both hungry and queasy again and, catching sight of Cecil with his friends, called him over. An extension cord run through the window of the moshav rec room was powering a small popcorn maker spewing warm popcorn into a clean feed bucket below. Natalie dispatched her obliging eldest son to bring her a bowlful, though she would likely only manage a few pieces before a wave of exhaustion overcame her and she was asleep, upright, in a plastic chair.

For her part, Charlotte had come to the movie night as the unexpected guest of Betsey Coffee, who had asked her just that morning whether she would do the book club the honour of joining their party. They'd all arrived to collect her in a crowded car – Betsey, Mac's Rachel, Dan's senior nurse Calla, and Dan's mother Lusi Zekri – and Charlotte clambered into the back for an unexpectedly raucous drive south. Once there, they positioned their huge picnic blanket close to the front, for Calla mentioned lightly that she'd broken her glasses some time back and had no hope of another pair for who knew how long. They'd not had an optician out these two years, and she was certain her prescription had changed; no sense spending good money on a mail-order approximation until she knew where she stood. Charlotte felt this explained a great deal of what she'd seen of Calla's suturing. She accepted a glass of fizzycan from Betsey, and turned around to survey the crowd.

The first person she noted was Katie Salmon close behind them, her knees drawn up beneath a pink gingham dress, her hair in perky, little-girl bunches incongruous with a sombre expression. She had been like this ever since the Island Council meeting. Now she sat with jaunty pom-poms in her bunches and her eyes full of sorrow, small hands gripping a large plastic cup. Occasionally she took a deep drink and shook her head at the film, as if it contained propaganda with which she entirely disagreed.

Then Charlotte's gaze fell upon the red-haired young woman who had argued against her on Island Council. She was barefoot and wore a tiny slip of a sundress, grass-green smocked cotton falling off one shoulder, at once almost ludicrously innocent and suggestive, and was gazing in adoration not at Billy Crystal, but at Levi Mendoza who was reclining on one elbow beside her, apparently absorbed in the film.

Tuga was small; possibly this girl was an old friend, or a cousin he had never mentioned. These possibilities evaporated when Charlotte saw the woman lean over him, cleavage first, and stroke the ends of her long rope of glossy hair down his jawline. It was both outrageously sexual, and outrageously annoying. Charlotte suppressed a violent urge to scream, both with thwarted possession, and vicarious itching. What the hell was that hair manoeuvre? Charlotte had already taken against the girl at the meeting, and now upgraded this position to one of instant, frank loathing. Could do better, indeed. It was a slight relief when Levi did not appear to respond – certainly he did not turn and dazzle her with the kind of seductive, playful smile that would have caused Charlotte to self-immolate with unhappiness right here, leaving a blackened crater at the centre of Betsey's picnic blanket. But neither did he swat her away. That girl was, apparently, permitted to touch his face. If he did not seem overly enthusiastic, still it was a bad sign.

Betsey followed Charlotte's eyes.

'Oh, *kerida*. Best you turn around right now, have some popcorn and forget all about that. He's trouble where the ladies are concerned, that boy, and always has been, however much of a tender spot I've got for him. And I do.' Here Betsey visibly softened, unhelpfully, at some remembered charm of Levi's. 'Oh, he was a devilish sweet little boy, that one. But I'd not trust him with a daughter of mine, if I'd had any. That Zimbul better watch her heart.'

Zimbul. That was it. Her name skewered Charlotte unexpectedly, a second wound after the first shock of seeing them. An island girl, a good match, a moshavnik, a councillor, which suggested she was a person of substance. In all ways an impressive partner for Levi Mendoza – except that she was monstrously irritating, and entirely detestable.

But how could it possibly matter? Why did it hurt, when Charlotte was leaving the island anyway? Did she expect him to pine for her after she'd gone, when it was absolutely certain they would never again set eyes on one another? Levi Mendoza was not suddenly going to appear in NW1. Charlotte told Betsey she was going to the rec-room window for popcorn and then rose, walking with erect and deliberate posture to the snack table, feigning an elegance incompatible with flip-flops on uneven grass. She hoped Levi was watching, and could see how poised she was, how independent. She smiled about her in all directions except his, a queen among her subjects, demonstrating her social confidence – her social *integration*, no less – and it was in this way, chin in the air, holding a cup of popcorn, that she bumped, heavily and painfully, into a stack of wooden deckchairs. Popcorn flew from her hands and scattered at her feet like flower petals before a bride.

28

'What do you mean, what am I doing here?' Charlotte hissed. 'What are *you* doing here?' She nudged Dan over with her foot and crawled into the dark space beside him.

They were in the shadows of the empty moshav rec room, a large rectangular shed with an eccentric trio of old sofas pushed against three of its walls, and a trestle table set up along the fourth displaying a collection of books, magazines and board games. Beneath this were two palm-leaf baskets of tatty and bright plastic children's toys, jumbled in among others that looked to have been carved from wood by Vitali Mendoza, or perhaps even the previous generation's carpenter. Dan had positioned himself not on any of these sofas but in a gap between two of them, sitting on the dusty linoleum floor. This was a hideout from which he was invisible and yet had an unimpeded view of the screen through the open windows. He had with him a beer, and a loaded plate.

'What does it look like I'm doing? I'm hiding, obviously. As behoves the chief medical officer and senior member of Island Council. I've got snacks, and I'm not coming out. We're not meant to be in here, just so you know.'

'Oh, call the police,' grumbled Charlotte, kicking off her flip-flops. 'And budge *up*.'

She too had fled, rushing through the first door she'd

spotted after her collision with the stack of chairs. Now she was stuck, because she was miles from home, had made the fatal error of coming out without a torch, and didn't want to drag any of the book-club members away until the film had finished. Nor could she bear to sit on a blanket at the front of a crowd, lit by the flickering screen, far too near her canoodling ex-boyfriend. And who knew? Maybe her weasel of a father was out there somewhere too, just to make the evening even better. Not weasel, she retracted, fastidious even in her own thoughts. Charlotte had a soft spot for mustelids – stoats and weasels and ferrets – who she felt got a bad rap.

'Ferrets are another thing,' she muttered to Dan now, as if he had been party to her inner monologue, which at present mostly comprised a mounting list of the things she missed in England. Reason to go home with her mother number nine million: mustelids. She took a few cashews from Dan's plate, and leaned back against the wall beside him.

'Ferrets,' Dan repeated.

'Yes, well they'd be catastrophic to the ecosystem, obviously.'

'Obviously. Are you all right?'

Charlotte shot him a withering look.

'My mother is driving me insane, my father is – who knows what he is. And Levi Mendoza is being felt up by your ginger councillor in the middle of that field, which is just distasteful, quite frankly. There are children present. Anyway, you're the one who's built a den.'

'I'm hiding from Natalie Lindo,' Dan told her, quite unembarrassed, 'together with every single one of her relatives. So many relatives.'

'Oh, no. Still no dice?'

'Nope. I've been told in no very polite terms that I'm

shirking my responsibility and shouldn't be trying to palm her off on to the NHS.'

'Lazy, lazy,' Charlotte smiled, teasing gently.

'I know. Lazy me, trying to save four lives. What would they like me to do if she stayed here? Fashion three incubators out of some washing-up bowls and a bit of pallet wood? What exactly is going to be the plan if she gets pre-eclampsia at twenty weeks? She's got a pair of monochorionic twins in there quite apart from the third baby – what course would she propose if they develop TTTS? I've been on the phone to the foetal medicine unit in London; they'd section her there at thirty-two weeks, latest, and that's with a theatre full of neonatologists and a month in NICU in the best-case scenario.'

'At what point do you start confronting her with true prognoses?'

Dan threw his head back against the wall, rubbing his eyes. On the screen outside, a sobbing Sally Albright was opening the door to Harry Burns in her dressing gown, about to go to bed with him in what Charlotte could only think of, scathingly, as a predictably abysmal idea. Their post-coital expressions she found almost too excruciating to watch – Sally naively blissful, Harry wide-eyed with terrified remorse. They had a good thing going until they'd crossed that line, and surely that was enough for anyone; solid, platonic, mutually supportive, and all without the fear and vulnerability of romance. Risk-free intimacy. Sally ought to have known that sex with Harry would torpedo everything. Charlotte averted her eyes from the screen and focused on Dan.

'Soon, I think. They already have four kids. Can you imagine if this lot came catastrophically early and they then had three more kids with substantial health complications? Or more to the point, no babies at all.'

'But surely once you've explained that, she can't possibly think it's a good idea to stay and risk it?'

'Oh, well,' Dan said wearily, and took a swig from his beer. 'She's no fool, Natty. She's just – she's fearful. She's never been off Tuga de Oro. And it's a lot to ask a mother to leave the babies she already has, for so long. But if I fail to convince her, it could be disastrous, and it will be *my* failure. Honestly, I can't think about it now; I think about it obsessionally almost every waking moment. All I do is imagine the boat leaving without her, and then unfurling disaster scenarios after that. I need an hour off. I've got till Island Open to work on my powers of persuasion. I'm just in here because I needed a break from the filthy looks. Anyway, distract me. Tell me about your work. What did Kew say?'

'Oh, it's good news,' said Charlotte, brightening, and Dan gave a soft laugh and shook his head. He made frequent jokes about her research curing insomnia. But deep down, she knew, he definitely loved chelonian data.

To understand better the diet of the gold coins and their role in the island ecosystem, Charlotte had begun an individual tracking study, following marked tortoises for up to fourteen hours as they grazed, napped, wallowed and mated in the dense interior jungle of the island. She'd spent long days in the jungle following individual tortoises, making a diary of their behaviour, and photographing everything they ate. But botany was not her strength, and the islanders themselves had not proven reliable witnesses on the identification of their own plants – or at least, not in a way that correlated with any wider system of classification. Mac's Rachel, it turned out, knew the local name and the medicinal properties of almost any leaf or fruit or tuber, but these names turned up nothing on the internet, and image searches were impossible on the limited Tugan bandwidth. Charlotte had instead shipped a memory stick to the team at Kew Gardens on the Island Close boat.

'She's started,' she told Dan, 'but she says she needs more time.'

'How many plant images did you send?'

'Twelve hundred,' Charlotte admitted, 'but loads of them are the same plant. Now I need to decide if sixteen case studies is enough or if I should do a few more while I'm still here. Then I can think about how to structure a korason germination study, beyond my initial messing about. But I've come up with a title.'

'Always good to have a title.'

'This is when you ask what it is.'

'OK. What's your title?'

'*The Role of Endozoochory in the Germination of Endemic Korason Palms on the British Overseas Territory of Tuga de Oro*. Or perhaps, *on the Isolated South Atlantic Island of Tuga de Oro*. Or even just, *on the Island of Tuga de Oro* – that might be snappier.'

'Snappier,' Dan agreed.

'The thing is, the next vet might not be interested in research, so anything I need to prep *in situ* has to happen soon. And I didn't feel like I could add a research interest as a stipulation, I don't think we're going to be overwhelmed with candidates as it is. No offence.'

She didn't add that she felt ambivalent about the arrival of another herpetologist on the island. What was best for the tortoises was clearly to attract as much academic interest as possible, but she wasn't yet ready to share.

'Any replies to your ad yet? Who's our next vet?'

'There's no need to sound so cheerful about it.'

'Oh, but I'm not. Truly, Charlotte, I will miss you. More than you can imagine.'

Dan was suddenly staring at her, steady and close in the

darkness. Neither of them spoke. Instead through the open door and windows came the sound of the film, the gentle dry snapping of the popcorn maker, as well as the low chatter of Tugans who talked, as was their wont, even through these last, climactic moments. Sally and Harry were fighting at a wedding, pain and passion in their voices, although the end of the movie would come soon, and would be a happy one. These two flawed humans would cleave together in a grand love, a true love, founding a lifetime of happiness upon their long years of friendship. But real life was not a romantic comedy. Charlotte, feeling new panic, quietly excused herself and went to find Betsey.

29

Charlotte sipped her coffee and watched the little theatre of the cuckoo clock as it called out the hour. She ought to have been studying the four CVs that had already been submitted for the role of island vet and which lay on the table before her, printed and stapled, arranged in an orderly fan. But she found herself unexpectedly hostile to these veterinarians from Edinburgh, Munich, Stockholm, Auckland. Each was manifestly more qualified for her current job than she was, each with years of practical farming and public-health experience beneath their well-travelled belts, each falling over themselves to exhibit their frankly excessive commitment in effusive covering letters. She felt suspicious of all of these people. What was it Dan had said when first she'd met him? *Folk are drawn to Tuga, running away, or searching.* What, one might ask, was driving Anders Lundgren to want to leave the bridges and saunas and advanced recycling facilities of Stockholm for the world's most remote populated island? What had gone so wrong in Auckland for Holly Wang that she was willing to abandon delivery services, anonymity, online dating, soft-serve ice cream, career prospects?

Dan was also hiring for the new contract doctor and had a larger number of applicants from whom to choose. But Charlotte had not advertised the veterinary post for a twelve-month or even a 24-month contract. She had provided only ad hoc care while she was here, without formal responsibility or manifesto, and whoever took over could make better progress simply by having a mandate. But with no one to manage staffing once she had gone, and no additional budget offered for annual berths and relocation costs, she had listed it as a permanent position. This would be Tuga de Oro's first proper vet. Soon would come a veterinarian who could shape the role, guide the island, and ideally safeguard the future. She wondered idly if Dan might come to Betsey's on his way to the clinic, and if he did, whether it would be wise or unwise to invite him to join her, given the strange tension that had fallen between them in the shadowed intimacy of last night's rec room. But instead Katie Salmon came in, wearing the same pink gingham dress she'd had on the previous evening, and looking like a woman who had recently been fished out of a shipwreck. Charlotte listened as Katie ordered black coffee and a vast breakfast, her voice a toneless croak. Charlotte resolved to be friendlier to a woman quite possibly in the middle of a breakdown, and so when Katie turned around she gave a small wave and beckoned her over.

Katie sat down heavily across from Charlotte, and the fraying rattan chair gave a creak of objection. She took a deep swig from a purple water bottle she was clutching, one that Charlotte recognised from Katie's desk at the clinic. It usually had a slice of fruit bobbing in it, prompting Charlotte to wonder how even a woman's drink could be irritating, under the right circumstances. But today nothing bobbed, and Katie drained the water and thunked the bottle down on the table. She had not removed her fuchsia sunglasses, and Charlotte remembered the previous night's pint glass of what had looked to be white wine. She now assumed that others had followed. Not a breakdown then, merely an advanced hangover. Katie nodded down at the CVs.

'How are they? Any front runners? Any of them engaged to marry a senior member of Island Council?'

Charlotte decided to ignore this. Her bright sympathy had flicked on and then off again like a light switch; wallowing in self-pity was tiresome, particularly when Katie was by now so clearly integrated and beloved, and the debate that had wounded her had been literally years ago. Since moving here she had started a geriatric clinic and a back clinic, had rehabbed farming and fishing injuries, launched several surprisingly popular fitness classes, and begun a programme of perinatal assessment and support that would change lives. The revelation about Katie's initial hiring had been undignified, but surely it paled into insignificance beside her concrete, obvious achievements. Charlotte too had been disparaged during the public meeting and had decided, not to put too fine a point on it, that she didn't give a monkey's.

'No idea how they are,' Charlotte said, deciding to reply in earnest in hopes of a real conversation. 'I can't help questioning the sanity of anyone who actually wants to move here. I mean, I know we did, but that's different, somehow. How can you tell who's mad from their hobbies and interests? Kite-surfing? Normal. Scuba-diving? Normal, normal. Theatre? Normal, although perhaps not much of it to go round on Tuga.'

'I've been thinking,' said Katie, entirely ignoring the information she had just solicited, 'I think I'm going to ask them to vote again on my appointment.' She smiled up weakly at Betsey, who had approached their table with a startling mound of scrambled eggs, fresh avocado and banana fritters. 'Oh, *thank you*,' Katie breathed, accepting this heavy plate with reverence.

'You're saying you want to reapply for your own job. That's insane, you know.'

Katie began to attack her breakfast with the speed and comportment of a finalist in a hotdog-eating competition. Charlotte kept her eyes primly on her own cappuccino.

'Is it?' demanded Katie, her mouth full. 'Insane to me is giving someone a job and a berth just to please the new doctor. I want to be hired, fair and square. I wanted to work here forever, I don't want my entire future life based on a favour to my ex-boyfriend.'

Charlotte resisted the urge to say: *you just need to get over it.* Then she stopped resisting and said, 'Oh, Katie, get over it.'

Katie paused, fork aloft.

'All I'm saying is,' Charlotte went on quickly, 'people questioned my role too. And in both cases everyone ultimately agreed we do good. It's OK for people to debate, isn't it? It seems a bit self-indulgent to make everyone go through a whole hiring process for a foregone conclusion. Who cares if one grumpy old man insults us?'

'Yes, thank you, I was there. They didn't insult you, actually; they questioned hiring someone *after* you, which is totally different from someone saying: *we made a job out of nothing for poor little Katie only because she was going to marry the doctor.* "Was" being the operative word there. Also, you're leaving, so why would you care? I'd say it's pretty self-indulgent to leave an island when there's actual work to do here for a threatened species, but never mind, that's your own business. Meanwhile I actually live here. Under false pretences.'

The bell above the door tinkled, and Lucinda Compton-Neville stuck her head in, wearing an expression of frank disapproval beneath an enormous palm-leaf hat, which she did not bother to remove.

'Hello? Service outside some time this century, please?'

Charlotte sank lower in her seat, feeling a ripple of returned disapproval pass through the cafe like a Mexican wave. From her position, quite literally darkening the doorway, Lucinda scanned the room.

'Oh, hello darling,' she said lightly, and then, as if anxious this had been too encouraging, added, 'So sorry, I'm with a friend just now, but perhaps after that? Do sit up straight.'

Charlotte gave a weak smile, ignoring Katie Salmon, who had cocked her head and seemed to be enjoying the opportunity to offer Charlotte her own expression of concern. Through the glass Charlotte could see her mother and Grand Mary settling down at a table beneath the wide red umbrellas, whose ratty scalloped edges fluttered lightly in a warm sea breeze. The two women sat with their backs to the cafe, surveying Harbour Street side by side, like an interview panel. Over their shoulders Charlotte could see Betsey with her notepad, listening, nodding, speaking, nodding again, while Charlotte imagined her mother making endless dietary modification to the simple menu. With some effort Charlotte brought her focus back to Katie.

'Have you got a clinic this morning? Why don't you go to bed for a bit?'

'I'm teaching a Pilates class at ten. Maybe you're right, I'll sleep after that.'

'Don't forget it's Friday lunch.'

Katie groaned and pushed aside her plate. Then she dropped her head backwards over the rattan chair, as if someone was about to wash her hair at a salon.

'I think I made a mistake,' she said, addressing the ceiling.

'You didn't,' said Charlotte firmly. 'You're feeling rotten, but it's going to be fine. I'm sure Dan won't mind if you miss Friday lunch on this one occasion; just survive Pilates and then go to bed.'

'Bed is where the problems started.'

'What?'

'I slept with Dan last night,' said Katie, in a voice so small that Charlotte thought she had misheard. But then Katie said it again, adding, 'Twice, in fact.'

Charlotte set her coffee cup down very gently into the cradle of its saucer.

'And?' she asked, carefully.

Katie finally took off her sunglasses and sat up to look directly at Charlotte, displaying remarkably tenacious iridescent pink eyeshadow, and last night's mascara still clinging to several lashes. Charlotte looked back, without blinking. Unlike lizards, snakes cannot blink. Charlotte tried to remember the different zones of refraction in the diurnal serpentine cornea. The specialised protective scale over the snake eye is called a 'spectacle' – a word she had always enjoyed. She tried and failed to enjoy it now.

'It was great,' said Katie, simply, with a brief ghost of a smile. 'As it always was. Great, and terrible. I needed to feel – oh, I don't know. I needed not to feel. And now I have to go and teach Pilates to his mother. Oh, shit, shit, shit.'

Quite, thought Charlotte, watching Katie rise with stoic determination, restore the pink plastic armour of her sunglasses, and set off towards the beach at a pace considerably slower than her usual needlessly springy and surely inefficient stride. No doubt Pilates would be a triumph, despite the hangover, as was everything that Katie Salmon did. Alone, Charlotte allowed herself to blink and blink. She was not a snake.

In the margin of Anders Lundgren, a large-animal vet who hoped to bring veganism to Tuga, Charlotte quickly sketched a little calendar, calculating the outer limits of her tenure here. For the first time, she thought that she would not disrupt Lucinda's mortifying campaign to scalp two berths on the Island Open ship. It would cease to be mortifying the moment they were safely at sea.

Grand Mary had gone. Lucinda turned and rapped on the glass. Charlotte rose to join her, unexpectedly grateful for the diversion. Anwuli Davenport caught at her sleeve as she passed.

'Tell your mother,' said Anwuli and Charlotte cringed, having grown used to these chastisements by proxy, 'tell your mother to stop hogging the phone box. Fifteen minutes or half an hour, fine. But she just come along and write her name at the top and draw a line through all the slots. Isa missed her weekly call with her sister in Stanley. It ain't right.'

Where a London equivalent might advertise a range of consolations and punishments, Tuga's only phone box instead displayed a large blackboard, with a little woven basket of moist chalk hooked on a nail beneath. On this board was a monthly calendar, and it was in this manner that Tugans without a telephone could book a time to make or await their calls. Charlotte agreed with Anwuli that it wasn't fair for Lucinda to exploit this system, but did not go on to explain that it would be hopeless for her to intervene. Instead she apologised and went outside to join her mother.

'Mary has been advising me on who among those with a berth would be easiest to persuade,' Lucinda told her, patting Mary's recently vacated chair. Charlotte feared this translated as who were the travellers most easily persuaded by Lucinda's chequebook.

'None of the berths are guaranteed until the doctors have assigned theirs,' Charlotte told her. 'It'll be quite last minute, but once they're finalised we'll know who's definitely leaving.'

'Medevac, you mean? That's a thought. Surely a pedicure counts as an urgent medical procedure, by this point.'

'No! Not for us. I meant, there are only eleven berths and the CMO can take up to four, I think – more if one of the patients is a child or someone who needs a chaperone. So no one knows till the last days who exactly is leaving, and some people who are packing now might lose their places. But –' Charlotte began to understand how heavily she was depending upon her mother's shameless bad behaviour to rescue her '– that still leaves lots of options, if you act fast.'

Lucinda sipped her Diet Coke and drummed her nails on the table. They remained flawless, Charlotte noticed. She must be painting them herself. She could do nothing about her growing roots, however, which perhaps even more than fear of sun damage accounted for her devotion to hats.

In the blissful heat of the morning Charlotte tipped her own face briefly to the sunshine, trying to soak its warmth into her bones. By the time they reached home, London would likely be close to zero degrees; long hours of damp and darkness wrapped around brief days of grey and dirty urban skies. If they found spaces on the Island Open ship they might be home for Christmas.

A slight figure approached from the west of Harbour Street. Zimbul Fairclough, still in last night's grass-green sundress, tripping lightly over the cobbles from what seemed likely to be the direction of the Rockhopper.

Charlotte and Lucinda watched her float past and into Betsey's, smiling to herself, a halo of red-gold curls escaping from a distinctly rumpled plait. Last night had been eventful for more than Dan and Katie, it seemed. As she passed she shot Charlotte a dazzling smile, which went unreturned.

'Ugh,' said Charlotte, before she could stop herself, though in any case Lucinda ignored her.

'You'd have thought that lummox Garrick could make himself useful, pull some strings. He certainly owes me.'

'Owes you for what?'

'Oh,' said Lucinda airily, 'I don't know, all of it. Imagine if I hadn't got pregnant? I'd have made QC five years earlier, at least. Perhaps I'd have been a judge. And meanwhile when I think about the cases I've missed these last weeks . . . anyway. I've emailed to reconfirm with Lars, and so failing Plan A, in worst-case scenario we will still have Plan B and a lift to Buenos Aires.' She nodded at the sheaf of CVs that Charlotte had forgotten she was holding.

'Do get on with that, it'll make you feel far less conflicted. Give those poor people a real vet. Don't look at me like that – I mean an actual vet, not an academic herpetologist.'

To Charlotte's horror she found that dangerous tears had risen, and had soon begun to roll freely down her face. Lucinda could never stand crying, even when Charlotte had been little. She turned to face the ocean, wiping her cheeks as best she could.

'Garrick hasn't spoken one word to me since everyone found out,' was what she heard herself saying, without any clear sense of whether or not this related to her crying. Snakes were so much more efficient. A film of tears remained concealed in the sub-spectacular space, draining invisibly, discreetly, into the oral cavity. A snake could weep and weep, and no one would know it. It was true that she was merely an academic herpetologist. But oh, she had loved the farm animals too. Probably they did deserve better.

'Effing Garrick,' Lucinda murmured. Then her expression changed and she rapped firmly on the table. 'Now I'm going to run, darling, because I've got a great deal to get on with and Evangeline is no doubt ringing and ringing that boiling little phone box. People do try and queue-jump even when it's quite clearly my reservation, and so I must press on. Mop yourself up, there's a good girl.'

And with that she rose, leaving Charlotte with the bill.

30

Since becoming chief medical officer, Dan had instituted Friday lunches for all staff. He made sandwiches and a fruit salad on Thursday evenings, and at midday encouraged everyone to eat together in the long garden that separated the clinic from the old Cole house. The nurses, Winston and Calla, physiotherapist Katie, vet Charlotte, and head of sanitation, Queenie Lindo-Smith. Dan had hopes of professional cross-pollination at these weekly gatherings; trust-building, the sharing of ideas across small but diverse departments. The reality was mostly a steady griping about who had used the last gauze without refilling the drawer, which nurse would deign to be on call with Dan the following weekend, and whether Charlotte was or was not entitled to take the portable ultrasound out of the clinic on weekdays. (Dan maintained that she was not.) Meanwhile, Charlotte had recently made them abandon the broad picnic bench beside the tree sorrel, because an inexperienced fairy tern had laid on too low a branch and would, Charlotte told them, feel threatened by lunching medics. Laying only a single egg per season and without even the protection of a nest, the tern ought to be left in peace. Until the chick had hatched, they ate on a blanket in the shade of an old tamarind, with Queenie positioned above them in a heavy wooden chair like the monarch for which she'd been named. She had not been able to reach the floor for two decades, she told Dan with some pride, as if working towards a world record. Dan felt this at least explained the eccentric cleaning system, whereby any debris too big to be sucked up the Hoover was simply pushed with the broom into a neat heap beneath his own desk.

Winston and Calla had taken the day off simultaneously, which was never meant to happen and always, always did, and Queenie had her great-grandchildren coming for dinner and was home, preparing her slow-cooked lamb with potato cakes. Today's Friday lunch was thus attended only by Charlotte, Dan and Katie. Dan felt karmically punished. In the last eighteen hours he had relaunched a tentative but ill-advised flirtation with one and then, almost immediately, slept with the other. Twice.

The three came into the garden from three directions: Dan from the clinic's front door, Charlotte crunching over the crushed-shell path from the vet's room round the side, and Katie from the old Cole house across the kitchen garden. (Still living with his mother, Dan daily regretted his magnanimity in ceding Katie this house after their break-up, while at the same time acknowledging it was the least he could do, having brought her here.) Then a fourth guest arrived, uninvited but welcome, as from the front gate a small mongrel slipped into the garden and headed straight for Charlotte. This was Long Dog, who seemed to belong to everyone and no one. The best Charlotte could surmise was that he was some sort of border collie/dachshund mix, a low-bellied, shaggy-coated gold and black beast who had always looked hot and matted on his perambulations around Town, until Charlotte could stand it no more and took a unilateral decision to shave him. Charlotte greeted Long Dog and then, with the fortifying slap of an undocked tail against her shins, told the other two humans that she would have to leave early, she had to go and meet her mother.

'Didn't you just see her this morning?' asked Katie. She had showered and changed and probably competed in a heptathlon since breakfast, her hair wet, her scrubs as pink as candyfloss, her hangover miraculously evaporated.

'Yes,' said Charlotte, prickly, though this had been asked without apparent judgement. She reached for a crab sandwich and sat down in the shade, wondering how soon she could politely leave. She had not wanted to cancel, fearing Dan might interpret this as relating somehow to events of the previous night. But it was impossible not to keep picturing these two people joined together in various athletically advanced sexual positions, like a sequence of animated Kama Sutra illustrations. Instead she tried to sound airy.

'She wasn't sufficiently insulting over breakfast, so we're meeting later for her to have another go. Probably too much iodine for you,' she told Long Dog, who was panting hopefully beside her, but then she relented and offered him a crust, which was swallowed whole. 'These are so much nicer than usual, what did you put in them?' She raised her sandwich at Dan, who had taken a seat far off the blanket, at such an odd distance from the two women that he would need a litter picker to reach his lunch.

'Thanks a lot. As it happens I didn't make them, I asked Marianne Goss this morning. Got back late last night and then I – got distracted.'

'Had your hands full?' asked Charlotte innocently, unable to stop herself, and on cue Dan began choking. Charlotte had never teased anyone so successfully. Katie snorted, and Dan looked between them with growing suspicion.

'You told her,' he said to Katie, accusing.

Charlotte rolled her eyes. 'What did you once say to me? *Tuga de Oro does a really good line in gossip.*' She waved a hand dismissively, as Lucinda might, a gesture indicating that nothing here was of any consequence, possibly including present company. Then she flopped back on the blanket and closed her eyes. 'If she hadn't I'd only have heard it later on the radio.'

'*Guay de mi*, don't even joke. This is . . . Friday lunch is meant to be a sacred professional assembly.'

Dan's cheeks had darkened with embarrassment, but then even he gave in and began to laugh. Katie threw a fallen tamarind pod at him and told him to get over himself. Then she too lay down, far from Charlotte, but in a similar position. She pulled off her sun hat and laid it over her face, and from beneath it said, 'God, I feel absolutely terrible.'

'Thanks!' said Dan. 'My cooking's no good and now this.'

'He does leave in too much shell,' Katie said to Charlotte, conversationally, and as if Dan wasn't there. They went on to discuss the ratio of lemon to mayonnaise, the many ways in which Marianne Goss's preparation was superior. Dan began to relax, fractionally, feeling that if they were mocking his culinary skills he was probably on the road to forgiveness. He had been duly ashamed of last night's actions, already planning his speech of apology, and so was relieved to see Katie seemed not just fine, but if anything in better spirits than previous days. She had taken the news about her hiring far harder than their earlier break-up (he tried his best not to find this insulting), and since then had seemed muted and vulnerable, uncharacteristically insecure. These were not a list of adjectives that suggested one should take a woman to bed. But she had drunk a lot of white wine in front of *When Harry Met Sally*; and afterwards in the dark field of cars had almost literally thrown herself at him, announcing, perhaps just one time too many, that she knew exactly what she was doing and that *I just for God's sake, just this evening, Dan, need to feel needed.* Katie could be very insistent. Still. It was not to his credit that he had failed to resist.

But here she was, apparently restored, and now asking him if he'd heard any more from Ruth's colorectal surgeon.

Charlotte lay in the warm shade, the small, bristled dog collapsed beside her, blissed out beneath her hand. Dan and Katie were now talking softly about Ruth dos Santos, whose life had been transformed with the completeness of a fairy-tale. Alex had never known his mother healthy until these last, miraculous weeks, but now Island Council had bought him a railcard, and he had been with her every weekend, visiting from his new boarding school. A recovered Ruth had been assigned a berth for the Island Open boat, and Katie was readying a physio programme.

Charlotte began to doze, listening to their low talk, and behind and beneath it, high above, the hoarse quacking cries of the fairy terns. She wondered how the clinic egg was coming along. She really did have to go and meet Lucinda, but she found that, for the moment, she was unexpectedly contented. And so the three were conveniently assembled when Oluchi arrived, out of breath, to say the doctor had to come now-now, Oscar Lindo had had an accident.

31

'He put some ewes out north-west last week,' Oluchi told Dan, as they scrambled up into the ambulance. In the absence of both nurses Katie jumped in the back, and Dan felt grateful to have her competent hands aboard. Hands whose competence, henceforth, he must strive once again to forget outside their professional context. He started the engine, and called to Charlotte through the window.

'Can you find one of the nurses to meet me back here? Or Saul?'

Charlotte nodded and then began to jog, Long Dog scampering gamely behind her.

'And then?' Dan asked, as they drove away.

'That rockfall last week made passing by land hard. Island Open almost come so we reckoned on good seas near the coast and went round in the RIB. And we did have good seas, mostly, just one bad wave. Oscar got a bar in the chest.'

'How does he seem?'

'I'd say he been better. We took him out at North Beach, Walter with him now.'

'Conscious? Awake?'

'Oh, yes.' Oluchi gave a brief smile. 'Swearing something awful, his mother'd be ashamed of him.'

*

Tugan roads were a tyranny. As FFA, Katie was not allowed to drive; Dan had had an unwelcome scolding from his uncle for allowing her behind the wheel on the day she'd first disembarked, in what now felt like another lifetime. Back then he hadn't known of a rule that had come in during his own years off-island, and that one illegal drive with Katie had been full of hope, touring the stage sets of their future life together – here the beaches, there the cliffs – and had culminated in his lifting her over the threshold of the home they no longer shared. She was now applying for residency on her own terms and with it, presumably, a driving licence, taking the obligatory six lessons from Taxi. But today she remained in the back to assist him, while Walter took the wheel.

Oscar gasped that the pain was in his left shoulder.

'Positive Kehr sign,' Dan murmured, not sure if Katie would know this meant he strongly suspected internal bleeding. She was holding Oscar's free hand in a firm grip and was talking to him, softly and steadily, while Dan focused on getting his oxygen saturation stable, and drawing up a dose of morphine. Oscar's pulse was rapid and thready. Dan needed to get him an X-ray and ultrasound as fast as possible, frustrated as a careful Walter took the elderly ambulance at the pace of a gold coin tortoise. But Elsie had been waiting for replacement air struts for eight boats now, and in the meanwhile the suspension was in poor condition quite apart from the terrain. Oscar groaned each time they jarred over humps and potholes. Finally they turned down the steep, rutted track that would take them back to the clinic, and in the front Walter's two-way radio crackled to say that the nurses had been found, and would be ready.

Scans confirmed a substantial bleed on the spleen. But for now Oscar was stabilised, Natalie and the nurses beside him, and Dan was taking a quick moment to write up his notes. When Saul arrived, Dan was surprised to see that he had brought Garrick with him, although until recently it would have seemed obvious to have the pastor's support during any emergency. Both men were in shorts and rucksacks, in addition to their bumbags, and looked to have come from a hike.

Saul approached and cast an eye over Dan's shoulder.

'*Ke haber.* Spleen?'

'Yes. Subcapsular haematoma of the spleen, where the eleventh rib has cut through it. Haemopneumothorax of about fifteen per cent with striking surgical emphysema.'

'*Guay de mi, ijiko.* Poor Oscar. Poor Natty, this isn't what she needs. Is she here? She been told he's had a bash?'

'Yes,' said Dan, wondering about the instinct that always made medics resort to nursery language when an injury was dramatic. In fact, 'a bit of a bash' had been precisely the term he too had used, to Natalie.

Garrick said he would go to speak to Oscar's parents who he had seen arriving, and coordinate a rota to help Natalie with the farm. He would head out to the waiting room. In short, thought Dan with grudging approval, he would come out of hiding and finally get on with his job.

'How's his pain?' Saul asked.

'Marginally more comfortable – I've put in bupivacaine intercostal blocks. But we'll have to keep him in a while, he's in no fit state to move. This isn't going to help my case to send Natalie. We've got to patch him up somehow so she'll leave the island.'

There was considerably more to say on this, but at that moment two children pushed open the door of Dan's office. One silently held a bag of sweet banana chips, and a crayon drawing of the *montaña*. The other held a ginger cake wrapped in a tea towel, on which was balanced a commercial greeting card, without an envelope. The card was one of about thirty that circulated permanently between islanders, heavily Tippexed. This one depicted a giraffe holding a bunch of violets and now read 'Get Well Soon, Oscar' where it had once, long ago, offered sympathy for a recent loss. Saul had received this very card for his retirement, and it had most recently been sent by Moz to Mac and Mac's Rachel, on the occasion of their wedding anniversary. News of Oscar's accident had spread, and island families were beginning to send their well wishes.

Dan directed these small carrier pigeons back out towards Garrick. Moments later Garrick himself appeared again in the doorway, holding chips, cake, card and drawing. He looked, Dan realised, ten years younger.

'Might you remember whether they were on their way there, or coming home?' Garrick asked Dan. Dan looked back, blankly.

'I mean, has anyone been to see to the sheep?'

'Truly I don't know.'

Garrick nodded, unperturbed.

'Don't worry, *ijiko*. I'll take care of it.'

Charlotte was closed into the vet's room, taking advantage of her mother's absence to make use of the computer, but mostly just keeping out of everyone's way. She had stayed in the clinic in case Dan couldn't find Saul or the nurses, but now he had a full complement of medical staff – Saul and Calla and Winston – as well as much of Oscar and Natalie's extended families in attendance, and a steady flow of visitors. Charlotte was not needed. From eavesdropping she knew the plan was not yet surgical but instead conservative management with fluid, pain control and symptomatic treatment.

Dan would remain on call, sleeping beside Oscar in the only other hospital bed, which he would wheel each evening into the waiting room, while Winston and Calla were to alternate keeping watch over Oscar on night shifts. Dan would make the patient's breakfasts, but Natalie would not hear of anyone else making Oscar's lunches and dinners, even if her own dinners were to be made by somebody else.

Charlotte was writing to her palm-tree expert at Kew Gardens, when there came a short knock and Garrick slid into the room with a look of guilty stealth, closing the door quietly behind him. *It's my father*, she thought to herself, in disbelief that she could have any association with this craven, bumbling man. He had not spoken to her since Lucinda's arrival. Not that, by this point, he could say anything that Charlotte wanted to hear.

'Charlotte.'

'Garrick.'

'Hello.'

'Hello.'

After that they both fell silent. This was already their most successful conversation since she'd found out who he was – possibly it was best to leave it there, she thought, and to move straight on to 'goodbye'. Instead she waited, trying to focus on the screen, reading and rereading her own sentence asking her research collaborator to clarify whether she would have to register as a plant importer herself, or whether a letter from Kew would suffice. *In either case I've submitted my application for a phytosanitary certificate for the first korason consignment.* She wondered, briefly, whether phytosanitary should have a hyphen.

'I have been made aware,' said Garrick, as if beginning a sermon, and then apparently thinking better of the volume and lowering his voice until it was a library whisper, 'I am aware that you might perhaps be experiencing some discomfort with regard to our – *association.* I recall that in coming to Tuga de Oro you had perhaps some expectations of finding . . . In light of subsequent events I wanted to relieve you of any lingering embarrassment.'

'I have absolutely no lingering embarrassment,' said Charlotte firmly, and at a normal volume. What had her mother said? *He doesn't want you within a hundred miles.* Well, the feeling was mutual. She wanted him out of her office. When he left she would open the exterior door and turn up the fan; she wanted the very molecules of the air to be cleansed of his presence.

'Well, but you had, in fact, visited the island in search of, ah, communion—'

'No. I came for answers, and I have them.'

The number and volume of voices in the waiting room suddenly increased, and Garrick's hand tightened on the door handle. Outside they could hear that Taxi had come, together with Oscar and Natalie's two eldest, and at the same time delivering what he swore blind to Oscar's mother was his last portion of a very strengthening stew – 'made with the old ways and means, if you get what I'm saying'.

Charlotte typed, *Have you determined how many seeds you will need for the first phase?*

'The Lindo children have arrived. I must go where I am needed, they will be upset about their father.'

The final word hung in the air between them. Charlotte said none of the things she might have said. Instead she added a hyphen to phyto-sanitary and then, after a second, removed it. And then, because Garrick had no view of her screen, she typed, *fuck off, fuck off, fuck off.*

'Right. Well.' Garrick adjusted the brim of his hat. 'Onwards.'

32

The children were wild. It happened that way – sometimes their minds were ripe for learning and other days, like today, the atmosphere in the classroom was charged with unspent energy. Legs twitched to climb; voices rose and rose, desperate to laugh and shout. Pockets of conflict broke out and needed, periodically, to be extinguished. Poor Cecil Lindo was already on to his second warning for burning the back of Hubert Spencer's ear with the scalding seed of a rubber tree, heated with friction by rubbing it against a little shard of granite. Moz herself had tortured her brother Garrick in precisely this fashion, and had in fact once applied the smooth, tiger-striped seed for a moment too long and left a mark on his forearm and been in all sorts of trouble with their mother. She remembered well the sharp thrill of glee when one's victim leaped up in brief but startled agony. Nevertheless, she had to come down on it heavily when it happened in her schoolroom, regardless of what a pupil might be going through at home. And there was no doubt, Cecil Lindo was having a harder time than most. His father was still in hospital with a nasty splenic haematoma, his mother pregnant with triplets, in urgent need of a medevac to England that she still nonetheless resisted. A week on, Oscar was out of the woods, the haematoma obediently shrinking. But he was in a lot of pain, and Dan wouldn't let him home until he was sufficiently recovered to go back to work. Whatever injunctions they might put in place, it was unrealistic to imagine that a father of four with a demanding smallholding and a pregnant wife would lie dutifully on a sofa. In the meanwhile, at school a frightened Cecil was monkeying. Miss Moz had stood at the front of this bright, modest room for more than thirty years, and she knew when times tables were a hopeless business.

She shooed them all out to the clove tree at the bottom of the lush school garden and put them to work harvesting some of the lower-hanging cloves into cotton bags. It was absorbing work for little fingers and would be excellent for practising their counting, later. Hubert had forgotten his shoes that morning and she dispatched him home to get a pair, for there were biting ants in the longer grasses. This gave him some time to breathe and to regain his dignity, and also perhaps to scavenge a rubber seed of his own.

Recently, Moz had led the children on a field trip to see a Tugan natural phenomenon – the blazing saffron-coloured marigolds that grew nowhere else on the island but the old cemetery, and even there, only in a strange, particular configuration. All the other older headstones were claimed only by scrub grass, but flowers encircled the grave of the pirate Benjamin Cole in a tall, bright ring.

For an island of secular humanists, there was a great deal of superstition surrounding both the cemetery and the ancient sycamore fig that reached huge sturdy branches over the pirate's headstone. Island children whispered that a dybbuk lived in the western boughs, and would take up residence in the body of anyone who scrambled within reach. It had been deliciously terrifying to gather with Miss Moz even far beneath these heavy dybbuk branches, where she instructed them in how to harvest marigold seeds.

The dybbuk marigolds, as the children insisted upon calling them, had all failed, taken as sure confirmation of their curse. They would not germinate at school under any experimental conditions. But the gerbera seeds brought as backup from Moz's own garden had flourished, huge saucers of vermilion and plum and garnet, and were ready to be cut. These would serve as the day's reward, one gerbera for each hundred cloves. Moz saw small heads draw closer together and the whispers begin, plotting victory.

To ready herself for the flowers, Miss Moz went in to get her favourite school vase, an outsized tin that had once contained green Provençal olives. Glossy bright crimson, this showed a black-haired girl in a buttery yellow dress, reaching up to pick the fruits above her with a dreamy smile on her face. Miss Moz treasured this tin. A former visiting teacher had sent her the olives on her return home ten years earlier, together with some French chestnut puree, and a beautiful waxed tablecloth that Moz had immediately given to Ruth and Marianne, something practical and decorative for a household that at that time had two raucous toddlers. Moz and Saul had eaten the olives on a holiday weekend to the Breaks with Garrick and Joan, and Joan had whipped the sweet chestnut paste into a Mont Blanc she'd apparently learned to make at finishing school, one of the periodic reminders that Moz's sister-in-law had lived, for a time, an entirely different sort of life. The chestnut tin, equally treasured, now held Moz's pencils.

When Miss Moz returned she was beaming, and had Walter Lindo-Smith beside her. Rebecca, on her knees before a tiny pyramid of clove buds, looked up to see her father across the garden, his weathered face alight with happiness. Father and daughter cherished one central objective, and when Walter nodded Rebecca rose and flew into his arms.

'Boat left,' murmured Walter into the cornsilk of his daughter's hair, 'boat left England and your mama's on it. She coming home.'

Rebecca released her father and threw her arms around her teacher's waist with such force that even sturdy Miss Moz staggered backwards at the impact.

'Mummy's on the boat!'

'I know, *kerida*.' Moz stroked her back. 'It's wonderful.'

'Ruth dos Santos staying longer in England, she gave your mama her berth,' said Walter softly, revealing the mechanics of the miracle. But Rebecca was barely listening. She did not care about Ruth dos Santos, a name she only vaguely knew. She cared only that her mother was coming home.

'How long? Did she get the message?'

'Three weeks, maybe. She got it, *mi vida*; Ovaltine is on its way.'

This was a happy day, but it was time to think of the others. Miss Moz's eyes scanned the garden to see which children had noticed this small scene; Cecil Lindo was occupied, but Annie Goss stared. Moz suggested that Walter take Rebecca home for the rest of the afternoon, and busied herself patrolling her clove-pickers, thinking hard. Rebecca had had a difficult eighteen months but Moz had no substantial concerns about the girl, beloved by two parents who loved one another. One did not, of course, get away with an eighteen-month maternal absence scot-free. But – it would be as fine as it could be, under the circumstances. And Rebecca was not the only child in her care who would be impacted by this ship, and its passenger list.

Each island event had repercussions in her classroom.

Cecil would be rightly anxious that, when the boat arrived, his mother would be forced to board it.

And Ruth dos Santos had stayed. The ripples from that decision would reach here, too. Across the garden Moz saw Annie had begun to slash at the gerberas not with yellow plastic school scissors but a ferocious penknife, the same size as the one Moz herself carried. Ruth dos Santos had stayed. Of course that meant that Alex dos Santos, also, could not be on-board the approaching ship.

Now ought to have been the time for Annie to come in from the wild, to seize with both hands as much as this island school had to offer, scant but solid building blocks for the woman she was fast becoming. After all, Alex was getting an English education. Annie ought to start helping the small ones with their reading and spellings, should be making use of all her manifest ingenuity to lead Scouts, and in general begin to shoulder some of the responsibilities expected of adult life in a collective. At the very least Annie should stop stealing fruit and terrifying all of Tuga by free-climbing the coconut palms. But without her twin, something in Annie was broken.

Moz made a note to stop at Marianne's cottage with some flowers on the way home, and to take another bunch round to Natalie Lindo. The woman had to go to England. And Cecil and his siblings were yet more island children about to lose a mother across the ocean for who knew how long. Their isolation sometimes exacted a hard price.

Moz allowed herself one final moment to savour Rebecca's pure, six-year-old joy, pleasure that evaporated when she scanned the garden and saw that Annie Goss had slipped away. Then she thundered through the raised beds to discipline that poor worried imp Cecil Lindo, who, thinking himself safe behind the wigwams of scarlet runner beans, was catapulting okra pods at the girls.

33

'*Paz*, Tuga de Oro, and it's all set to be an easy Island Open. Smooth seas, light breeze, good visibility, and all cargo onshore later today reckons Little Doc, he's running ship inspection with Big Doc, who ain't doing much to convince me of retiring, I tell you that, with all that hard labour Little Doc got him doing. A big welcome home to Maia Lindo-Smith, and here's hoping you brought us all some Ovaltine. Scouts and Guides would like it known they made extra fig jellies, raising money for a proper good charity called EDGE they been learning of. EDGE do all the taking care of the world's most endangered animals that represent – hold on, let old Taxi get this right –' there was audible rustling of paper, which sounded on the radio like static '*– few close relatives on the Tree of Life and are often extremely unusual in the way they look, live and behave, as well as in their genetic make-up.* That's what my paper says, so that's what they do, and Dr Vet tells us that our very own gold coins are an EDGE species, so buy an extra fig jelly and raise money for them tortoises. What do you think they'll spend it on, eh?'

Listeners were here forced to wait until Taxi's laughter and subsequent coughing fit subsided.

'So. Scouts and Guides charity stall outside the Old Kal till first bat. Customs officer has the postbag, anyone wanting to collect can call by Customs House four o'clock, and all else will go out to be delivered tomorrow. Little Doc informs us that anyone waiting on a prescription refill best call by the clinic after lunch tomorrow, he reckons. There's a pup on-board need checking for ticks. And once that's been *ticked off* . . . ha. Anyone needing pallet wood is to put your name down on the board today, and then go see Levi Mendoza day after tomorrow who kindly agreed to be in charge of distribution this ship. I'm eyeing some up for a new rocking chair, myself. When I made my last one this next track was top of the charts, a good song for a bit of carpentry is what I recall thinking, and I'll give my offcuts to anyone guessing the year it came out . . . ' and thus began 'Wooden Heart' by Elvis Presley. Charlotte stopped packing, switched off the radio and headed into Town to help Elsie, as she had promised.

Beside the harbour wall a child of about seven was clinging to her mother and weeping, though Charlotte could not hear her torrent of words, for the sound of Rebecca's sobs was swept out to sea by a stiff wind, and the Brassy Ladies now struck up at an ear-splitting volume, inviting the island to come on and celebrate good times. Island Open was indeed a time of exuberance and promise. Miss Moz led on the French horn, and Maia bent to whisper while small, sturdy arms locked around her neck, two heads together, long hair mingled. Then Maia straightened, lifting Rebecca who rose up in her huge flounced dress of rainbow tulle and sequins, wrapping her legs around her mother's waist. The two rocked together side to side, in time to the music. Behind the pair stood Walter with a hand over his mouth, for he too was crying. Then he laid down the sign that Rebecca had flung aside at first sight of her mother's approach: a painting of the ship, and beneath it the three words, WELCOME HOME,

MUMMY. He went over, embracing wife and child. Other travellers were stepping ashore to joyous calls of 'What, ho! What, ho!' for the ship took eleven passengers, and the other ten were looking around at the low, candy-coloured buildings of cobbled Harbour Street, accepting fig jellies from Hubert Spencer, the child selected to do today's honours.

Soon the lighters would unload much-needed island supplies. The clinic had run out of haemoglobin test strips, and had so few remaining pairs of surgical gloves that Charlotte had been relegated to the horrible, sweaty reusable ones kept in reserve for precisely these circumstances. It was always a relief to exchange the empty oxygen tanks for full.

But for now all eyes were on the little huddle of Lindo-Smiths, a family reunited, the final puzzle piece found, and clicked back with relief into its place. Charlotte felt burning in her own throat and turned away only to find that immediately behind her stood Levi, his arms slung around the shoulders of his parents, the three waiting their turn to welcome Maia home. If Levi noticed Charlotte, he did not show it. His eyes were fixed on his sister and her family, his handsome face alight with joy. Charlotte composed her features, and set off back down Harbour Street. The puppy could wait for its tick check until she'd had a fortifying cup of tea. But as she approached Betsey's she saw her mother through the window, standing with her back to the coffee bar wearing a straw boater and what appeared to be a tablecloth, and addressing the entire population of the cafe. Here then, Lucinda's campaign to buy two berths had entered its final, nuclear phase. Charlotte backed away from the window and cast about in despair. Short of hiding in the phone box there was nothing for it but to help process customs and excise, and hope against hope that her mother would discover two Tugans who had never really wanted to travel, anyway.

34

Annie rode Alex's bike now. Her own had been too small for them both for years, while this one was too big. But it was sturdier, had a fixed gear, and with practice she was managing greater speed and power both up and down the uneven island tracks. It had been Alex's older brother's pride and joy, and only a growth spurt had prevented Caleb from taking it with him when he moved to Slough, to apprentice as a roofer.

The old bike was fit for scrap. But Annie had still managed to sell it to Cecil Lindo, who would take anything of hers and would now be condemned to servitude until he had cleared his outstanding debt, which was to ride out and water her apple seedlings morning and evening for a month. Only later did she realise her mistake, putting Cecil on wheels. When they tired of him, she and Alex used to shake him off simply by riding; now, she had given the smaller boy a fighting chance to follow her.

Alex's bike was heavy. Annie stood on the pedals, pushing and pushing as fast as her legs could move until she was far beyond Town, beyond Mac's Pantry, beyond Lemon Tree Valley. Her eyes were stinging and her lungs burned, and still she did not stop. She needed not just temporary solitude but assured isolation.

At Go-by-Donkey she dropped the bike into a straggling mintberry bush, kicking it further until it was invisible and the scent of crushed leaves rose, sweet and sharp. She crossed beneath the trees, pushing through dense, knee-high ferns until she emerged back into the blinding white light of the beach, which stretched in a crescent around the gentlest of bays. Remote, she could seek refuge. It was a Ship Day, and no one else would come.

Here, long, horizontal sea hibiscus curved towards the shoreline, trunks dipping into the sand and rising again, like the humps of a sea serpent above the water's surface. She sat down on one of the thicker arches and looked out across the ocean. The sea was pale verdigris and turquoise, and a ribbon of indigo marked the horizon from the clear and cloudless blue of the sky. From here the ship was invisible, anchored at the northern kelp beds. Not far to the east lay Conch Island, cut off now by a high tide, but anyone over on Conch would be busy, tending their gardens, minding their own business.

Marianne had brought them here to Go-by-Donkey when they were children, had shown them the magic clock flowers of the sea hibiscus – petals etrog yellow in the morning, bright raspberry after lunch, and already a faded, papery poppy red by the late afternoon. At dusk they fell and scattered upon the warm sand, a flower that teaches not only the time but to notice, to pay attention, to cherish the ephemeral.

Now, it was mid-afternoon and the hibiscus blooms were sun-faded, an early few beginning their noiseless drift. It was mid-afternoon at the Fabian Academy in Kent, too, which Miss Moz had called the Garden of England, and used as the beginning of a lesson on English counties. Tuga de Oro kept Greenwich Mean Time and therefore half the year – this half – shared its time zone with mainland United Kingdom. Annie had slipped out of that lesson, when it turned into

English geography. It was stupid to learn the attributes and character of places you would never go.

In her hands she held eighteen letters and two postcards, bundled together in a cross of elastic bands. Here was more post than she had received in her lifetime; but then anything would be, for Annie had never before received any. She began to organise them by date until she had a stack, oldest to newest. The first, in Alex's familiar uneven print, had been written on the ship, while still in sight of Tuga. The final missive was one of the postcards, sent only six weeks ago. This surely had been written by someone else. Small, even, elegant script, which Annie struggled to read. Well. She would get to that in time, whatever it was.

When the first, lone bat crossed the fading sky Annie barely glanced up. She read, and read, though the light was failing her. Twenty messages, sent over the course of five months, each ending with a version of the same thing. *I'm sorry. I miss you. I'm lonely. I miss you. I'm sorry.*

She would need to preserve her waning torch battery for the long way home. She looked around the debris at the base of the small beachside trees, a tangle of sea hibiscus, sea grape. The palms were a little further back. She found several of the coconut husks she needed, dry and splitting, and carried an armful of these to the sand. From within she pulled some fibres and separated them out, and then began to roll them back and forth between her small hands, into a slim, tight cigar. As she rolled she concentrated, scanning for two flat rocks. Then she laid her fibre cigar on one stone and began to rub it back and forth with the other, as if she were sanding down a piece of wood.

It did not take long. After a few minutes she could smell the first hint of smoke; pulling apart the fibres she saw one winking spark: one was enough. She blew tenderly into her spindly strand, and soon it had the strength she needed. This tiny taper she returned to the inside of the coconut husk, and blew, and blew. The fire caught, filling the bowl, and soon she had a heap of six coconut husks aflame. By the light of her bonfire she could finish reading.

The final letters had indeed been composed by a stranger. They had been written with a new fountain pen by Alex dos Santos, a real Kentish scholar since only September, but a boy who now joined up his letters and wrote of his football team, of the unimaginable wonders of the tuck shop, of breakfast, lunch, dinner served in the dining hall, and even an afternoon tea of packaged white bread and a caterer's tub of strawberry jam. *The bread tastes like clouds*, he wrote. So grand now, eating clouds, in a hall. A hall! He sounded breathless with it, a little punch-drunk. The homesickness to which he professed had not prevented him showing off. *I'm on the swim team*, he boasted, in one later message, *and the coach says I am an unusually strong swimmer for our year, he reckons it's growing up outdoor swimming.*

Annie curled her lip in disgust. Alex was the one who fretted and got into stupid troubles at sea; it was always Annie having to right him. *She* was the one who had taught him. She was the stronger swimmer. And where on earth would a person swim except outdoors?

She considered sleeping on the beach, but Marianne made her life difficult when she stayed out all night. Instead she would have to walk the bike home, navigating in the weak beam of her torch, if it held. But for a moment she stayed by her small fire, relishing the brightness of it, and the grey smoke that spiralled upwards in the windless night. Its low, crackling ferocity was hers, for she had brought it to life. To make fire was to become as powerful as a dragon. One by one she dropped the letters into its flames.

In letting Marianne send him Alex had shown himself a traitor, and England had erased whatever traces of him remained, with its boarding schools and grand halls, its football teams and fancy pens. Annie did not know what a tuck shop was, but she knew that she could never again have any use for Alex dos Santos.

When the last fragment had drifted upwards on a curl of smoke she used two coconut bowls to put out the fire. The seawater hissed and spat, and all went dark. By flickering torchlight Annie made her way back to the mintberry bush by the track, scanning through the leaves for centipedes before she waded in to retrieve her bicycle and begin the long hike home. It took courage to hold firm to the belief that you lived in the best place on earth. But Annie knew that she had courage.

35

Charlotte heard about it on the radio. A medley of the Shadows came to an abrupt end and Taxi's voice replaced it, addressing the island with the authoritative calm appropriate to an emergency.

'Sorry to interrupt, *haverim*. Dr Vet, you're needed at the clinic. We've a tortoise in trouble. Anyone out there see Charlotte Walker, tell her come to the clinic now-now.'

Charlotte quickly laced her hiking boots, and was throwing items at random into her backpack when she saw Levi emerge from within his workshop, crossing the yard towards the open kitchen door. He looked so very much like himself – tall and muscled, moving with his familiar, easy stride – and her heart lifted at the thought that perhaps, finally, he had come to talk. Instead he stopped a way off, beneath the spreading avocado tree. Charlotte came to the stable door and tried a tentative smile, unreciprocated.

'Tortoise trouble at the clinic,' he said, and then turned and began to walk away.

'I know, I heard, I'm ready. Wait, Levi! It must be Martha. Please – I'm sorry to ask you. Will you give me a lift?'

Charlotte had put her arms tentatively around Levi's waist, but when he roared off she was forced to grip tighter, breathing in the scent of him, wood and earth and ocean, his back hot against her chest. He was going too fast for the bends, certainly too fast for conversation, and she had no choice but to lean with him as they slalomed, leaving a dust trail behind them on the steep track. She rested her cheek between his shoulder blades and closed her eyes. Outside the clinic Levi barely stopped for Charlotte to dismount. He circled round her and accelerated away, back up the way they'd come. She took a steadying breath, then another. Then she ran inside to find out what on earth was going on.

In the vet's room Charlotte found an odd crowd assembled. Dan, Miss Moz, and Levi's brother-in-law Walter kneeling in a ring, and Lucinda in her usual station at Charlotte's desk, busy with something on the computer. When Charlotte entered, the three on the floor looked up at her with varied expressions of worry. Her mother continued typing.

They had wheeled aside the stainless-steel exam trolley, and on the floor sprawled not Martha but a mid-sized gold coin tortoise, motionless in the centre of a traditional Tugan blanket. Presumably this had been used to carry it, and concentric rings of marching donkeys and tortoises surrounded the patient like a tiny defensive army. Charlotte rushed to the sink to scrub up, and then dropped to her knees between Dan and Miss Moz to examine the wounded animal.

It was horribly fractured. It was hard to fathom the blunt force that must have done this – its domed shell was cracked from head to tail in the shape of a lightning bolt, several pieces clearly missing. Charlotte studied the damage from every angle. Rose-pink resin on a back scute, so this was a tortoise she had tagged, a robust female, almost certainly of breeding age.

'It was hit by a car,' Dan said quietly. 'I know as a rule you don't interfere with wild animals – but this one, I mean, cars aren't a natural phenomenon, we felt we had to bring him to you . . .'

'Her,' said Charlotte reflexively.

'What?'

'Her. This is a female. How long ago did this happen? Who found it?'

Walter, Moz and Dan seemed to be exchanging glances.

'It was hit by a car,' Dan repeated, unhelpfully. 'Out near the taro fields.'

'Can you move please, so I can have some light? Did anyone see what actually happened?'

An awkward murmuring began. No, none of them had seen what happened, no one could rightly say. Charlotte gave Dan a questioning look but he shrugged and looked back down at the blanket between them.

'Oh, for goodness' *sake*.' Lucinda spun round on the office chair until she was facing them all. She was dressed in the tablecloth again, white robes to which she had added a white crocheted cap, to hide her now extensive grey roots. She looked like a vengeful cult leader, Charlotte thought, about to exact a punishment upon a follower who had displeased her.

'I ran over the fucking tortoise. None of them will tell you because they're all too *honourable*, but honestly it was hardly my fault, those roads are in an appalling state, potholed to within an inch of their lives, I mean, they're hardly roads at all, trying to drive here is like playing a bloody computer game. How is one to tell the difference between any one of the massive boulders and a bloody tortoise?'

Through the uppermost crack in the shell Charlotte could

see a wet bubbling, and felt certain that the tortoise had a punctured lung, possibly two. The animal that wheezed between them was drowning.

'FFA aren't meant to drive,' Charlotte said softly. She too was having trouble breathing, her own chest constricted. 'I've been here more than a year, and I've never driven. Not once.'

Lucinda crossed and recrossed her arms, and then her legs, huffing. 'Well, I mean, but that's ludicrous, who's going to stop you? There aren't exactly officers on every street corner. There aren't even any street corners. Or any streets, come to that. And if they valued you as any sort of an emergency responder then they really ought to have given you a car, darling . . . '

If anything, the damage looked worse the more closely Charlotte studied it. The tortoise would be in pain. Her mind went to the sodium pentobarbital, high on the shelf, and she thought, *intravenous, via the caudal tail vein*. She would ask them all to leave, and she would put this animal out of its suffering. All but Dan, maybe, who could help her, the only one in the room whose presence she could bear while she ended the life of a tortoise she had come here to save. Charlotte lowered her head, just for a moment, her gaze upon the dusty dull scales of the dinosaur leg beside her. Then she raised her head to look directly at her mother.

'You can't just follow the rules, even when everyone else somehow manages, you always have to be special. There are two hundred and seventy-eight gold coin tortoises in the world, and now thanks to you there will soon be two hundred and seventy-seven.' She was shaking, and yet the words, once begun, were pouring from her now. 'You've never cared about anything that mattered to me and this is just – I mean, it's actually hilarious now that I think about it, it's like a bad joke, I've devoted my life to reptile conservation and then you come halfway round the world and you judge everything and know best about everything and you destroy *everything*, and then you literally *run over* – the thing I most care about, it's like, if that's not a metaphor I don't know what is. Just come out and tell me that you don't give a shit about me and you've never given a shit about me, that you wish I'd never been born so you could have *made QC five years earlier*, and you're desperate for me to move back to London not because you actually want me there, but because you want me to, I don't know, become a banker or marry a banker or whatever the hell would be most impressive for you to talk about at the chambers Christmas party. If you loved me you wouldn't have taken Joan away . . . ' Charlotte was crying freely now and couldn't seem to stop, though she was surprised to find that it was this particular injustice, perpetrated twenty years ago, that had surged back, painful as a fresh laceration. 'You took Joan away just because your boyfriend didn't like her and it broke my heart –' here some confusion was sown among the increasingly uncomfortable onlookers, to whom Joan was not the beloved bearded dragon of Charlotte's childhood, but rather the minister's recently deceased wife '– and you could have just told me that my father was married and useless and would never want me, instead of leaving me with this big mystery my whole life. It would have been much easier, honestly. "Your father won't care, I don't care, get on with it." At least I'd have known where I stood.'

Lucinda opened her mouth and then closed it again. Her face had paled. And Charlotte found – clear as ice, sharp as ice – that she did not care. She was alight with anger so vast that it razed all else to the ground. No anxiety, no need, no fear was greater than the pain that had surged when she saw the mess of this tortoise, crushed by her mother's indifference, emblematic of everything. Actually – she was damned if she would euthanise this animal without a fight. Her mother only destroyed, but she could heal. She lifted her hands from the tortoise to wipe her tears away, and then turned to Dan, speaking fast.

'See that bubbling? There's communication with its airways. Tortoise lungs are high, below the shell here and here. We need to pack this central wound with gauze, then I'll try to repair the rest of the shell with epoxy resin. That's step one. Oh, would you just *get out*!' This last was to her mother, who had risen and begun to approach, peering.

'Gauze we have,' said Dan, snapping on a pair of surgical gloves and glancing uneasily after Lucinda, as she left. 'Epoxy resin, not.'

'I've got some for tagging but it's in my kit box in the jungle, and probably not enough. I don't think we have time to get it.' Charlotte was thinking fast. 'It might be used for boats, I don't know.'

She looked at Walter, who nodded.

'Oh, and maybe some glass fibre?'

'Back in a tick,' said Walter, and was gone.

'And a Dremel! Or any multi-tool!' Charlotte yelled after him, and heard his shout of assent. The thud of quick footsteps told them he was running. Miss Moz also took her leave, saying that she would send them a child on a bicycle, so they might have a useful messenger.

'What's next?' Dan asked.

'Antibiotics. I'll need to run a feeding tube, so if you could grab me a paediatric NG tube at some point – but that's secondary for now. The main thing's to get this packed and closed as soon as possible, every second that it's communicating with the airways is a risk of asphyxia.'

'Or infection, presumably.'

'Yes. Can I borrow some tramadol?'

'Of *course.*'

Usually Charlotte did her best to avoid depleting the human pharmacy, but this – a long shot, which possibly she shouldn't be taking – deserved pain relief. She reached to cup the head of the tortoise, which was far extended, and resting immobile on the floor. A bad sign. Dan headed for the pharmacy, but in the doorway he paused.

'Two minutes. I'm here,' he said. 'I'll help.'

36

Charlotte had already cleaned and packed the deepest wound with sterile gauze pads when Walter returned from the boatyard with a mid-sized bottle of epoxy and hardener, a sheet of chopped-strand fibreglass, and a small cordless multi-tool. Charlotte measured and mixed the resin and hardener. Then she gently sterilised what she could, showing Dan where she needed him to hold pieces steady. She began, painstakingly, to glue the fragments back together. Where shards were missing she packed the gap with gauze, painted resin around the perimeter, and then covered this with a thatch of glass fibres, tamping them down with the brush of epoxy until it soaked and formed into a light protective shell of its own. Dan nodded down at the resin, not colourless as they'd expected, but instead the glittering turquoise of a California swimming pool.

'Fancy.'

'Mmm.' Charlotte was not in the mood for banter. 'It's setting, we have to be quicker.'

Together they worked. Dan, in gloves, was shaping small pads of glass fibre, ready for her to use. When he saw Charlotte's urgency he picked up another brush to help repair the other side, but she snapped, 'Not along the scute lines!'

and he stopped, realising that in his ignorance he could only make it worse. He went back to assisting, stirring the stiff and thickening gloop with a stick to keep it useable as long as possible.

It took them two hours. There was gravel and sand in the wounds. Above the back left leg the shell had separated, and a sharp pebble stuck fast in the gap. The edge above that same leg had broken and splintered, and Dan held one side still while Charlotte sanded the jagged shell with the Dremel so that as the tortoise walked it wouldn't stab into the leg beneath. Miss Moz had sent them Annie Goss, who indeed proved herself invaluable when they ran out of epoxy, cycling to the boatyard and back at a speed only attainable in the tropical heat for a determined and energetic twelve-year-old. This second batch proved to be silver, and even Charlotte allowed herself a despairing laugh.

'Disco tortoise,' she said, bending over the animal, looking into its hooded black eyes. And then to Dan, 'Sorry I was short with you. You see here, these lines between the scutes, they're growth lines, we have to do our best not to impede or disturb them. Obviously where it's really damaged that's impossible. You do this one.' She tried to hand him the brush but Dan shook his head, more than content to remain her scrub nurse.

When the shell repairs were over, they regarded the tortoise. It was no longer bloody. Now it was a strange patchwork, swirls of iridescent aquamarine and glistening silver, many with long flossy white fibres sticking out on all sides. Charlotte had been working quickly and there were blue and silver drips around the lower edges of the shell.

'What a dog's dinner. I'll sand down those fluffy bits eventually but not yet. She deserves a break.'

'Maybe a dog's dinner, but you've saved it.'

'I've a long way off saved her, but at least she's all closed up. Right. Last thing is we get this tube in. Then I'm going to take her home for some rest.'

'Home the jungle?'

'Obviously not. Home my house. Levi's house. Wherever the hell I live. She needs intensive care, I'll have to put her in the bath. What I really need is a UV basking lamp.' She thought for a moment. 'What about a blacklight, has anyone got a blacklight bulb anywhere, for parties?'

'You've been at island hops. Not really a blacklight sort of vibe.'

'But there are teenagers here, doesn't anyone have, like, a garage somewhere? Illegal raves, or whatever?'

'I truly don't know, I'll ask around. Are you telling me something about your own teenage self?'

'Ha. Can you imagine? I was reading about non-native newt invasion while they were all snogging in blacklit garages. Let's get this oesophagostomy line in.'

They brought the tortoise home, very slowly, in the ambulance. Out of respect for Charlotte, who seemed distinctly wobbly beneath a deliberately steely professional exterior, Dan did not even try a salmonella joke.

For her part, now that the adrenaline had begun to disperse, Charlotte felt oddly hollow, a strange sense of disengagement about what was almost certainly a catastrophic rift with her mother. The grand work of her life had been to avoid upsetting Lucinda, fearing banishment to the chill, lonely tundra of her disapproval. Now that Charlotte had screamed – spectacularly, irrevocably – she was fairly certain Lucinda would never speak to her again.

She had no parents. She had no berth off the island. Her fellowship was over, the fellowship administrator dead. She wouldn't even have a job here much longer, for she had already begun contacting references for her three shortlisted candidates to replace herself. How much longer could she possibly stay a squatter in her ex-boyfriend's cottage? She had a disco tortoise to save. That was it.

Dan backed the ambulance up close to the cottage and Charlotte jumped out to prop open the kitchen door, and to shove the little table against the sink to clear a path. Together they hoisted down the turquoise- and silver-patched tortoise, still on its Tugan blanket, and carried it through to the living room.

'Where to?'

Charlotte gestured behind him with her head.

'Bathroom.'

Charlotte lifted the listless animal from beneath its plastron, and set it gently into the bathtub. To the blue and silver had been added the putty-peach of surgical tape, four strips holding the end of the violet-capped feeding tube in place. The animal stayed very still, and Charlotte and Dan also stood still, regarding it. Then the sound of footsteps on the stairs made them each turn.

Lucinda surged towards them, tablecloth trailing, white knitted cap slightly askew on her blonde hair. If anything it was more astonishing than her first appearance on the island. Lucinda had not disowned her. Lucinda was waving.

'Oh, welcome back, darling. You must have left in such a rush this morning, I've just been having a little tidy-up.' She peered between them into the bathroom. 'Very good to see, it's still going, well done. Goodness, what a jolly colour scheme. Festive.'

It was as if their last conversation had been about housekeeping. Charlotte was saved from replying, for at that moment Annie Goss also came in, holding a white plastic box.

'I got the nail lamp, she said it's in two parts so you can open it up, like you asked.'

'Isn't that Katie's?' Dan asked.

Charlotte was dismantling the lamp, triumphant. 'Yes, I just – took a punt, her nails are always too annoyingly perfect, I was sure it had to be UV gel. Annie, well done, thank you so much.'

Annie bobbed a thank you. Then she looked with anxiety over Charlotte's shoulder at the gold coin in the bathtub.

'Will she be OK?'

'I am going to do all I can, I promise you. And I need your help, still. Can you get me an extension cord for this? If we can angle it on a chair . . . ' Charlotte had begun to mutter to herself. It would not be the ideal wavelengths but surely it was better than nothing, if they could fashion a stand for it. Dan squeezed her elbow and took his leave, ushering Annie out with him. A moment later they heard the ambulance driving back up the stony track to the main road. Charlotte and Lucinda were alone.

'Goodness,' Lucinda tried, brightly. 'Those islanders are full of surprises. If I'd known someone had a lamp I'd have been round like a shot.' She extended her hand to look at her own nails. 'I'd give a kidney for a good gel manicure.'

'Why are you here?' asked Charlotte, shortly.

'To see what I can do, darling, to see you.'

'You never want to see me. I've got work to do.'

'Well, I shall roll my sleeves up, give me a task,' said Lucinda, and Charlotte felt an inner scream rising that she could not make this all – stop happening. She wanted to be flushing out the endotracheal tube and giving a bolus of antibiotics and tramadol to her tortoise – whom she had already privately named Gloria Gaynor. She did not want to be discussing manicures with her mother.

'This animal needs round-the-clock checks, heat, antibiotics, fluids, ultraviolet light. I don't even know if this nail lamp is UVA or UVB or just purple rubbish. She's going to need 24/7 intensive care, probably for weeks.'

'Surely I can do a bit of that,' said Lucinda. She crouched down and patted the tortoise awkwardly on the head with a bouncing movement, as if ringing the bell on a hotel reception desk. 'Hello,' she said, and then turned her back to the bathtub and returned her attention to Charlotte. 'I mean, not weeks, obviously, because we will be leaving sooner than that, thank goodness, but certainly until we go.'

Lucinda began to bite a cuticle in an uncharacteristically nervous gesture.

Charlotte walked away, so that she would say nothing else. She flung open the fridge in search of tortoise sustenance, and found some cantaloupe, and a precious head of newly imported Island Open romaine. She had begun to feel wobbly again, and realised she herself hadn't eaten since early that morning. She sliced bread for toast, and began to liquidise some lettuce for Gloria Gaynor.

37

Lucinda expressed her determination to stay at the cottage in order to be nebulously 'helpful', and so Charlotte assigned her once again to the bedroom upstairs, in the hope that she would soon retreat to it. In any case Charlotte would not sleep much, for Gloria Gaynor needed hourly observation and fluids. She shoved the sofa closer to the bathroom door so that she had a view of the bath from her pillow. She was curt in her explanations, and aware of speaking with a pious solemnity. It was possible that she was making a bigger performance of this than necessary. Nonetheless, a petty yet irrepressible instinct impelled her to demonstrate the gravity of Lucinda's transgression and, more to the point, exactly how competent was veterinary surgeon Dr Charlotte Walker, BVetMed MSc MRCVS PhD, when it came to cleaning up and repairing the resulting mess. For the first time in her life, Lucinda was compelled by proximity and liability to pay attention to her daughter's job. Charlotte felt the warm glow and certainty of the righteous. She flushed the tube with saline, she listened to Gloria Gaynor's heartbeat with a Doppler swiped from the clinic. She busied herself, her back turned to hovering Lucinda. At midnight her mother murmured something about feeling a touch faint in the heat, and retreated upstairs. The house fell silent.

At three a.m., a drowsing Charlotte heard footsteps on the stairs again. It was Lucinda, pale hair loose, a spectral apparition. Charlotte shook herself awake, determined not to have been caught sleeping. Lucinda floated towards her.

'I came to see if I might be useful, darling.' Her voice was quieter than usual, almost quavering.

'It's fine,' said Charlotte tightly. 'It's under control.'

'I must say I do feel rotten about this.' Lucinda's hands fluttered at her stomach. 'I feel positively ill with it.'

'Mmm,' Charlotte said, and then stood and went to the kitchen sink to wash her hands in Hibiscrub, before checking again on her patient. It was typical of Lucinda to compete like this. Charlotte was the one who felt sick with sorrow, quite frankly. But at that moment Lucinda clapped a hand over her mouth, and with an indistinct gurgling surged forth into the little bathroom. Seconds later came the unmistakable sound of retching and Charlotte knew, with a sudden rising, roiling inevitability, that she too was going to vomit. She grabbed desperately for a saucepan as the contents of her stomach erupted, hot and acidic.

Once it began, it was as if the vomiting would never stop. Charlotte hung over her saucepan, unable to lower it for more than a few seconds before the next wave; across the room she could see in the purplish light of the nail lamp her mother kneeling over the loo, gripping either side of the seat. Charlotte staggered into the bathroom, but Lucinda would not cede her place. Charlotte bent to drink from the tap, but no sooner had she swallowed a teaspoon of lukewarm water than it came back up again. At her feet Lucinda wrapped her arms grimly around the toilet, like a child refusing to release a toy.

'Fuck,' Lucinda managed, and Charlotte opened her mouth to reply, and instead was sick again. If Lucinda did not move out of the way soon the saucepan would overflow, or the sink block. She felt lightheaded and clammy with cold despite the temperature which was, on the tortoise's behalf, close to forty degrees. They had not turned on the fan or opened the windows, and the air was humid and still.

'Fuck,' Lucinda said again, hoarsely. 'This is how it ends.' She released her grip on the toilet bowl and listed sideways until she was lying in the foetal position on the bathroom floor, her cheek against the tiles. Charlotte staggered forward gratefully and upturned the contents of her saucepan. In the sink she rinsed it, and then clunked it down on the floor. She hugged her knees to her chest and moaned, the room spinning. In the bath she heard a faint scrabble of claws, but couldn't raise her head to check. Let the poor animal die, she thought, as she herself was surely dying.

'Euthanise me,' whispered Lucinda, with uncanny telepathy. 'Put me out of this misery. What's *happening*?'

Charlotte gave a grunt of reply.

'Salmonella,' she managed eventually, and then closed her eyes, exhaling slowly while the room lurched and spun. It was as long again before she could say anything further. 'Salmonella. From . . . it's on their shells. I was upset, I – I – maybe I touched my face.'

Lucinda was in child's pose, forehead down, against the floor. Then she rose with a sudden surging desperation and all but elbowed Charlotte out of the way. Charlotte crawled to the far wall, embracing her saucepan again. For a long time, neither spoke.

Through the tiny bathroom window the dawn came, faint pink and a slowly deepening rose beginning to creep across a sky washed palest grey. Soon, a buttercup sun would warm the island back into vivid colour, the birds begin their chorus, the flowers would unfurl. It promised to be a beautiful day. Meanwhile, in Charlotte's cottage, the diarrhoea began.

38

It was mostly over by lunchtime. Charlotte was lying curled on the loose pebbled floor of the outdoor shower. Standing seemed impossible, but a particularly sharp rock was protruding uncomfortably into her shoulder, and it did not seem sensible to lie in direct sunshine when, despite the falling water, she was no doubt severely dehydrated. Over, or maybe never over, for while her shaking body was clean again, her mind was polluted with squalid memories she feared she might carry with her forever. Eventually she turned off the tap and dried herself, struggled into knickers and a vest top, and made her way back into the cottage and up the stairs.

Lucinda had already showered and lay curled on one side of the bed wearing a pair of Charlotte's pyjamas, her hair wet on the pillow. Parted from the cosmetic dermatologist, her face had become increasingly expressive during her weeks on Tuga, as if the longer she stayed, the more expansive became her feelings. At present her newly mobile features were screwed up in a picture of acute distress, eyebrows raised, as if demanding an explanation from the universe. Charlotte collapsed on the bed beside her and groaned.

'Are you seriously telling me the tortoise did that to us?'

'Most of them carry salmonella on their skin, their shells, in their digestive tract. It's our fault for poor hygiene.'

‘I have a newfound respect for tortoises. I thought they were just animated side tables, but no. You run one over, and it decides to effect karmic retribution. Like a golden poison frog, but stealthier.’

Charlotte gave a surprised laugh, which twinged in her strained stomach muscles.

‘How do you remember about golden poison frogs?’

‘*Phyllobates terribilis*,’ recited Lucinda without hesitating. ‘Darling, you talked about nothing but frogs for about a decade, I’d have to have been thick as a plank not to absorb some of it.’

‘Tell me about golden poison frogs?’ Charlotte asked. She wriggled beneath the light covers, readjusting the pillow beneath her.

‘We must keep sipping water. God, as if my complexion hasn’t suffered enough in this infernal place, I feel a husk. All right. Golden poison frogs are the size of a fifty-pence piece and contain enough poison to kill ten humans.’

‘That’s amazing. Habitat?’

‘Amazon rainforest.’

‘What about . . . the tomato frog?’ Charlotte tried, not testing exactly, but intensely curious. Until seconds earlier she would have said that her mother couldn’t tell a frog from a fruit fly. She could not quite believe this conversation was taking place.

‘*Dyscophus*. When threatened they secrete some ghastly something-or-other. And I distinctly remember that they can live for up to eight years. They had one at Palmer’s Pet Shop and you wanted it desperately, if you recall. A year or two, and I might have at least heard your case, but eight years was unthinkable. You intended to call it Pomodoro, I believe.’

‘It would have been Pom-Pom for short,’ said Charlotte, remembering. ‘I thought that was such a clever name because they can puff up. Like a pom-pom. They're the most beautiful frogs in the world. Apart from the mimic poison, of course, but that's in a league of its own.'

Lucinda gave a small, sad smile. 'Your ability to find beauty in slime is truly remarkable. I am sorry about Joan. It wasn't my finest hour, getting rid of her. In my defence, you'd managed to name her after your father's wife, and that part was just terribly odd, and the final straw with a creature I hadn't exactly adored to begin with. I did wonder at the time if somehow you knew.'

'I didn't know anything about *that* Joan, it was after Joan Beauchamp Procter.'

Lucinda flapped a hand at her, indicating that she had no wish to cover old ground.

'I know, I know, the zoo woman with the Komodo dragon and the haircut. The first female curator of tennis elbow in salamanders, or whatever it was. I might have managed it differently, with hindsight. Adrian didn't like animals and when I married him I thought, well, she's going to have a bit of a life now, a family of sorts, she's taking Adrian's name, and those boys of his will be playmates so she won't need the sad little menagerie. It hurt me, that those were your friends. Slimy things and stick insects and all those hours you spent cultivating horrible bugs, and I thought maybe without all that you might . . . You were such a quiet, solitary little girl. I wanted you to have real friends.'

'They were my real friends, then. I loved them.'

'I know that. I did see after I'd done it that I'd made a mistake, you weren't going to suddenly develop social confidence and wherewithal just because I'd sent away the animals. And it wasn't actually the point that those strange tanks and ponds and God knows what were your world, which I found agonising. They were your *work*, which I didn't see, because you were a child, and one doesn't think of children's work . . . But Adrian wouldn't have the dragon in the house, and by the time I wouldn't have Adrian in the house you'd stopped asking for it. I thought perhaps you'd forgotten. I don't know what to say. I made a lot of mistakes.'

'It's OK,' said Charlotte, finding, with surprise, that it was. Hearing her mother speak the words *Phyllobates terribilis* had realigned something within her cells; it had worked a deep, strange magic upon her, like an incantation. *Phyllobates terribilis.* All those years, her mother had been listening.

'Get some rest, darling.'

Lucinda's hand fluttered, as if she might raise it to reach over. But she tucked it under her cheek and closed her eyes again, and soon they were both, mercifully, asleep.

The ship's horn sounded, and as Charlotte awoke the island bells were ringing out in reply. She opened her eyes to see that a bottle of Mac's coconut water had appeared on her bedside table. Cold and sweet, it was just about the only thing she could imagine wanting to consume, possibly for the rest of her life. Beside her, her mother was propped up in bed, drinking from her own bottle with tentative sips, grimacing.

'That ratty child came again,' Lucinda said, by way of explanation, raising her drink as if about to propose a toast. 'She'd made a get-well-soon card for the tortoise, and brought you a KitKat. I sent her off for electrolytes and she came back with this. It helps, but one mustn't overdo it.'

'Oh, lovely Annie. She probably pinched the KitKat. How is Gloria?'

'Who's Gloria? Oh, yes. Alive. Scrabbling. I can't say I'm lining up to get particularly intimate with her.'

'She'll need fluids too, in a minute.'

Lucinda took a final, microscopic sip of her coconut water and then lay back down gingerly, beside Charlotte.

'That racket was the boat leaving, I presume. So on that account, at least, we are no longer against the clock.'

'Yes. That's it, now.'

'I don't suppose it matters really, a few days here or there. I couldn't persuade any of those stubborn bloody islanders in any case. For people without a bean they've proven remarkably resistant to bribery. Lars is on his way for us, thank goodness. I had hoped for something a little more comfortable for our return – the journey here, I must tell you, was something of a trial. But a boat in the hand, and all that.'

'When will he get here?'

'I don't know, darling. Soon, I think, don't worry. Two or three days, I'd expect. He was in radio contact with your hulking customs woman the day before yesterday. The one who's in love with the skippy little physiotherapist.'

'In love with Katie? Is she?' Charlotte had never considered Elsie having room in her heart for anyone besides a considerably slimmed-down Argentinian red tegu.

'Goodness, yes. Positively moony-eyed.'

'I'm not sure that has legs. Katie Salmon came here engaged to Dan Zekri.'

'The hunky doctor with the nice bottom and all that brooding angst, yes. I know all the dramatis personae now. He chucked her because he's got a thing for you.'

'No he doesn't,' Charlotte protested. 'Well, definitely not any longer.'

'I can't be expected to keep up. Though I must say at your age Levi would have been far more up my alley.'

Lucinda looked steadily at Charlotte, who flushed and busied herself with her coconut water. After a moment she said, carefully, 'I'd have thought you'd be Team Dan all the way. Doctor, studied in England, proper career, etc.'

'Oh, don't be so suburban, Levi has more sex appeal in his little finger. And he is charming in his own raw, rough-hewn sort of way; I entirely understand why you had your fling, or whatever it was. But neither of those men is an actual viable prospect for any sort of real *life*, so how could it possibly be relevant if one happens to have a medical qualification? It doesn't matter if one is a doctor and the other is an astronaut, neither is right for my daughter. You'd never be happy with some eccentric little islander – butcher, baker or candlestick maker. Bonk Levi to your heart's content before we leave – and Dan too, for that matter; I can hardly see that it makes much difference.'

'Absolutely not Dan, he's my friend.' Charlotte paused. 'And Levi's got a girlfriend.'

'Oh well, then.' Lucinda waved her hand, dismissing even the idea of him as she would a bothersome housefly. 'Onwards. You've had your grand catharsis with your father, that's what you came for. Now you'll come home to London and work. You can despise everything about me, and it seems that you do, but for the record I do feel I must clarify that I have never wanted you either to be, nor to marry, a banker. I have only ever wanted you to do good work well, and that you already do. In that sense you are my child through and through, by the way, reject me as you might. Your drive and your work ethic are pure Compton-Neville. The only route to fulfilment for women like us is to do *hard, engaging work that matters*.'

For the rest of the day they lay in bed, two survivors. Often they were silent, dozing, occasionally prompting one another to take small sips of coconut water; discussing, with trepidation, whether they were out of the woods. Charlotte made lightheaded, careful excursions downstairs to tend to Gloria Gaynor, who seemed stable. At nightfall each tried to eat a dry cracker, and was successful. The turmoil of Charlotte's guts had finally quietened. Her mind too had more and more lucidity: a rock pool stirred, the sand slowly settling. It was new clarity, perhaps her first.

Because, of course, her mother was right. Lucinda had shaped her by example, far more than she had known. Work as pleasure, work as fulfilment; vocation as self. Those were lessons driven deep; shaping a core that now had, Charlotte realised, more solidity than she had ever imagined. She too was passionate and single-minded. Meaning came from hard, engaging work that mattered. Seeing that, Charlotte saw everything.

39

In the morning, Lucinda awoke a new woman, and announced that she was ravenous, in a voice loud enough to fill a courtroom. After her final check of the tortoise in the early hours Charlotte had not been downstairs again but had stayed the rest of the night upstairs in her own bed, with her mother. This declamation came surprisingly close to her ear. She dragged herself from the submarine depths of heavy sleep.

'Shall we have a bit of toast?' Lucinda was asking, brightly. Yesterday's infirmity seemed a distant memory, but of course she had not been running obs and fluids every ninety minutes, till the small hours. Charlotte felt jet-lagged and slow; she could never match Lucinda's pace at the best of times. Her mother was sitting up cross-legged, brushing her hair with Charlotte's hairbrush. As her hand moved something blue caught Charlotte's eye.

'Do nip down, darling. Some person or other had left you a crock of new butter when I arrived yesterday, I forgot to mention. Crock! What a wonderful word, one doesn't usually have call for it.'

'What's that on your hand?' Charlotte mumbled, half into the pillow.

'Oh, yes. I intended to ask you about this.'

Lucinda clattered the hairbrush on to the bedside table

and threw back the sheet, coming round to stand next to Charlotte. She extended an elegant arm, and Charlotte saw on her middle finger an enormous ring of rich blue enamel, patterned with tiny gold stars.

'Where did you get this?' Lucinda demanded, in the manner of an interrogating officer displaying evidence.

Charlotte felt she herself might well ask the same question, had she dared, for this ring had been hidden in a small box at the bottom of her own washbag. It had belonged to Garrick's wife, who had left it to Charlotte in her will, an oddly excessive bequest from someone she had known only slightly. At the time she had felt the honour of it, without entirely understanding. Now, simply owning it made her feel guilty.

'Joan Williams left it to me in her will. Obviously she didn't know I was Garrick's illegitimate daughter.'

'You do have a way of making everything sound so sordid, I wish you wouldn't. You are the legitimate daughter of me. I see. So this was given as a mark of her esteem for your – tortoise-ship. What a woman.' This without apparent sarcasm. 'I see there's a stone missing. Do you think she wore it farming?' Lucinda extended her hand again, turning it side to side.

'I don't know what to do with it, it just makes me feel complicit, somehow. I can never wear it.'

'I'm not sure whether feeling complicit in one's own conception is narcissism or solipsism, but either way, perhaps don't. This ring is somewhat in my style, in fact, don't you think? Now get up, darling. Yesterday I spotted you had some bread in the fridge.'

Charlotte closed her eyes again. 'I don't think we should eat anything in there.'

'Nonsense. Marmite toast cures all.'

'Betsey has Marmite,' Charlotte suggested, battling to sound enthusiastic. She forced herself to sit up. At present the idea of leaving the cottage was about as appealing as scaling Thursday's Peak. 'But please don't forget to take that off before we're in public, everyone will recognise it.'

'That's absolute madness, we're not going out anywhere. Nip down and pop some toast on, darling.'

'Gloria Gaynor died,' Charlotte said softly. 'About two hours ago.'

'Oh, darling, I am so sorry.' Lucinda seemed to sag, and sat back down. 'I'm truly sorry. But what has that to do with—'

'I wrapped her in a bin bag and put her in the fridge.'

Charlotte flopped down in bed and, just for one blissful moment, turned her face back into the pillow.

There was some stale ginger cake in a tin, and they ate this on the sofa with mugs of black tea. Neither felt ready to face dairy, and in any case, the milk was now inaccessible behind the chilled corpse of the two hundred and seventy-eighth gold coin tortoise. Lucinda sat as far away from the fridge as possible, though she gave it intermittent nervous glances. They talked, and talked.

'And you are quite certain,' said Lucinda, after a time.

Charlotte nodded. 'Yes. I can't keep staying here, and of course you were right about what you said. I need to get on and email the vet candidates. But you're sure Lars will be fine with this?'

'Darling, he's been saying from the off that he'd take us both, and he knows you've been here a year, I'm sure he's expecting a few boxes. I must warn you that it's an absolute tin can, but I assure you there's enough space. I shall go back to Mary's, and get out of your way while you finish the last bits of packing.'

Lucinda shot a final, queasy glance at the refrigerator and stepped out of the door. Under the avocado tree she stopped, and turned back. At her feet the overripe pears lay smashed and splitting; seething with ants.

'I've no doubt all your lab people at ZSL will be overjoyed, darling. Shall we meet this evening for a very light supper?'

'I'd like that.'

'A bowl of plain pasta with butter, maybe, and some fresh ginger beer.'

'The ship's been,' Charlotte told her. 'Betsey will want to serve us baked beans with Cheddar.'

'Oh, don't, I shall be sick again and never stop. We'll go to the Rockhopper then, we can have that glowering woman's delicious bread.'

Charlotte laughed. 'Marianne Goss.'

'That one. We shall have salted butter and her miserable, delicious sourdough, and show off your new cheekbones. I must say, a day of vomiting suits you.'

'They do amazing chicken soup with ginger, too; it saved me when I was seasick. Can I ask, why were you actually driving near the taro fields?'

Lucinda gave a heavy sigh.

'As it happens, there's a girl on the moshav who gives an excellent deep-tissue massage, and Katie Salmon chats too much. It seemed prudent before a long and confining sea voyage. Mary offered me her car, as I had not felt inclined to take the girl's direction and "catch a donkey".'

Something caught her eye, and she peered through the window, around the side of the cottage.

'Look at that, your bougainvillea's in flower, it's the most glorious bright pink. We must be sure to take a cutting before Lars comes. I will concede this infernal island has some attractive flora.'

40

It was a pleasure to visit Sylvester's after the Island Open ship had cleared its cargo. Shelves that had lain empty for long months were now replenished with apples and washing-up liquid and packaged noodles; toilet bleach and hairbrushes and bagged raisins and brown sauce. The usual scents of island citrus and cinnamon and vanilla were today overlaid with others; nets of garlic heads filled two baskets, and a box of washing powder had spilled behind the counter. Wheat and oats had come in sacks of twenty-five kilos stacked on a pallet in the store's backyard, and drums of vegetable oil were lined up in the shaded passageway, brought in for those who considered it superior to the island's own plentiful coconut oil. The drums and the sacking were also useful items, sometimes earmarked by a different customer from the one buying the contents. These were pleasurable days and trying ones, as Sylvester worked to satisfy everyone, and to ensure a fair distribution of necessarily limited resources. Tugans had a collectivist spirit, and on the whole little intervention was needed. Most would never dream of buying more than a fair share of rice or fresh vegetables. But where confectionary was concerned generosity was tried to its limit, and Sylvester felt obliged to remain vigilant. The last box of Cadbury's chocolate fingers had induced some inelegant behaviour, that memorable year they'd contained both white chocolate and milk.

This particular ship had brought a wonderful glut of celery and leeks and brown onions, promising months of fragrant soups ahead; all these grew on the island, but never in large enough quantities. The wrong brand of cornflakes had come, and what seemed an excessive quantity of barbecue-flavour Pringles, to the disappointing exclusion of ready salted. Some of the AA batteries had leaked. But they had a solid shipment of Cs back in for torches, as well as waterproof sunscreen, and a larger quantity of nail polish remover than usual. Sylvester was writing a sign when Charlotte entered. He looked up.

'*Paz*, Charlotte Vet. Ain't no pink wafer biscuits come.' He shook his head slowly. 'It say twenty boxes right on the order slip, and they've charged me and all. Elsie says she'll take it up with Bucknall & Porteous and they'll be on the next ship, but Elsie ain't going to have to tell the children now, is she.

'Of all the things. Now, if it was Jammie Dodgers forgotten that ain't a problem, because our Marianne can make just about anything and the jam here's better and all. I'd be the first to enjoy a papaya Jammie Dodger, myself. But I can't go asking her to make me two hundred pink wafers.' He turned his page around so Charlotte could admire the large-print NO PINK WAFERS COME and beneath it Sylvester's own illustration, a puce rectangle, with a sad face. 'What can I do you for? I got your printer paper set aside, and them sticky notes you wanted. Don't break my heart and tell me it's wafers you've come for.'

Charlotte looked at the posters behind Sylvester. Subject to the arrival of the casings, Burt would be making sausages next week, and anyone wishing to put in an order was to leave a note with Sylvester. Volunteers were needed to run next week's clothing swap at the Old Kal. There was an advert for Katie's Pilates, printed on mauve paper and containing many athletic emoji. Charlotte admired her own notice regarding her new and improved flea initiative, Flea and Easy.

'No biscuits. I actually wondered how much vodka you had?'

Sylvester sucked his teeth.

'As I recall from the doc's retirement party, you ain't a one for vodka.'

'It's not for drinking, it's for a work thing,' said Charlotte, flushing. Then Annie Goss stepped from behind a bank of shelves holding a KitKat, and Charlotte was saved from further explanation. Annie came over silently to queue behind Charlotte.

'Morning. You look like someone who's been adventuring. Can I get that for you?'

Annie gave a rare grin and slapped it down on the counter.

'Yes.'

'Please,' Sylvester prompted her.

'Yes, please,' Annie repeated dutifully. Charlotte noticed she held one hand behind her back.

'Anything else?'

Annie casually handed Charlotte a can of lager and gave her a breezy look, chin lifted. Charlotte looked steadily back at her.

'I'm not convinced your mum would thank me if I got you that,' she said, setting it down gently.

Annie began to scratch an angry-looking mosquito bite on one shin with the grubby heel of the other foot. Charlotte saw a bead of blood form, then smear. She longed to take the child to the clinic for some antiseptic.

'She don't get to decide my life. All she does is try to ruin it.'

Charlotte felt a new pang of sympathy for cool, remote

Marianne Goss, repository of all this resentment. Marianne had always repelled intimacy, repelled even the lightest of passing conversations. And yet Charlotte remembered the warmth between Annie and her mother, and the quiet shared, exclusive laughter between Marianne and the girl and boy she'd raised together as twins. Perhaps because of Ruth's illness, theirs had seemed a household apart. But within it, behind whatever invisible pane it was that separated them, there had been tenderness, and play. Charlotte had barely ever seen the children without one another until Alex had sailed.

'I promise you lager is disgusting, take it from me. It is not the answer to anything,' Charlotte told Annie, resisting the urge to push the child's hand from her mouth, to stop her from tearing at a fingernail.

'Oh, I'd beg to differ there,' Sylvester interrupted and Charlotte frowned, to silence whatever inappropriate advice was to come. 'A bit of flat lager on a rag'll bring back the shine to a hardwood in no time.' He winked at Charlotte.

'There you go. What about a Mars Bar?' Charlotte turned back to Sylvester. 'A KitKat and a Mars Bar for my friend, please, and if you have it I need twenty litres of unflavoured vodka, the highest proof you have.'

Sylvester disappeared into the yard, where he could be heard moving boxes around and muttering. Annie snatched up the chocolate bars and raced out of the door, her progress only slowed by arriving customers who stepped aside to let her pass. Maia Lindo-Smith entered with Rebecca, who slipped her hand into her mother's and smiled at Charlotte with shy pride. Behind them an impassive Levi stood with his arms crossed, unsmiling, as if he were Maia's personal protection officer. He was wearing a familiar T-shirt, one Charlotte had loved to borrow, worn to softness with age and washing. She met his eyes only for a moment, and then he looked away.

'*Ke haber*,' said Maia, offering her hand.

'Hi, I'm Charlotte. So nice to meet you.'

She did look like Levi, Charlotte realised, despite the fairer colouring. The wide dark eyes, and thick long lashes. The strong jaw.

'Rebecca has been so helpful,' Charlotte told Maia. 'She's taught me all about plants, and all the local fruit, and gardening, haven't you?'

Rebecca gave a serious nod.

'I've got a new tooth wobbly. It's on borrowed time, Mama says.' Rebecca pulled down her lower lip so Charlotte could see. 'And Mama's brought loads of fabric bits from England and we're going to make a rabbit.' Rebecca had become taken with rabbits recently, having never seen a real one, and had even launched a tentative and doomed campaign for Charlotte to sanction the import of one as a pet. It was hard to think of a greater ecological catastrophe on Tuga than rabbits.

'Uncle Levi is going to take me and Mama camping next weekend,' Rebecca added, beaming up at Levi, and apparently content to make conversation for all of them. 'He's got a tent that goes on the roof.'

'Well, that all sounds very exciting,' said Charlotte, fighting vivid memories of that same roof-tent. She was aware of Maia's steady gaze upon her. It was not exactly unfriendly. Appraising, perhaps. She wondered how much Levi had told her. At that moment Sylvester reappeared carrying a case of bottles, which he heaved on to the counter.

'That's a dozen in there of 70cl, and you're wanting twenty litres, so by my cal-calations, you'll be needing two and a half more cases, have I done that correct?'

Levi and Maia both turned to look at the cardboard box, stamped with 'Smirnoff Red Label', together with a sequence of legal health warnings. Levi raised an eyebrow.

'Having a leaving party?'

This was the first direct sentence he had spoken to her, and yet 'ha, ha' was the sharpest answer of which Charlotte felt capable. Then she glanced anxiously at Maia. Nothing about this encounter seemed designed to improve whatever impression she might have.

'I'll pass, if that's all right. Busy that night. Be careful with my house.'

Charlotte, who had been about to say something entirely different, instead snapped, 'Don't worry, you'll have your house back soon enough.'

Then she told Sylvester she would call back for the rest later, picked up her case of vodka and left, with as much dignity as she could muster. It was a shorter walk to the clinic than the cottage and so she stopped there first, shoving the crate beneath her exam table. On the printer in her office lay some papers, the details of her chosen candidate for the permanent vet's role. These she checked through once, twice, a third time, before signing them and taking them over to Customs House for the island councillors.

41

The cottage was as bare as the day she had come. Until only a few months earlier the heavy mango-wood bed had been downstairs, filling the kitchen and leaving only a narrow channel in which to get to the sink, or to edge open the cupboards. For a year she had slept within arm's reach of kettle, hob and bin, and the bed's absence still made the small room feel bigger than it was.

Now her bags were stacked neatly on the little porch, beneath the spangled vine of pumpkin-coloured spider-flowers that most nights insisted on curling new tendrils through the kitchen window and once, when she had not interrupted its progress, had gone on to encircle the handle of the washing-up brush, as if it had only come in to help. The pair of slim frangipani trees that flanked the tiny house seemed always to be in bloom, and today each thin branch was topped with a heavy pom-pom cluster of velvety white flowers, smudged yolk-yellow at their hearts. How Charlotte had loved this house. She had been happy here.

On the kitchen table she left Levi's lurid, hibiscus-printed bucket hat, and a bunch of wild calla lilies that she'd picked by the roadside, tucked into an empty bourbon bottle. There were no keys to return, for the cottage had no locks. She left, gently closing both halves of the kitchen door behind her.

On the porch a Tugan blanket was rolled up neatly on top of her few bags, another gift from Joan Williams when Charlotte had first arrived, thick wool in primrose and saffron and chestnut, its design of rudimentary donkeys and tortoises not entirely dissimilar from the one they had used as a stretcher for Gloria Gaynor. Beside it stood only a 25-litre paint bucket with a metal handle, its seal wrapped around and around in silver gaffer tape. She had not, in the end, acquired much.

Any minute Dan would be here to collect her suitcases. He would have happily given her a lift to the harbour too, but Charlotte felt too raw for small talk – or worse, for real talk – and so she left the cases and picked up the paint bucket. This she began to haul with her, the tub thumping painfully against her shins as she walked the sandy track from the Mendoza cottage to the harbour, for the last time.

The romance of the gesture had dissipated by the time Charlotte had lugged her bucket all the way. It wasn't an unreasonable distance but it always came as a surprise, how much harder the heat made physical labour. She should have waited for a lift. At the end of Harbour Street she stopped, thudding the sloshing tub down at her feet, rubbing her hands, her palms raw from the thin plastic of the handle. Her sunglasses slipped down her nose.

As expected, Lucinda was already waiting. She wore the clothes in which she had arrived, ironed and pristine, with the towering addition of a stack of three nested palm-leaf hats, as if she had come to the harbour to hawk them to passing tourists. Her lavender pashmina was folded over her arm in the manner of a sommelier with a napkin, and as Charlotte approached, Lucinda extended the corner of this scarf to show that the monogram 'LCN' had been embroidered in silvery thread. Beneath it was a small green tortoise, a golden coin at the centre of each tiny scute.

'Your hulking customs officer has hidden talents.'

'That's very beautiful, I didn't know you'd asked her to do that. Why are you wearing so many hats?'

'A woman must, darling. And also because they'd be crushed beyond recognition if I tried to stuff them into something. Look at this work! She has the most exquisite touch, with those giant hands of hers. She's going to embroider a set of napkins and some linen hand towels for the downstairs loo – Evangeline is having them sent here direct from Liberty. Perhaps I shall have them ready for a dinner five years hence.'

Sea spray on the breeze cooled the air and Lucinda shivered, and arranged her pashmina around her shoulders for the first time since she had arrived on the island. A slim, barefoot young man with a halo of blond curls and a sleeve of tattoos stepped forward and stood beside her like an attendant squire. This, presumably, was Captain Lars.

'Your mother is a remarkable woman,' he said, pumping Charlotte's hand up and down as if to congratulate her for being related to Lucinda. Charlotte noticed a large dragon wrapped around his forearm, its clubbed tail ending between his thumb and forefinger. 'I wouldn't sail so many extra weeks in the middle of a race for many people.'

'How *is* your race going?' Lucinda enquired. 'And I presume you still have my luggage aboard?'

'We think we're in sixth place, out of twenty. The *Lucky Devil* smashed up off Tristan da Cunha; the crew were rescued by the islanders but they're disqualified now, of course. Not so lucky, in the end. Also very stuck. We might go rescue them, if no one else is closer? Only three weeks extra, maybe four.'

Lucinda's expression was not one of a passenger enthused about a detour to Tristan da Cunha.

'But also maybe not.' Lars gave a shrug of reassurance, or perhaps fatalism. 'There's another crew not far past Gough, they might do it. In these seas we all have to help one another. Who knows?'

Fear, and hope. Shipwrecks and rescues. Separation. Everything was happening very fast. For now what Charlotte most wanted was this boat safely docked in Argentina. Yesterday, if possible.

'They've only tested DNA persistence in vodka for up to forty-two days,' she whispered to Lucinda, who nodded, imperilling the tower of hats.

'Captain Lars, my daughter thinks it best to sail straight for Buenos Aires.'

Lars turned a dazzling grin on Charlotte. 'Ah, it's an honour to help a scientist. I hear from your mother you're a fellow conservationist, you may not know we're on the same team. This whole adventure is raising money for EDGE.'

'Wonderful,' said Charlotte, unable to stop herself from adding silently, *unless it sinks.* She glanced involuntarily at the rust bucket, anchored a mile offshore. It looked small and vulnerable in a huge sea.

'Also, it'll be great to carry so much vodka. Only in case of emergency, you understand. And now –' he spread his arms, joyful, expansive '– now I've been ashore on Tuga de Oro! How many can say as much? I must grab a photo in the phone box. I'll be quick –' this to Lucinda '– and in a few moments we'll go to sea. I've loaded the supplies in the lighter so only two minutes, OK?'

Lucinda and Charlotte were left alone together, standing beside the harbour wall.

'Well, darling. Have you told Levi?'

Charlotte shook her head. She was finding it hard to speak. 'He's with Zimbul now. It's over.'

'I have always had a profound antipathy to any adult woman who wears her hair in plaits,' said Lucinda, dismissing Zimbul with a gesture so slight it was barely perceptible. Then her expression altered, as if several instincts were doing battle within her. Finally she said, 'I've seen the way he looks at you, darling, it's far from over.'

Then she cleared her throat, once again businesslike. 'Now, to other matters. I'm not overly enamoured of that Marianne misery-guts. Will you really be comfortable all the way out there? Is it safe?'

'All of Tuga's safe. I won't actually be living with her, it's her neighbour's house. She just takes care of it, and they share a yard.' Charlotte swallowed with difficulty, trying to smile through the hot pressure of sudden, rising tears. 'I wish you'd seen it.'

This last thought, that her mother had not come to see her new home while she'd had the chance, brought on a sort of rising panic. What other chances had they missed? And now there was no time left.

'I can well imagine the splendour. No doubt it's all Georgian mahogany and Colefax and Fowler. Has it an indoor loo?'

'No,' Charlotte admitted.

'I have no words. Now.' Lucinda threw back her shoulders. Then she extended a hand for the white plastic bucket. 'Give me my albatross. Come on, hand it over.'

'It's really heavy.'

'*Instead of the cross, the Albatross / About my neck was hung.*'

'Mummy.'

'I'm only joking, Lars will heft it for me. And I shan't be

a greybeard loon much longer, thank God, the first thing I shall do on dry land is a colour and a trim.' She put a hand on her hip and regarded the bucket at Charlotte's feet. 'You've absolutely ensured it won't leak? Without a wish to revisit painful memories, I urge you to consider what salmonella would be like at sea.'

'I promise I've sealed it. But obviously if it gets bashed about you might want to check on the tape, periodically.'

Lucinda looked as if Charlotte had suggested that she might like periodically to take over the navigation of the ship.

'And what is it precisely that I say about this item, once I attempt to disembark with it?'

'In the next ten days I'll have the paperwork ready, I promise. Someone from ZSL will have the licence in your email account long before you get there.'

'I'm telling you right now that without paperwork Gloria Gaynor goes overboard in Buenos Aires.'

'That's reasonable.'

They exchanged a smile, and Charlotte felt vertigo. She wanted to take her mother's picture as she stood in the cobbled Main Street, to capture her here on the island, in her monogrammed pashmina beneath the huge crowned Victorian lamp posts, behind her a host of tatty Tugan flags whipping and snapping in the wind. She would never be permitted such a photo. Lucinda's grey hair, the free movements of her forehead, her increasingly eccentric island attire would become a thing of myth, a secret known only to the islanders of Tuga de Oro, who were unlikely to forget this particular visitor for some time. In Buenos Aires Evangeline had booked not only hairdresser but also manicurist, dermatologist and even hygienist; Lucinda would land back at Heathrow as polished as if she had merely hopped to a weekend conference in Manhattan. But Manhattan could be reached in only seven hours, scarcely a breath over the Atlantic. It was not likely that Lucinda Compton-Neville would ever come back to Tuga.

Lars jogged towards them, and they all walked together down the dock. Lars leaped nimbly into the launch to join Walter who was waiting patiently, and now turned a questioning face to Lucinda and Charlotte. Charlotte hauled over her sloshing specimen and Lars set it steady, between his feet.

She had managed, in the end, to fit in the entire tortoise. She had pierced its soft tissues over and over with a long, fine needle, in the hope that the twenty litres of vodka in which it was now soaking would penetrate, preserving the body for science. Her colleagues in London had grand plans for Gloria Gaynor: her DNA would be sequenced; her death would benefit her two hundred and seventy-seven remaining cousins. Lucinda might even have advanced the cause of science, in the end.

'*The ship was cheered, the harbour cleared*,' Lucinda quoted, and briefly wrapped her arms around Charlotte who took the opportunity of slipping a small box into her mother's pocket, quickly, before she lost her nerve.

All too soon Lucinda released her and, taking Lars's hand, stepped nimbly into the boat. For a moment Charlotte feared her mother wouldn't turn back, but Lucinda took a seat on the central bench and then looked up towards the dock.

'I'm glad you came,' Charlotte said, but this came out so softly that she then had to repeat it in a strange, hoarse shout.

'Yes, well.' Lucinda looked down rather pointedly at the brown water swilling at her feet. 'As you know, my usual policy is only to travel to cities in which there is a Four Seasons, so you must take this adventure as the compliment it is. Do remember to be a bit more fastidious with sunscreen, darling.'

And with that Walter cast off, and Charlotte watched her mother grow smaller and smaller until the lighter drew up near the kelp beds. She had gone, a far-off figure, wearing many hats.

42

Twenty-five years earlier . . .

On a street in north London stood a woman, watching a house. She wore a navy dress with balloon sleeves, white-collared, white-cuffed, and which the inhabitants of the street would be surprised to learn that she had made herself, from a pattern said to evoke the silhouettes currently favoured by Princess Diana. She carried a sturdy leather handbag, old but well polished, in a rich maroon. It had belonged to her mother, who had schooled her in the importance of correct and appropriate dress for all occasions, even and especially in adversity.

The house was very clean buttercream stucco, Regency, with a great many square, white-framed windows around a glossy black front door, on either side of which loomed a sentry pair of ornamental orange trees in huge, zinc planters. It stood in a long terrace of identical houses within the perimeter of Regent's Park. From within the capacious bag Joan Williams took an envelope and held on to it, together with her resolve. Then she crossed the road and rang the stiff brass bell.

The door was opened by a woman, and through an unexpected blurring of her vision Joan received an impression of shoulder pads, an ash-blonde chignon, a black and purple silk scarf knotted at a white throat, a frosted pink mouth. Against all this Joan raised up her letter, and thrust it forward, like an identity card.

'Good God. Where on earth did you get that? What do you—'

'I'm Garrick's wife. I don't want to cause trouble –' from which soap opera had she absorbed such a phrase? '– I'd like to talk. Briefly, I promise.'

Joan lowered her letter and blinked, and Lucinda Compton-Neville swam into focus.

'One moment.'

The front door was slammed shut, and Joan was left standing between the unexpected orange trees. From within the house she heard running, a calling voice, and then more footsteps, approaching this time.

When the door reopened Lucinda appeared to have composed herself, and led Joan past the gilded mirror of the hallway and on into a grand drawing room, quite as if she had been expecting her. She indicated a pair of mustard silk armchairs in a bay window. She did not offer her a glass of water. Instead she sat and crossed her legs, leaning forwards only slightly. With a manicured hand she swept a long blonde fringe to one side, and waited. It was as if Joan had come to interview for a household position. The silence would extend, Joan saw, until she herself was able to break it. The time had come to speak.

'I need to tell you – Garrick doesn't know I'm here. He doesn't know that I know anything about you at all. I took your letter, and he's never seen it. He is in total ignorance. About everything.'

An expression of what might have been surprise flickered like passing light across the other woman's face, and then vanished. She was once again cool, and impassive.

'I've come—' Why had she come? It had all seemed clear, on Tuga. She'd come to safeguard her own future. She had come to make things right. She steadied her gaze and stared at the sweep of cobalt eyeshadow, shimmering up over the socket.

'I'm here to return this, and to ask you to give me your word that you will never write to him again. I've come to tell you that if I can help it, he will never know about the child.'

Lucinda raised an elegant eyebrow.

'I don't make promises, as a rule. Certainly not where I owe nothing.'

Joan felt her breath come faster. She was prepared to fight, if necessary. But before she had a chance to reply Lucinda seemed to reconsider, and change course.

'In actual fact I regretted that letter the moment it was posted. Before I even posted it, if such a thing is possible. It was the greatest act of self-destruction of my life. I had become consumed with the fear that he would somehow find out about her, and it felt desperately real and frightening. I had that terrible impulse to realise my worst fear so it would be over, or so it seemed to me afterwards. You know what it's like, the post-partum insanity.'

To this Joan made no reply.

'Of course when I had slept a bit I was rational again, and how on carth could he have found out anything? It was quite literally impossible, he might as well have left the planet for all it mattered. But by then it was too late. If that's really all you've come for then you and I have aligned interests.'

As she spoke she rose, crossing the room to a bookshelf and returning with a packet of cigarettes and a box of matches fished out from behind a row of paperbacks. Joan watched the ritual: the match struck, the elegant hands cupped, painted lips closed around a gold tip. Lucinda inhaled deeply and sat back.

'Christ, all those hormones, I was awash with them. And so many, many drugs, I wasn't in my right mind. I'd had a fairly awful time of it. Show me?'

She reached for the letter which Joan dutifully surrendered to the hand that, five years earlier, had written it.

> *Dear Garrick,*
>
> *I am writing to notify you that I've had a baby. I had no intention of ever telling you, but I almost died and if I had I don't know what would have happened to her. ~~How strange to think that~~ But I must tell you a truth I've discovered this evening. It is that she is mine. Do you understand? I almost died, and I hadn't planned to write this. I feel actually quite* [a lot here was crossed out and illegible] – *I have come to understand that she is as much mine as if I'd had her by parthenogenesis. Maybe I did. Now you must instantly forget I have written. She is nothing to do with you. I alone am on her birth certificate, and I alone have legal rights.*
>
> *Lucinda (Compton-Neville)*

Lucinda gave a short laugh, and tossed the letter on to the small polished table between them. 'Christ, it's unhinged. I knew it was bad, I had no idea I sounded raving. All that underlining, and repetition. Compton-Neville. In parentheses!'

'You'd just had a baby,' said Joan, oddly defensive of the letter-writer, her shadow companion these last years. She could not laugh at the words that had riven her life.

'Yes, and it did get rather sticky at the end,' Lucinda said, her voice thickened with smoke. 'I was actually in intensive care for a night and a day after she was born, heart business, I don't know, all a big fuss, they were all quite sombre about it. Goodness knows what they did with the baby while I was a vegetable. Anyway, once I was cogent again I hired a maternity nurse and recovered, and recovered my wits, more to the point, and that was that.' She paused. 'But, hold on, sorry, I'm confused, why do you have this? Did he give it to you?'

'No!' Joan almost shouted. 'I have already said, he's never seen it.'

'Ah. You open his post.' An awful note of amusement.

'Garrick is a leader in the community and on the Island Council; there's a lot of unofficial diplomatic work, fundraising, work on behalf of the island. I help with his correspondence.'

Joan looked down at her hands, resting on the bright leather bag that sat primly in her lap. Her mother had also taught her always to wear gloves in the sun, but she had now lived for almost twenty years in the tropics. One could not live a life in gloves.

'But in any case I just – I *knew*, long before you wrote. He came home . . . wracked. And after the initial – oh, shock, anger, grief, call it what you want – I had to –' She took a deep breath. 'I had to face some hard truths. There have been – mitigating circumstances.'

That, she had not meant to say.

Lucinda leaned forward, searching for somewhere to stub out her cigarette, and settling on the inside of a delicate, olive-green china jewel box on the table beside her. Joan resisted the urge to wipe the tiny ornament with a handkerchief.

'You've come to extract a promise that I'll never be in touch with Garrick.'

'Yes.'

'I give you that promise.'

'Thank you.'

'That's it. There's nothing further?'

Joan shook her head.

'And you, in your turn, will you promise never to tell Garrick that my daughter exists? Can I be safe in the knowledge he will never try and stake a claim?'

'Oh, I can absolutely promise. I just—'

'Yes?' asked Lucinda, quite sharply.

'May I see her? Just for a moment. I've brought her something, a little toy. From the island.'

'When you arrived, you know, I thought you'd come to try and take her.' Lucinda said this lightly, but there was unmistakable challenge in the eyes that met Joan's. 'That remained a late-night fear. On the bad days.'

'She isn't mine to take.'

'No. She isn't his either, you know. I was right about that part. All right. You may see her.'

Lucinda held out a hand and Joan placed her gift upon it humbly, awaiting judgement. Lucinda peered inside the bag.

'A walnut.'

'There's a miniature creature inside, a tortoise. It opens. Look, here.'

A few minutes later Lucinda returned, pushing before her a little girl of almost five. She was dressed in clothes from another century – a smocked white blouse, Black Watch tartan kilt held with a big gold pin, grey tights, a red velvet hair ribbon from which stray wisps escaped. Lucinda tucked the little girl's tresses behind her ears and lifted her chin with a forefinger.

'Mrs Williams, may I introduce my daughter, Charlotte. Charlotte, this is Mrs Williams.'

'How d'you do,' the child mouthed.

'Goodness, only bats can hear that. Mrs Williams has come from the ends of the earth and brought you a present.'

'Thank you,' said Charlotte, only a fraction louder.

Joan held out the gift and the little girl looked to her mother, uncertain. Lucinda gave her a brisk shove between the shoulder blades. Charlotte stepped forward and her small hand closed around the walnut. Then she retreated. Garrick's daughter.

'There's a dolly inside. Now run along, go on. Go and take it in the kitchen.'

'Thank you,' said Charlotte again, reflexively, and slipped away, without once having glanced at Joan.

'We didn't show her how to open it.'

Lucinda waved a hand, dismissive. 'She's an enterprising child, she'll work it out. Christ. I've a trial starting the day after tomorrow and stacks to do, but I do think I need a drink.'

She closed the door firmly and then threw open what turned out to be a mirrored bar cabinet, and proceeded to mix Martinis. After handing one to Joan she raised her glass.

'What does one say, on your island? Cheers?'

'*Salud*. She's very beautiful.'

'Do you think?'

'She looks like you.'

'She does, doesn't she.' Lucinda sounded gratified. 'There you go. Parthenogenesis after all.'

Something had released between them, a tension dispersed and an air of conspiracy arisen, inspired by the adrenaline of Charlotte's appearance, the covenant of mutual promises, and by the late-morning cocktails. Lucinda sat back in her chair.

'So what have you told him that you're doing in London?'

'I manage the donations of an anonymous benefactor, so I said it was for that. And . . . I invented a dead aunt.' Joan clapped a hand over her mouth, stifling an inappropriate bubble of mirth. In the grandeur of the room, this delicate glass in her hand, she felt slightly crazed. Lighter, too, having disposed of the walnut, which she had carried in her bag for months like a tiny grenade.

'It was easy, really, in the end. I was born here, my parents were English. My father was the Tugan administrator, that's how my family first came to the island. I was sent home to boarding school, and then when I was eighteen I met Garrick on the ship, when I was going out to visit my parents. Needless to say, they did not approve. I wasn't quite truthful before, there was something else. I had this idea that maybe you hadn't any money – that you might need my help. I have come with my chequebook.'

She looked from the antique Persian rug to the heavy-swagged damask silk curtains.

'I'm fine in that regard, thank you,' said Lucinda, failing to conceal her amusement.

'Yes, I see that now. I had an idea that you were a struggling ingénue, but I see in that I underestimated you.'

'Or underestimated him.'

Joan felt the sting of this, but accepted it.

'Perhaps. Everything I imagined has been – but it is a relief to know that she will always have all she needs.'

Joan's only adornment was a slim ring of copper alloy, in which was set a chip of matte teal-coloured stone. She took this from her finger and set it between them on the table.

'Perhaps I might give you this, it was Garrick's mother's. It's a local stone, I don't know its chemical composition, Tugans call it peacock stone. I'm sure it's called something else, too, though I'm afraid I don't know what. Garrick gave it to me when we married.'

'You can't possibly give that away!'

Joan drew herself up. 'I'd like her to have it. You needn't tell her whose it was.'

Lucinda looked at the modest trinket on the polished surface of the table, and then glanced down at her own hands. She wore a huge cocktail ring, round as a penny, royal-blue enamel starred with gold and encircled in tiny diamonds. She slipped this off and reached for the other woman's hand, pushing it on to Joan's finger with a gesture so like a wedding that they exchanged a brief, scandalised laugh.

'A trade,' Lucinda said, and when Joan seemed to hesitate added, 'say the dead aunt left it to you.'

Joan extended her hand to study it.

'It is beautiful. Was this very expensive?'

'Very. My parents gave it to me. Don't get the wrong impression, they were bloody awful people. Paloma Picasso, from Tiffany. Thousands, I should think.'

'What a generous aunt.'

'Aunt Lucy,' Lucinda added, flashing a wicked grin.

Suddenly both women were laughing, and Joan fumbling for a handkerchief to wipe the tears that rose, too easily. The huge ring caught on the zip of the bag as she opened it. She would have to learn to move her hands differently, to accommodate such a piece. She stood, signalling her departure, and Lucinda walked her out the way they had come. The gleaming hall was just the same, but for a child's bracelet of purple glittery acrylic beads shaped like daisies, dropped or abandoned in the middle of the carpet. Joan, walking behind, watched Lucinda nudge this to one side with her foot as she passed.

On the doorstep Joan said, 'I am glad I came,' and looked, earnestly, at Lucinda. But whatever had been briefly between them had gone.

'Goodbye,' said Lucinda, rather too brightly, and with

obvious relief. She had left the copper ring where it lay on the table and Joan understood, with absolute certainty, that she would never pass it on to the girl. 'East is East, and West is West, and never the twain shall meet.' Lucinda closed the door firmly upon Joan, and all she represented.

Joan still had most of the day before she was due at the little clinic on Harley Street. She needed a guarantee, she had told Saul firmly, and he had bowed his head, without argument, and had arranged it all on the telephone. One more letter remained in her handbag, Saul's referral for a quick procedure that would forever put an end to all the false beginnings. She could return to Garrick and be, for the first time in many, many years, a wife to him again. Indeed, her plan for these intervening hours had been to go to Liberty for lawn cotton, and on the ship home to make herself a new nightgown. But for just a moment longer she stood between the potted trees, wondering if the pallid fruit was edible, and listening in vain for the sound of a child's laughter from within the vast silence of the house.

43

Sylvester had sold six jars of cashew butter, half a carton of Lotus biscuits, some washing-up liquid, powdered milk, a case of Red Stripe, and twenty-four rolls of loo paper to Captain Lars and his rust-bucket challengers. He'd even persuaded them to take the tinned small potatoes which had some time ago been delivered to him in error, and after the morning's excitement, he came into the Rockhopper looking forward to a snakebite and black. It was quiet, and he took a seat at the corner of the bar.

At the other end, Levi Mendoza was chatting to Zimbul Fairclough, who was giggling and twirling a long red plait around her fingers. Sylvester raised a hand in greeting and carefully began to set up a chessboard, while Levi reached down a pint glass from the shelf behind the bar. Then the music faded out and Taxi came on-air, oddly adenoidal.

'Afternoon, folks. Fair sea conditions and a strong day for the fishermen, I'm hearing, back with a quota-busting catch, so let me be the first to say well done, *haverim*. I'm after making crab cakes for me supper, if anyone fancy laying by one or two good specimens. I need something to look forward to because that cold come in on the Island Open ship has knocked me for six, I tell you. I hear it took out half the moshav, and so I'm hoping all you lot are faring better than old Taxi. You Conch lot might want to steer clear of town till it's burned out. Now for the news and you ain't going to Adam-and-Eve this one, but a little birdie tells me that the new vet joining the island clinic come sooner than planned, and might be a familiar face.'

Levi paused, releasing the pressure of the cider tap but not, to Sylvester's disappointment, moving on to add the lager. Intent upon the Réti Opening, Sylvester moved his knight to F3. Levi appeared not to notice.

'Doc Charlotte Walker has been overseeing the appointment of the new vet to replace herself, and has officially appointed –' here Taxi left a dramatic pause '– Charlotte Walker. That's right, Tuga de Oro, our tortoise-loving Dr Vet is staying on, and I'd like to be the first to congratulate her. Hope the move south goes well, and your ma got off all right. Reckon a vet's job'd be a whole lot easier if we could just –' and then he left Sammy Davis Jr to finish the sentence, with 'Talk to the Animals'.

Sylvester nodded encouragingly at the lager tap, willing Levi to get on with it. Instead Levi put down the half-filled pint glass.

'What he on about?' he demanded. He shoved a pawn to F5, without seeming to have glanced at the board.

'Just what he said, I reckon. Vet lady's staying. Fine by me. Better the devil you know, and all that.' Sylvester, considering, set down a pawn in B3. Levi seemed irritable, and the game was likely to be aggressive.

'We voted day before yesterday,' Zimbul said, addressing Sylvester rather than Levi. She too sounded congested, and in fact paused now to blow her nose. 'Island Council called a meeting.'

'You ain't told me about it,' said Levi.

Zimbul sniffed, and tucked her handkerchief back into her bumbag. 'Wasn't public business yet. What's it to you what she does?'

'It's to me if my tenant ain't leaving, is all,' Levi said, bad-tempered. He picked up the glass again. 'What were you doing with her suitcases, then?'

This was louder, addressed to Dan Zekri, who had been sitting in the booth at the far end of the Rockhopper with a crab salad and a copy of *The Da Vinci Code*. He looked up from his book, startled. He had presumed Levi already knew, and wasn't thrilled to have to be the one to transmit it.

'Just helping her move. She's renting Ruth dos Santos's place.' Dan didn't think it helpful to add that council's only dissenting vote on Charlotte's appointment had been Zimbul's.

'Lucky her,' Zimbul said now, 'renting a family cottage all for herself. Maybe I should become a vet.'

'You fine just as you are,' said Levi vaguely, but it was clear his heart wasn't in it. She rolled her eyes and slid off her stool, announcing that she had a lot to do, and her cold was giving her a headache. She would probably not see him later.

'Lager, *ijiko*,' Sylvester prompted, unable to wait any longer, and Levi snapped back into the room, topping up the pint glass, adding a dash of blackcurrant cordial. His form was off, Sylvester thought, after a disappointing sip. It was far too much cider, and nowhere near enough blackcurrant. They'd not had blackcurrant all Island Close and, with stores replenished, it was not the time to stint. But Levi didn't seem in the mood for complaints, so Sylvester left him to frown over the chessboard, and retreated to the booth to join Little Doc who was only, after all, reading a paperback. While he was here he might as well ask about his piles.

44

Charlotte was making her way back from the west of Tuga when a rustling in the undergrowth made her turn. It was Long Dog, scavenging further from Town than usual. He leaped and pranced across the track like a spring lamb, apparently overjoyed to see her, but his pant had a rasp to it and he looked hot, she thought, stopping. She dismounted, and poured some water from her own bottle into a clean milk-testing dish, waiting patiently while he lapped. When she set off again, the little dog fell into step beside her donkey.

Charlotte too was far from home, returning from a smallholding near the taro fields after treating a sow with mastitis. She'd given a dose of tetracycline and corticosteroid and felt fairly confident the pig would do well, but the two smallest piglets still worried her as it was thirty degrees, and she feared swift dehydration. She'd encouraged the farmer to transfer this pair to another sow with a strong milk supply. This meant taking them right across the island to his sister's pig, he told her, for no one out west had had a recent farrowing, but he had wrapped them up and headed off in the truck without complaint. Now she was going to the clinic for a few hours, and would call back again tonight, to check on the mother.

This stretch of track was usually deserted, but when she

passed the Rupert Whitten Library she heard loud piano music and saw that the doors were hanging open, and the twine that usually secured them lay in a tangle on the ground. Intrigued, she tethered the donkey to a palm and climbed the steep path, flanked with waist-high agapanthus, their fluted petals striped in bright red and white like a circus tent. A huge red crab glared at her from between the thick stems.

Inside the library was a hot and bothered Garrick, on his knees, and pushing a small, tan-coloured hand-held vacuum across an expanse of very dirty floor, a Bach partita playing at full volume on what looked like, and indeed was, a portable MiniDisc player. He looked up, startled, wary as the crab.

'What are you doing?' she asked, curiosity for the moment overcoming resentment, repeating her question when he'd silenced the deafening music.

'Cleaning. This place is a disgrace.'

'You can't clean a whole shipping container with a thirty-year-old Dustbuster.'

Garrick made a harrumphing sound. He sat back on his haunches and did brief battle with the machine's off switch. She noticed he wore navy trousers better suited to the pulpit. His white shirt, unironed, was streaked with grime. The room smelled of dust and lanolin, recalling its previous incarnation as a storeroom for unprocessed sheep fleece.

'What might you suggest I do instead?'

'I don't know your objective,' said Charlotte, reasonably.

She felt oddly buoyed, encountering him like this. Garrick had been out and about much more of late, back to something that approximated business as usual ever since Oscar's accident, and he himself had taken over Oscar's shifts at the taro fields. From necessity, it seemed that everyone else had moved on. He never addressed Charlotte, and she no longer feared that he might. But still. She felt an unpleasant jolt whenever she saw him. This was the first time they'd been alone since he'd sidled into her office.

Whatever abstract grief she might have about her paternity, no one need overthink their feelings about this particular person who was grovelling about on the floor, unthreatening, undignified. Beside her Long Dog panted, and she bent to pat his flank. Then, loyal to no one but himself, he slipped out into the heat of the afternoon. Charlotte felt a flicker of betrayal, left alone, without a teammate.

Garrick stood stiffly, brushing down his shirt front, instantly less harmless. He was eye level now and was, in fact, a real person. A real, craven, harm-doing person. Charlotte took a small, involuntary step backwards.

'I am *trying* to take this library by the scruff of the neck. It is a source of great shame, to have a public institution in this condition. It is an insult to the island, and an insult to Joanie who did all that work cataloguing, and who wanted this place to be used. To be – to be *enjoyed*.'

At one time, Charlotte and Garrick had agreed to do this work together. They'd agreed that this unprepossessing space could become a place of real value to the islanders, and might also become a resource for scholars, if they achieved their dream of digitising Grand Mary's collection of Tugan writings, and housing that digital archive here. But all that camaraderie had been before.

Garrick gestured around at the shelves of swollen paperbacks, most of their titles illegible on broken spines. 'I'm concerned that we have not made adequate provisions to guard against infestation.'

'I'd say the silverfish could do better than a load of 1980s pulp horror and six copies of *Endless Night*. It's all junk.'

'It's what we have. For now. But we must try, I must try.

She wanted it better. We must do better. Just to leave it is – is an insult to . . . I promised Joan.'

Charlotte summoned the good grace not to say aloud that he had promised Joan a lot of things, fidelity not least of them. She saw that this library had become entwined with his guilt and, for the first time, did not experience his guilt as a personal affront. Here was a man who suffered. He had loved his wife and now he grieved for her, and for a wrong impossible to right. The insult to Joan for which he wished to make amends was not the state of the public library. Garrick's thoughts must have run along similar lines, for the next thing he said was:

'Your, ah – she had a trial beginning, I believe. Did the rust bucket make it back in time?'

'How on earth do you know about her trial?'

Garrick had been pressing and releasing the catch of the Dustbuster beneath his thumb. Now it sprang open, disgorging its contents. Dust and hair floated down at his feet in a grey cloud. He frowned, but made no move to pick it up, merely closed the compartment again with a click. Charlotte itched to find a wet cloth, less from an impulse to help Garrick, and more to solve a simple problem. She restrained herself.

'She did make it back in time. Thank you for asking.'

'She paid me a visit before she left, in fact,' Garrick went on, looking down with resignation at the filthy floor. 'The morning of Oscar's accident. She suggested I had been – she thought an overture to you would be advisable.'

'She read you the riot act.' Charlotte was unexpectedly delighted.

'In fact. That is a better characterisation of our exchange, yes.'

Garrick's inexplicable sidling into her office now made

perfect sense. It had been on Lucinda's command. If he wished she had never been born, still she pitied him, she realised, compassion enabled by the truth that she had no need of him. She had found her way, and Garrick, still, was lost. She said, more gently, 'I'm sure once it's cleaned and painted we could get some books sent. Better ones. Contemporary stuff. Every Camden Town charity shop is packed to the rafters with more books than they can sell.'

'Nothing inappropriate,' said Garrick, gruff. He was kneeling down again, preparing to begin his Sisyphean mini-hoovering. And then before Charlotte could protest this outrageous ingratitude added, 'Thank you, ah, Dr Walker.'

'You're welcome. *Pastor.*'

They exchanged fleeting, awkward smiles.

'Now I have to go and milk a pig,' she said hurriedly, and left, before the conversation could go wrong.

45

Over the last weeks Charlotte had grown used to opening the door of her new cottage to find Annie on the sofa feeding banana chips to her little caramel nanny goat, or sprawled on the floor playing solitaire with a pack of ancient, softened PG Tips promotional cards retrieved from Alex's old bedroom. Annie and the goat appeared to come with the house. There had been several brief moments of tension between them after Kidda had been allowed in unsupervised and had each time wrought havoc, destroying two notebooks, blessedly unfilled, and consuming all but the underwire of a treasured bra. Toffee-coloured lace and mulberry silk, it had been Charlotte's favourite – beautiful, horribly expensive and, now that she had chosen to make her life on a tiny and remote tropical island, all but irreplaceable. Drawn sodden from the pharynx of the retching goat, its mangled remains seemed somehow to represent the state of her romantic possibilities. But Annie had been wide-eyed when confronted, and the giggles she'd failed to repress had soon forced Charlotte to see the funny side. During a second break-in, the animal had ripped Charlotte's washbag to rags, smearing the bathroom with toothpaste, and crunching into splinters a miniature tortoise inside a hinged walnut shell, a carving Charlotte had treasured since childhood. The next day Annie had picked her a bucket of mangoes, by way of apology. Now Elsie had arrived, and Charlotte was taking several of these mangoes from the fridge.

'You said picnic. There was no mention of taking to the high seas.'

'Oh, we'll picnic, all right,' said Elsie happily, accepting and admiring the fruit. On her own account Elsie rarely took a day off, but this trip was a treat for the vet, meticulously planned as a thank you for saving Hilary's life. The tegu was now in fine fettle – slim and sleek, and on Charlotte's advice Elsie was determined to keep her trim, and increase her outdoor basking.

'What a day for it, don't you reckon? I've been waiting for just the right Sunday. Seas are fair, I thought I'd take you FFA out round the old lighthouse in Oluchi's boat. You seen it?'

'Seas are fair,' Charlotte repeated. She felt she could live quite happily without sight of an old lighthouse, especially one she knew to be positioned far out on the island's most treacherous western rocks. She had, in fact, already seen it – from a very long way off, her boots planted sturdily on dry land up the north-western flank of the *montaña*. Close up, she could only presume it looked the same, but larger. She stared down into her open rucksack, which she had earlier readied for a hike. She had been looking forward to a hike, in fact. She'd had gecko-watching plans, and snail-spotting. She hadn't even begun to think about the snails here, and they called to her. Twelve endemic species had been identified by a naturalist in the early 1800s but locals only talked about three, when she probed, and so far she herself had only spotted one, *Insulidiscus laura*. Now, today too would offer no snail progress. She consoled herself with a snail's-pace joke. What did people on boats need? Swimsuit. Life jacket. Paper bag? Diazepam?

'Seas like a mirror,' Elsie reassured her. 'Plain sailing, else I'd not take you out, I promise. We all heard tell of your crossing.'

It was a surprising relief to be out of Levi's cottage. She had not known until she was freed from it how wearing it had been, trying to look blithely busy and effortlessly attractive whenever she was in her own kitchen. But now, in the weeks since Lucinda had sailed, she had barely had to see him; the new cottage was much further out of Town and, between Marianne's baking next door, and the continual flow of farm produce delivered by grateful islanders whenever she treated an animal, she'd found no need to venture to Betsey's, or the Rockhopper. More to the point, she'd had no time.

She owed her ZSL colleagues a draft of two gold coin papers: one a provisional population survey; another in collaboration with a scientist at Kew Gardens, drawn from the first round of tracking studies. Her lab supervisor agreed that she could remain a valued remote member of the team, but of course it would be incumbent upon her to publish regularly, as before. But beyond and above her academic responsibilities came the pleasure of laying claim to a clinical role that was officially hers, now. She would soon start a canine neutering clinic, with Long Dog her first beneficiary, and switch them all to a broader-spectrum antiparasitic. Many of the older donkeys needed urgent dental care. She felt certain that sheep better suited to the humidity could one day be imported and, in the immediate term, she would redesign the vet's room.

The commitment to stay had freed her imagination, and with it her ambition burgeoned and stretched. Evening command centre was at her new, bigger farmhouse table in Ruth's cottage, Kidda collapsed in the open kitchen door, watching benignly from her length of rope, rising occasionally to try and eat something else that she shouldn't. Now that Charlotte had all the time in the world, it was clear there would never be enough for all her plans.

And still, there was time for beauty. That morning on her way back from a successful twin calving she had stopped on the cliffs near the Boatmen's Memorial, suddenly arrested by the dawn. The clouds were lit flamingo pink in a sky burning from plum to lavender to lilac as the sun rose over a boundless gold-washed ocean. She had stood and watched and felt, for the first time, *Here I am. This is where I live.* The island itself was a revelation and a joy, again and again. Fresh from this epiphany, she had been excited for a day exploring Tuga. On land.

Charlotte followed Elsie out into the yard, where another unwelcome element of the plan revealed itself. Katie Salmon sat in the passenger seat, wearing bright pink sunglasses and a Care Bear T-shirt, waving with the toothy and exaggerated smile of a children's television host. Charlotte waved back in silence, and clambered into the truck, readying herself for a day at sea with two of the world's most competent women. They would sail and tack and boom – was that even a verb, or a thing? The truth was she had no desire to find out. If forced to take a day off, all she wished to do with it was to photograph or better still audio-record some lover-girl geckos, be the first to rediscover a mollusc thought extinct, and then lie in the sunshine and eat lychees.

At the back of Ruth and Marianne's shared yard, Elsie reached a stick up through the glossy leaves of the heavily laden starfruit tree and knocked two down, catching them easily. She inspected them, lobbed a reject into the dense jungle, and reached higher for another. Then she leaned in to arrange them on the dashboard, climbed into the driver's seat and sat contentedly with the door open, her smiling face tipped to the sun. They waited in the hot truck in silence until Marianne's kitchen door opened and Marianne came out, wearing a floury apron and a frown, carrying a box over to Elsie.

'I've done the roasted aubergine you wanted. I've got no orders for tomorrow and I had three tomatoes turning, so I did you some goat's cheese and tomato tarts as well.'

Good tomatoes were a rare treat on Tuga; imported, expensive, easily bruised. Elsie expressed appropriate gratitude, and Marianne gave a stiff nod. Charlotte had never seen Marianne relax with anyone, she thought, though like almost everyone on the island, these two women must have known one another all their lives. Now that she was living next door, Charlotte was often around when rare visitors called to place or collect orders, and it was always the same. Marianne betrayed no sign of particular familiarity. Not exactly hostile, but seemingly impossible to draw.

It was a Sunday, but there had been no sign of Annie since early in the morning when Charlotte had been woken by the sound of her bike on the loose gravel of the track. Marianne went out little, and lived and worked very quietly. Meanwhile for Charlotte came the stream of farmers' children on bikes and donkeys, dispatched to summon her to a calving, or a downer sheep. She willed one to come for her now, to rescue her from this impending boat trip, but the track remained empty and silent. Elsie handed the box to Katie, who turned and extended the Tupperware behind her to waft gleefully in front of Charlotte. How could one person be so relentlessly enthusiastic? Then she leaned over Elsie towards Marianne.

'You should come with us,' Katie called out of the window, beckoning. 'Elsie's taking us round to see the old lighthouse. There's a good swim there, apparently.'

Marianne demurred. She had laundry to bring in, and the kitchen to clean. Charlotte glanced through the open stable door where she could see the small table and work surfaces, pristine. She often felt somehow silly around Marianne, and on guard lest she cause offence. But Katie's openness was contagious.

'Come,' she said. 'Come on, Marianne. Please.'

Marianne hesitated. Then she said, 'All right,' unexpectedly, and flushed. Katie whooped, as if this was the fulfilment of her dearest wish, and Charlotte thought she saw a faint look of panic crossing Marianne's face.

'I'll just write a note,' she murmured, returning quickly to the house. Charlotte wondered if she was in fact going to make a run for it, but a moment later Marianne returned with a small bag over her shoulder, and without the armour of her apron.

46

Oluchi kept a little inshore workboat, currently moored at Go-by-Donkey. Charlotte had to admit it looked picturesque where it bobbed beside two other small craft in the middle of the bright and placid bay, its hull a faded spearmint green beneath a little moulded cuddy of primrose yellow, recently hand-painted with pink and red hibiscus flowers and already fading in the wind and the salt spray. To a Londoner it was a postcard boat, one to admire while sipping from a fresh coconut, from the safety of a landlocked beach towel. But to say so was not in the spirit of the day, nor in the spirit of her recent determination to embrace what was now her island. Instead she helped Elsie unload two big waterproof bags from the back of the truck, together with a heavy cool box. There were ferocious urchins in the rocks at this season, and so Marianne and Charlotte and Elsie kept their sandals on to wade out to the boat. Katie had come in hiking boots, and Elsie gave her an effortless piggyback through the warm, shallow water.

Once aboard there seemed to be a great deal to do. Elsie and Marianne set about a sequence of incomprehensible boating tasks, while Katie secured the cool box below a narrow bench with a length of bungee cord, and unpacked into various cubbies and lockers. On Marianne's instruction, Charlotte took up a position on the engine in the middle of the boat, facing forwards. Soon Elsie weighed anchor and they motored out of the bay, as Elsie began to speak at length upon the horsepower of boat engines; about the need to protect the integrity of the hull by staying not only within the lower but also the upper limits of these ratings. It was surprising, she said, partly to Katie, partly to herself, but more was not always better. Charlotte looked up at the wheeling terns, and breathed, slowly.

They went south-west, hugging the coast at a little distance. They would pass the Breaks encircling the lagoon, Elsie told them, and from there make their way around the gentle southern tip of the island near Out the Way beach, passing over wide seagrass beds, one of the old breeding sites of the Tugan conch before its extinction. (It was a disappointment that Elsie could answer none of Charlotte's questions about Tugan conch breeding age or lifespan, nor the speed of population decline during the middle and final days of the nineteenth century. It would be interesting to know how it compared to the Caribbean queen conch, another gastropod mollusc now under threat of extinction from over-fishing. 'I don't reckon I could tell you any of that,' said Elsie, quite cheerfully. 'But I can tell you some of them bigger conch grew pearls the size of rubber seeds. Rich folk would sail half round the world for them, long after the conch was gone from these waters.') Then they would carry on until they reached Papasiegas at the north-west, dropping anchor not far from the rocks that encircled the old lighthouse.

Elsie and Katie were keen to snorkel in one of the offshore wrecks that lay as eerie testament to the treachery of Tuga's changeable and capricious seas. These artificial reefs could be home to the odd giant octopus, Elsie announced cheerily, but as long as one swam in pairs, there was little to worry about. An unperturbed Katie revealed a diving knife on a neoprene leg strap, much admired by Elsie who had brought something similar of her own devising. Charlotte took a deep breath and closed her eyes against the glorious sunshine, and all this excessive survivalist competence. Beside her she was aware of Marianne, silent and unsmiling, her hands folded in her lap like a novice.

They dropped anchor near the lighthouse. They were in shallow water, sun-warmed and clear. The anchor groaned and chinked on the sandy bottom and before long Katie was asking whether it was possible to swim out to what looked, to Charlotte, like a distinctly uninviting rock. Elsie, enthused, confirmed that it was. Katie lifted her T-shirt over her head in a single, fluid movement, revealing a white bikini, and a set of abdominal muscles to rival Levi's. In yellow board shorts and a floral rash vest so well worn it was translucent in patches, Elsie was already dressed for the sea.

'Who's coming?'

Charlotte said that for now she would just enjoy the view, and the novelty of being off the island. Marianne shook her head, saying they should go and have fun, she would get lunch ready.

'Oh, no,' said Katie brightly, 'you won't. Today you're not feeding anyone else, or clearing up after them. Here, take this.' Katie opened Elsie's cool box and extracted a tin of Red Stripe, cracked it open, and then placed it firmly into Marianne's hand. Marianne gave a faint smile, and raised the can to Katie.

'Here's to a glorious day,' said Katie, and slipped into the sea.

Marianne drank her beer and watched the water. When after a few moments it seemed she did not mean to break this silence, Charlotte took out some work. The *African Journal of Herpetology* had published a paper entitled '*Agama agama*: a charter tourist in the Cape Verde Islands?', an article of the sort to give pause to anyone now officially responsible for biosecurity. Recently introduced to Santo Antão, though no one knew how it had travelled, the diminutive, tangerine-splashed lizard was successfully spreading to other Cape Verdean islands, preying on vulnerable endemics. Without intervention, the impact on local reptile populations could be devastating. There would be no Tugan charter tourists on her watch, Charlotte resolved. Her border checks would have to be impregnable. In the margins she scribbled: *Re: vehicle imports, check tyre treads for mud. Nematodes!!!*

Marianne spoke.

'Look at them.'

Charlotte glanced up. In the far-off distance were two small figures, waving hugely. As Charlotte and Marianne watched, Elsie stood, one arm raised, pointing towards the lagoon. Katie watched beside her, mask and snorkel on her head, while Elsie no doubt spoke of tide patterns or perhaps, judging from her current movements, successful techniques for fishing in the lagoon with spears of different lengths.

'It's like they're a superior species of human,' said Charlotte, squinting at them through her sunglasses.

Marianne adjusted her skirts.

'The athletics, you mean? Or the optimism?'

Charlotte smiled, surprised.

'I had meant physically. But I see what you mean. Maybe a lot of exercise makes you unusually cheerful.'

Marianne drained her can, shook the last droplets over the side, and crushed it, carefully.

'In that case maybe I should give it a go.'

Before long Katie and Elsie were on their way back, a pair of strong, steady swimmers, lithe as porpoises. Then they were calling from the water.

'You have to come in now,' Katie shouted. 'It's obligatory.'

Marianne took Charlotte aback by standing up without protest, and stepping out of her dress. Beneath it she wore a plain red swimsuit, sun-bleached, fraying at the shoulder straps. She tipped her head back and began to plait her long blonde hair, securing it with an elastic from her wrist. Then she stepped elegantly on to the gunwales, surveyed the water beneath them with a practised eye, and dived in with such precision that she barely made a sound. Charlotte looked after her in astonishment. It was easy to forget sometimes that Marianne was young; that as a native Tugan she was almost certainly as easy in the sea, on the *montaña*, in the jungle, as Elsie herself. Marianne surfaced further away than Charlotte had anticipated, treading water effortlessly while she fitted the snorkel mask that Katie passed her. Through this she looked back at Charlotte, expectantly.

For a vet Charlotte was not intrepid. She loved to be outside, but she was not a thrill-seeker. Her most familiar bodies of water were the English waterways: ponds and sluggish rivers; still murk in which she could stand in waders, a podcast playing quietly in her ears beneath the insulation of a woolly hat, chemical hand warmers tucked into the backs of her gloves to fend off frostbite. Ponds were sensible, and generally behaved and contained themselves. No self-respecting vet she knew would miss the opportunity to snorkel in Tuga de Oro's crystalline waters and most, indeed, would never get the chance. And it was true that it would be a pleasure to see the marine life. These waters were as clear and unpolluted as any on the planet, and it would be a rare privilege to bear witness where an unspoiled ecosystem remained. But also, she really liked to stay dry.

'Someone should be on the boat,' she called to the others.

'Why, what exactly were you planning to do if it started sailing off?' Katie called back. Charlotte was beaten, and from her bag reluctantly drew out her swimsuit and towel. Once changed, with a tentative and inelegant slither overboard, she joined the others in the warm, clear sea.

'And what was the huge crazy lime-green and yellow one that looked furious?' Katie asked. She squeezed her hair out over the side of the boat, and wrapped it neatly into a bright pink microfibre turban, Velcroed into place. She then reached behind her back to undo the strings of her bikini top, which fell to the deck with a wet slap. The bottoms followed shortly afterwards, and then Katie lay face down on her towel, pillowing her forehead on her crossed arms. 'It had bits of bright blue on it as well,' she went on, muffled.

Charlotte stared down at the naked body, spreadeagled, unselfconscious, in the middle of the sun-warmed deck.

'I'm no marine biologist,' she said, pulling herself back to the question with a touch of false modesty, for in fact she knew precisely what it was, 'but I think it was a dolphinfish, or mahi-mahi. Also known as dorado.'

'Maybe so,' said Marianne, 'but it's just a prettyfish, round these parts.' She too seemed unable to take her eyes from the sight of Katie's pert bottom, glistening in the sunshine. They were transfixed less by the nudity than by the confidence it represented, Charlotte thought, wondering again what it must be like to be Katie, and to move through the world impervious to the very concept of embarrassment.

'My mama used to cook one for us to share each year for Santa Esterica,' said Elsie. 'In butter and coconut milk. You ain't ever tasted anything like it.'

'I do the same,' said Marianne. 'Ocean Rodrigues gets them in, it's Annie's favourite, stuffed with rice and mintberry.'

'Esterica? Like, hysterical?' Charlotte asked. 'I've been here more than a year, I don't remember Santa Esterica.'

'Saint Esther,' Elsie told her. 'Happens at home, is why you ain't seen it, it's a festival for mothers and daughters, private, like. A whole load of cooking and preparation for a special feast. Day after tomorrow, as it happens. That was a fine big one we saw, should have grabbed it for Annie.'

'Not necessarily one to celebrate if your mother is on the other side of the world, then,' said Charlotte, trying and failing to imagine Lucinda stuffing her a fish.

'Or on the other side of the world working cruise ships and also a raging alcoholic,' Marianne agreed.

Katie raised her head. 'Oh, same!' she said cheerily. 'Not the cruise ships bit. Although mine's also a depressed nymphomaniac alcoholic. In a cult.'

'Mine was great,' said Elsie, thoughtfully. 'But, she's dead.' Into the shocked silence she began to giggle. Watching her, Charlotte felt a bubble of laughter rising in her chest, and on the deck between them Katie's shoulders had begun to shake. Marianne snorted, and spat a mouthful of beer out over the side.

Eventually they subsided. Marianne looked at the lengthening shadow of the lighthouse where it fell across the still water.

'I should get back. I got dough to prove. And cooking for Santa Esterica. I want to get my eggs in colour for the *folares*.' She picked up her dress and stepped back into it, now that her costume had dried. 'Not that Annie lining up to celebrate anything with me. But I should be back first bat, that's my rule for the children.'

'Does Annie follow it, these days?'

'Not these days. No.'

'Well then,' said Katie, sitting up and handing Marianne another beer. 'Seems to me it's about time you take off that hair shirt and had a break.'

47

When Marianne got home, long after darkness had fallen, Annie was sitting alone at the table, her delicate sunburned shoulders hunched, her tangled hair falling forward, almost into her bowl. She had left on her bike early that morning and Marianne could no more imagine where she'd been than she could read the future. When Alex had been here they'd also disappeared for long weekend hours, but their morning departures had been raucous, joyful affairs, two rambunctious puppies tumbling out towards a day of adventure, begging treats, calling farewells, knocking the best of her ripe fruit from the trees as they passed them. Marianne had stayed with Ruth knowing the children were taking care of one another. Their mutual devotion gave her confidence when they were ranging across the island. At first bat they would reappear without fail, dusty and ravenous, and over dinner their day would come spilling forth, turned out for display like the treasures hoarded in their pockets. Two of their seedlings had failed but another had true leaves, now; Mac's Rachel had given them each a soursop ice lolly in exchange for stacking some shelves; Cecil and Hubert had started a war, but Natalie Lindo had caught them all and hauled Cecil home for lunch, and then Hubert had cried and had to be comforted by Betsey with a muffin, and Annie and Alex had then left the war and gone up to feed some of Betsey's melon rind to Martha over the wall of Martha House. All those words, Marianne remembered, now. Streams of stories ended only when she stemmed their flow with bedtime shushing. She had not known their chatter was a precious commodity. Those breathless, beautiful words had been offerings, entirely withdrawn now by her silent daughter.

Annie looked almost guilty. She had been soaking up the remains of Marianne's ginger chicken soup with a handful of soft fufu, and had thus been caught in the act of accepting her mother's cooking, her mother's care.

Marianne moved forward, dropping her bag on the floor. She sat down opposite Annie, each in her usual place at the kitchen table.

'I'm glad you're here, I want to talk to you.'

A conviction in Marianne's tone made Annie glance up.

'It can't go on like this, *kerida*.'

Annie rolled her eyes. She stuffed the remaining fufu into her mouth, the meal now finished, and with it her reason for remaining in her seat. She chewed, staring, cheeks huge. Under other circumstances it might have been funny, but Marianne did not smile. Annie then rose to put her bowl in the sink and Marianne reached out, touching only the tip of her fingertips to her daughter's arm. Annie flinched away.

'I need you to understand, finally, and to listen to me. I didn't do this to hurt you, *mi vida*, I did what – I had no choice.'

Annie began to wash the bowl and spoon, noisily, and Marianne rose and went to stand beside her. When Annie could no longer extend this task she placed them on the draining board and Marianne resumed speaking, more quietly.

'It was birth gave Ruth all that trouble, and Alex spent his whole life thinking it was his fault. Then Katie came and told us they could maybe fix Ruth up if we could get her to England, and it was Alex had to take her. And that school still had a place just waiting for a Tugan child . . . ' Here she drifted off, sensing she should pursue this no further, though each knew precisely which Tugan child the school had actually been expecting. 'It was the only chance to set him free.'

Annie seemed about to speak, and Marianne held her breath. Since Alex had gone she had heard her daughter's voice only in the vivid passions of her dreams. She spoke to others, Marianne knew. She spoke at school, and she chattered away to Charlotte. But after all these mute weeks, still she said nothing to the one person who most longed to listen. Annie closed her mouth.

'Can't you see this is better? Can't you see –' and now Marianne tried a last attempt, a risk '– can't you see what your letting go gave him? It's the greatest gift, his mama getting well.'

Annie was inching closer and closer towards the door. Marianne felt the urge to fall to the kitchen floor and kiss her daughter's dirty bare feet and plead and beg; an impulse of equal force made her long to grab the girl and trap her in a steel bear hug with the violence of possession, with the terrible assertion of her superior strength. She felt crazed by the silence, and quick words began to spill from her that she barely knew to be her own. They seemed to come through her, unfurling the secrets she kept even from herself.

'Do you think,' she whispered, urgent, 'do you think if I'd known this would happen I'd have done it? You are my world, you are my *everything*. I'd have sooner had Ruth here forever just as she was, Alex stuck, us washing sheets and Ruth's endless pills – I'd have it all back tomorrow and all their suffering with it if you just forgave me, can't you see that?'

Annie took a few steps forward and as she drew closer Marianne opened her arms. But Annie pushed past her into the dark yard and then she was gone again, out into the night. Marianne wrapped her arms tightly around herself. Beneath her clothes she still wore her swimming costume, a relic from another, glimpsed life.

48

'Go away.'

Cecil dropped his bike and risked a step closer, and then another.

'You ain't at school.'

Annie didn't look up. She was tending to her beloved apples, saplings now, two feet tall and flourishing under her obsessional care. She had spaced them well. Initially, she'd worried they were too distant from their siblings for they looked vulnerable so far apart, but since then she had interspersed some other seeds and these were already catching up. Each apple now had its own tall ruff of marigolds, standing golden guard.

'You coming in this afternoon?' Cecil persisted.

'No. I'm done with all that.'

'What you doing?'

'None of your business. You need to go back, you'll get in trouble.'

'No I won't. Now I got a bike I go home lunches.' Cecil looked pleased. 'Miss Moz think I'm on the farm and Papa think I'm at school.'

He stared around at the plot, which had more infrastructure than his last visit. After running from her mother Annie had not come straight here but had crept into Ruth's cottage next door, Charlotte's cottage now, and had taken all she needed from Alex's room. Cecil saw a sleeping bag, a tin kettle, and the remains of a small fire.

'You making camp here?'

'Made it last night.'

'You sleep here? By yourself?'

'Yes.'

Cecil looked impressed. 'All night? Don't your mama care?'

Annie stabbed with her fork. She had stolen a tub of chicken manure from Levi Mendoza and was turning it into the soil in tiny amounts, wary of burning tender roots. One day this would be her apple orchard, frothing with pale pink blossoms, thick with bushes of golden marigolds she would sell on market days, and to passing tourists. Pirate flowers. Miss Moz couldn't make a single seed start from the cemetery, and the children whispered that they'd been cursed by the dybbuk. But they burst willingly to life for Annie, as if they knew her. Already she had bright saffron globes, tight-frilled between her saplings. Companion planting, Marianne had taught her, going on like a broken record to say that, like all else worth knowing, she had learned it from Ruth. Ruth knew everything. Ruth cared for everything. Ruth had been the perfect, perfect, perfect mother, till she wasn't. Unlike Marianne, Annie thought, fiercely, stabbing, who had never been anything but wild to be rid of her, with her boarding-school plans cooked up since babyhood. Marianne who claimed that true love lets go, which only proved that Marianne didn't know how to love hard enough.

'She won't come looking,' said Annie, shortly. 'She never does.'

Trusting Annie's competence, it was true that when she had stayed out in the past, her mother had not gone searching. She omitted to say that each time a blanket and pillow suggested Marianne had slept on the sofa, facing the half-open kitchen door.

'She don't care what I do,' Annie added, with slightly less conviction.

Cecil looked down doubtfully at the sleeping bag, from which emerged the paw of a stuffed toy sheep, once white, now an indeterminate matted grey.

'What about centipedes, at night?'

'Getting a chicken.'

Centipedes had only occurred to her when it was too dark to relocate to the safety of the huts of the Breaks, with their reassuring raised bed frames. The moon had risen, the temperature fallen, and the cocoon of her sleeping bag had begun to feel vulnerable to writhing, slithering, skittering things. But then by moonlight she had come up with the chicken plan and found it comforting. A tame chicken would be pest control, egg-provision and company. In her mind she had already named this animal Brownie. She would buy a pullet from Mac's Rachel, in exchange for errand-running or garden-work.

Cecil sat down at a safe distance and pulled a tiffin tin from his backpack. Annie watched. The provisions she'd swiped from Charlotte's kitchen had been ginger cake and walnut biscochos, and earlier she'd split open a fertilised coconut for the sweet sponge within. She'd not have to go far for avocados, and she knew several places to collect fresh water. Armed with only a very little local knowledge, it was not hard to survive forever on a lush tropical island. But surviving was not the same as a thick tuna mayonnaise sandwich made by Oscar Lindo on rye bread, and studded throughout with bright gems of imported, coveted tinned sweetcorn. She began to see that Cecil might make himself useful, held out her hand for the tiffin tin, and sent him off home with a list of requirements.

49

First thing on Monday morning, Charlotte had arranged to meet Walter at the clinic. On the boat on the way back home she had sketched various shelving configurations advised by practical Elsie, with Katie and Marianne chipping in, increasingly enthusiastic and ambitious in their interior design as the afternoon heat rose and the cool box filled with empties. By the end, Katie had proposed installing a tank to offer canine hydrotherapy, and Marianne was insisting that no self-respecting medical establishment should be without an adjoining cafe–bakery, which she herself might run. Charlotte had fantasies of more modest expansion, but even these she would keep for further down the line. For now the new office would be functional and beautiful; no longer the clinic dumping ground, but a legitimate and organised country practice. She had commissioned the schoolchildren to paint her a series of animal portraits for the walls, and if she ever worked up the courage to talk to him, she would ask Vitali Mendoza to make some proper picture frames.

When she arrived Walter's truck was beside the ambulance and Walter was unloading, the exterior door of the vet's room standing open. He called out a *paz*.

'Honestly,' Charlotte told him, grabbing a stack of dust

sheets and following him up the crushed-shell path, 'I cannot remember the last time I was this excited about anything.'

'That a sad story,' said Levi, who she found unexpectedly, standing in her office. He seemed amused by her surprise. She would not grant him the pleasure of wrong-footing her, she thought crossly, determined to be casual. Levi was holding his toolbox, which he set down with an emphatic thud.

'Are you going to be here all day?' Charlotte asked, dropping her bundle on a chair.

'You lucky enough to have the honour of my carpentry services, yes. To make all your wildest storage fantasies come true.'

'Sorry. I just – thank you. I didn't know. I asked Walter.'

'Matter of fact, I volunteered. Sounded like exciting shelving. In fact, I can't remember the last time I was this excited.'

Charlotte turned her back on him and began to shuffle papers at her desk, needlessly, to recover from what had surely been flirtatious emphasis on the word 'excited'. Then Walter joined them again, this time carrying Charlotte's sketch and his own version. These he laid out side by side on the exam table. She stood next to him, offering what she hoped was a businesslike expression.

'Are you wanting this open shelving here, or cabinets?' Walter asked, tapping the page.

'Is it much more work to put some doors on?'

'More work? Yes. But that ain't the point if you want them.'

Charlotte tried to ignore the fact that Levi stood listening a little behind Walter, arms crossed, obviously finding her entertaining.

'Then I think cabinets here and here, and just some bookshelves at this end, over the desk? And can we put a cabinet near the top inside the main cupboard, too, with a lock on it?'

'Lock with a key needs ordering from off-island. Combination padlock I have.'

Charlotte agreed this would be easier in any case and Walter drew some quick amendments, handed the plans to Levi, and made as if to leave. Charlotte gave him a questioning look. Levi with Walter was unexpected. Levi without Walter was an entirely different prospect.

'Maia and I going over to Conch for the night, we setting off in a bit. We got enough Brilliant White for woodwork and walls, I reckon, unless you wanting colour – that might take ordering. Levi'll measure up and get started.'

Charlotte agreed that white was fine, and Walter touched fists with Levi.

'Relax, *badj*, everything in hand. Rebecca and Uncle Levi got picnic plans after school.'

'Thank you,' Walter said, with unexpected feeling. In case they needed a moment to talk, Charlotte tried to make herself helpful and occupied, and so began to move the furniture out of the way. She unlocked the wheels on the exam table and gave it a firm shove out into the garden, but she had misjudged the height of the steps, and it clattered down at much greater speed than she had anticipated. When Walter left she followed him, mumbling something about getting out of Levi's hair, and going to work at Betsey's.

50

Annie was beside the saplings and packing her bag again when Cecil returned, his own rucksack heavy. He was tired now, not yet accustomed to long cycles in the heat of the afternoon. He hadn't enjoyed such large-scale theft from his father's pantry. It had left him guilty, and cross.

'What you doing now?'

Annie shouldered the backpack. 'Riding up to the Lakes. Going up round Thursday's Peak.'

Lindo family parties were often held at the Lakes, and Cecil knew his father disliked anyone travelling there by Thursday's Peak unless absolutely necessary, preferring a longer route to the south, through a cinnamon plantation. It was true that the elderly or infirm went round Thursday's Peak by donkey, but that was a different prospect from wheels, whether two or four. Tugan donkeys were basically mountain goats, nimble enough to pick their way unscathed through a landslide.

'That ain't a good road.'

'So don't come.'

'Shouldn't you take a donkey?'

'You a donkey,' Annie said, with scorn. 'I ain't going into Town just to catch a donkey and bring it all the way back here. I'm going round Thursday's Peak and if you coming for a swim you coming now.'

Cecil did not ask why Annie was so determined to go swimming when so little of the day remained. He merely dropped the bag of contraband and clambered back on to the big bike, perceptibly weary, absolutely determined to keep up. Annie seemed to relent somewhat, and they rode the first distance at an easy pace, side by side.

'What were they all doing when you were back?'

Annie sounded as if she had been away from society for years; nostalgic for dispatches from a life she'd once known.

'Small ones with chickens. Papa mucking out. I'm meant to be mucking out too, helping him extra till Mama home.'

Annie snorted. 'Why'd she want to come back here?'

Cecil didn't understand the question.

'She live here.'

'People can change where they live, *hamoriko*. Ruth ain't ever coming back, now.'

Cecil didn't know Ruth, and had nothing to say about this. Annie went on, pedalling harder.

'She say just a bit more time, just a few months, maybe, but everyone know she ain't coming. She give up her Island Open berth and she ain't even put her name down for another.'

They were climbing now, the tops of the cinnamons far below, over the crumbling edge. Cecil was beginning to get out of breath as the road steepened and narrowed.

'Alex will come back?' he panted, an exhalation between each word.

'We got no use for *him*,' said Annie fiercely. 'Folk go to England and it change them, they learning stuff that messes with their brains, makes them think they got no place on Tuga. Probably your mama will decide to start over, raise those three new kids proper English, that's all everyone wants here, English school, opportunities, blah, blah, blah. Why'd she come back to you island donkeys?'

She left a silence for this to land. The road was too narrow for them to ride abreast and Cecil was behind her now, breathing hard. But after a moment he said, 'You wrong.'

Annie did not turn, and made no indication she could hear him. She had never cycled this track before and the gradient was an unpleasant discovery, especially when combined with potholes, and patches of rockfall and fallen palm fronds left uncleared by the usual roadwork teams, who did not often reach this altitude. It was too late for the Lakes, where in any case she no longer even wanted to go. She did not want to go anywhere except to outrun the shameful chaos of her own self.

'You wrong,' Cecil said, louder, increasingly robust as his conviction clarified. Round his wrist was the knotted bracelet of crimson embroidery thread that Natalie had tied there, a love token, the night before she sailed. 'Our mama loves us, she didn't want to go, and when the babies are safe she'll come back. I got the best mama in the whole wide world.'

At these last words Annie sped up, faster and faster. Fighting, it seemed, to shake free.

On one side the mountain rose above them, concealing from view the gentler terrain of the familiar Lakes. On the other it fell away, a steep ravine. Before long the creaking bike behind Annie was slowing, but then came a new sound, a loud thud, and then a crashing of branches, a tumbling and scraping of metal on rock. Annie braked and spun round, but the path behind her was empty. She called out. Then she heard, far off, the sound of Cecil crying.

'Annie!'

His voice was small, and echoed.

'Where are you?'

'Here. Annie, I'm scared!'

'Where's here? How far down?'

'I – I don't know.'

Annie knelt at the edge and looked over, scanning the steep flank. There was Cecil's red head, just out of reach, for he had caught in some high protruding brush.

'I – I can climb up.'

'No! Don't move. You proper stuck.' Annie looked at the smooth rock face on either side, with no visible purchase. He was closer than she'd feared, but the bottom of the ravine was far below. 'Don't you shift, do you hear me? You'll fall.'

'Don't leave me here!'

'I got to. I won't be long, I promise. Just promise me not to move.'

Cecil whimpered and shifted.

'Stay still. Don't move.'

His breaths were shallow and audible now, a wheezing sound with each exhalation. He tried to straighten, to reach upwards. A branch beneath him cracked, and two stones dislodged, rolled, fell.

'Cecil! Stay still.' Annie had begun to cry. 'Stay still. I'll get a grown-up. *Stay still.*'

51

In the forked branch of the nearby tree sorrel the fairy tern chick had hatched. All day it waited without complaint, clinging on with scaly feet, scanning with beady black eyes for its mother to return with a beak full of tiny fish skimmed from the ocean surface. It had been a vulnerable nesting site, but the little family had made the best of it.

Charlotte was sitting on the outdoor steps of her office with her binoculars, watching for the mother bird's return, and admiring the pleasing chaos left at the end of the first day of renovations. Levi had gone. He had chased some extra wiring into the walls for more sockets, and for better lighting, and the first set of shelves had been cut and primed with undercoat, laid out on dust sheets to dry in the sunshine. Tomorrow Levi would fill and plaster the cracks in the walls. Inside, Charlotte could faintly hear that the clinic waiting room was busy, but none of it was for her. She was not officially at work today.

In a minute she would begin the long walk back to Lemon Tree Valley where someone had probably left her a milk bottle of fresh lemonade, or three perfect eggs laid by a hen she had treated, or she would find a gawping fish, whole and startling inside the fridge. For now, she moved her gaze from the fairy tern to an iridescent skink making its silent way along the humped root of the tamarind. By focusing on the lizard she hoped to displace the image of a shirtless Levi crouching on her desk with a tape measure and a spirit level, making pencil marks on the grubby walls and singing along, loud and heartfelt, to 'Dancing on the Ceiling' by Lionel Richie. This was how she had encountered him earlier, after lunch, and when he'd noticed her standing in the doorway had not stopped but had grinned and begun to sing louder, drumming with his free hand on the actual ceiling, for emphasis. He had been inexplicably ebullient all day. She found herself wanting and at the same time not wanting to know why, just in case the answer had something to do with Zimbul. Instead she hauled her mind back to the subject of benches and, more specifically, whether she ought to ask Walter to make one to put outside this garden door, as Dan did not permit her larger patients to wait inside. Then came the sound of a bike and Annie Goss approached, riding right into the garden and stopping with a screech in between the drying planks. She bent forward, grabbing Charlotte's hand and hauling her to her feet, and began pulling her and then pushing her round the corner towards the ambulance bay.

'Please help, oh, just *come*.'

'Is someone hurt? I can't drive that. Annie, what's happened? Shall I get Dr Zekri?' As she said this she remembered that Dan was over on Conch, and the waiting room was full of patients only for the nurses' clinic. 'Dan's off, I'll get Dr Gabbai.'

'What's Dr Gabbai going to do? He can't climb!' Annie was shouting. 'Cecil down over the side of Thursday's Peak. Come, come, oh, please!'

'Shh, shh. OK. Can we get to him from below?'

Annie shook her head. 'No. If I had a rope I could climb but I'm not big enough to lift him. Please!'

'How far down is he?'

'Not that far.'

'Is he hurt?'

Annie shrugged, helplessly.

From beneath a dust sheet Charlotte grabbed her smaller vet's bag, a rucksack in which, among other emergency kit, were bandages and sutures. Then she climbed on behind Annie as once she had ridden with Alex, on her first official visit to Martha House, to give the tortoise her first check-up.

Soon they were turning down the familiar track. Annie stopped short, almost tipping Charlotte to the ground, and Charlotte ran towards her beloved little cottage. Levi's cottage, she corrected herself.

In the front yard, Rebecca was on a new tyre swing lashed to a thick branch of the spreading avocado tree. Levi was facing her wearing a pink straw hat, wide-brimmed and frilled, frothing with paper roses and strawberries, and listening intently to the little girl's chatter. At the sound of their approach he looked up. Charlotte almost collided with him and reached out for his arm, as much by old instinct as to steady herself. Then his other hand was at her elbow, strong and solid. He took off the hat and handed it to Rebecca, who had come to stand close beside him.

'Go in, *kerida*, OK? Tell Nonna I got to help my friend.'

'Nonna staying with me tonight at my house,' Rebecca said to Charlotte, twirling her hat, 'and she brought three puppies all the way from Conch in a cardboard box.'

'Tell her I'd love to visit them tomorrow,' Charlotte told her and Rebecca nodded, pleased, and disappeared obediently into the house.

'Dolittle,' said Levi, and Charlotte couldn't help but notice that he still gripped her. 'What is it you need?'

*

Soon they were in Walter's truck, barrelling along a shaded road that led south into the interior of the island. Annie and her bike were in the back. Although they'd briefly considered going out to the farm for Oscar, they had immediately dismissed the idea. For now, they still had light, but night fell quickly on Tuga.

They were not yet climbing; they would make their way through a cleared jungle track and then come out near the eastern foot of the *montaña*, and begin a careful ascent. There were no crash barriers; there were only a few on the island, and these in whimsical places – one alongside the entirely straight, flat length of paved road by the new cemetery; another positioned on what had long ago been a bend of Lemon Tree Road and was now marooned in the middle of a field, appropriated by Mac's Rachel as one side of her pigsty.

'How he end up over the edge?' Levi asked, after a while.

'I was mean to him,' said Annie, sounding wobbly. 'Then he just – fell.'

'Be honest. You push him?'

'*No!*'

Charlotte could hear from Annie's voice that he had won a small smile. Then Levi glanced over at her and their eyes met. This mission had an intimacy that felt dangerous, and Charlotte looked quickly out of the window, as the road began to climb and narrow. It was urgent she remind herself that Levi had come not for her, but for Cecil.

They were passing grazing land, rugged and uninviting, and in the distance what looked, inexplicably, like a crop of English saplings standing in a fairy ring of golden flowers. She pointed these out to Annie, who frowned and returned her anxious gaze to the road ahead.

'She get back OK, your ma?' Levi asked, lightly.

'Yes. She survived the rust bucket. And she got my tortoise to the lab in one piece. Some colleagues in Buenos Aires got her into proper cold storage and flew her back.'

'Your mother?'

'Very funny.'

'And the clinic renovations. Hold on.'

The track here was rarely used, and narrowed in places by debris. A rotting branch ahead barred their way, fallen from a huge old starfruit, and Levi stopped to clear it.

'The clinic renovations,' he repeated, when he climbed back in. 'What's that, a boat-to-boat thing? You doing all this for who's next?'

Taxi had made several references to her formal employment on the radio, so Levi surely knew this. Everyone on Tuga knew everything, whether you wished them to or not.

'No. I've signed a permanent contract.'

'For your *actual life*,' Levi repeated, innocently, as if merely confirming. Charlotte felt the heat rise to her face, remembering her own words to him on the beach. Annie's presence behind them was a constraint, and probably a blessing.

'My actual life turns out to be here, it seems. I was wrong. About a lot of stuff.'

Between them there fell a sudden charged silence. Charlotte considered saying several things and found, when it came to it, that she was capable of saying none of them. She feared exposure, transgression, possibly both. Levi seemed about to speak, but then Annie sat forward to say with urgency that they should go slower, it was somewhere around here, and Charlotte recalled herself, grateful for the interruption. There remained the immovable fact of Zimbul. Perfect, appropriate Zimbul, who had probably been inside the cottage when Charlotte had come just now, chatting to Levi's mother, playing with Rebecca, already part of the family. Looking out on Charlotte's pink bougainvillea. Sleeping upstairs in Charlotte's – but she would not think any further about that.

'You ever belayed?' Levi asked in a totally different tone, dislodging this last, unwelcome thought.

'Outdoor pursuits were never exactly my thing. I'm sorry to be useless.'

'You many things, Dolittle,' said Levi, giving her a grin he must have known would be devastating, 'but you far from useless.'

Charlotte allowed herself both the pain and the pleasure of this compliment. Then Annie gestured, and they pulled over. Annie scrambled out and stood beside Levi's door, jigging from foot to foot with anxiety. Levi cut the engine and jumped out, and Charlotte watched him rest a hand on Annie's shoulder.

'Come on, *kerida*. Let's go fishing for your pal.'

52

'Cecil?' Levi had his hands cupped round his mouth, hollering. 'Cecil? We here now, *kerido*. Cecil?'

When the silence extended Levi called, and walked, and called. There was no trace of panic in his voice, no rising pitch. He just tried again, and again. They needed Annie to direct them, but she seemed uncertain about exactly where it had happened, and was no longer leading but following. Charlotte shouldered her kitbag, beginning to feel frightened. The bottom of the ravine was a narrow valley of dark, lush foliage. Much too far to see anything so small as a bicycle, or a boy. The only way to know if the child had fallen would be his silence, Charlotte realised. Then they heard a whimper, then another.

'Papa?' And then again, frantic. '*Papa?*'

'It's Levi, *kerido*. We going to get you to your papa.'

'I'm scared.' This last word was a shudder, extended over many syllables.

'I know. We know, it's all right. Squad's here now, hang on.'

At the top the sides were steep, almost vertical in places, a mixture of loose dull earth and glinting rock. Spindly vines provided patches of ground cover, and here and there a few scrubby, tenacious ferns projected. Some woody shrubs had taken root on small ledges, while others had made their lives almost perpendicular to the rock face, and on one of these Cecil Lindo had snagged, hung out like a dish towel. He had been here, alone, precarious, for what must have been more than an hour. Levi's calls drew forth a long, hoarse wail.

'*I want my ma-ma.*'

The little boy began to sob, and the sound located him a bit further up the road. And then he must have shifted, perhaps straining to scramble up again in desperation to reach their voices, for there was rustling of leaves, a creak of branches, and a distinct, sharp crack, followed by the sound of tumbling scree. Charlotte ran, dropped her bag and lay on her stomach in the dust, looking over. She could see him, and she gestured to Levi. Then she called very gently to Cecil, not wanting to frighten him.

'Cecil, it's Charlotte Walker, I'm with Levi and we're going to get you up very soon. Annie's here too.' Charlotte looked over her shoulder and gestured to Annie who took a tentative step closer. 'It's going to be all right very soon. Not long now.'

Levi jogged back to the truck and nosed it carefully forwards, his eyes upon Charlotte, indicating that she was to guide him to get the wheels close, but not too close, to the edge. He parked up and then clipped his ropes to the tow bar.

Levi was stepping into a harness, and positioning over his shoulder several looped slings, presumably to anchor Cecil. Charlotte fought the image that arose: Levi tugging the whole huge truck after him down the side of a mountain. Then she watched as he stepped backwards, one foot on the edge, looking down. Charlotte stood up and put an arm firmly around Annie's shoulders, as much to reassure herself as the child.

'Cecil. I need you to be brave for me, *haver*, OK? I need

you not to move.' Levi's voice was easy and unhurried. 'When your papa and I were just about your age we got stuck over the rocks at Papasiegas high tide, you know that?'

'Cecil,' Annie called out, 'Cecil, if you stay still you can have my bike.'

There was a silence. Then a small voice answered, 'Alex's bike?'

'It ain't Alex's, it's mine. If you do as Levi say, I'll give it you.'

Levi, now invisible from the waist down, gave Annie a grave nod. Charlotte watched him step lower. She tightened her grip and Annie squirmed away from her.

They watched the ropes moving and straining, and listened for Levi's voice. He was level with Cecil now and was explaining to him what would happen next.

'Hold on,' he kept saying, 'that's right, tight-tight. Keep holding.'

It seemed to go on forever. Charlotte watched as slowly Levi came back into view with the boy clinging to him, and carefully unclipped the carabiners on the straps that bound them together. He pushed Cecil back over the ledge, hard, first with one hand and then reaching out with a boot to shove him away from the edge. Charlotte took Cecil beneath the armpits and pulled him further in, on to the path. A moment later Levi was up and safe, kneeling beside them.

Cecil's teeth were chattering, and across his shoulder he had a fresh graze; very fresh, Charlotte realised, for this had come only when Levi had shunted him. She pulled her water bottle from the mesh side pouch of her bag, and the boy gulped from it. Then she stripped the wrapper from a Dairy Milk and pressed it into his hand, but not before breaking off a square and slipping it to Annie.

'Have a little sugar and let me take a quick look. You're OK.'

Annie stood close at Charlotte's elbow while she cleaned Cecil's shoulder, staring at him. Charlotte saw Annie take in the torn shirt, the shorts caked in dust and grime, and wet with urine. She took a few steps back. Then she turned and began to run down the steep track. Cecil struggled, roused.

'I ain't telling!' he shouted. 'Annie, I ain't going to tell!'

53

By the time the truck pulled into Oscar's farm it was long gone first bat and, while not worried, Oscar had begun to consider whether he might possibly start worrying, in a bit. On the whole, island children were independent and skipping school, while not to be encouraged, would not put in mind anything more sinister than a little light truancy. As a child Oscar himself had not been an assiduous attender of lessons. But staying out past first bat was unusual for a boy who was always ravenous. Oscar was grilling in the backyard and would have expected Cecil sniffing around, staking a claim on the biggest lamb chop.

Cooking was not Oscar's domain, but he was making do. Since Natalie had gone he had tried various techniques, the most successful of which was to make only one item per meal but in hearty quantities; sometimes potatoes, at other times two roasted chickens. This simplified the clearing up and also avoided the need to get the beans done at the same time as the fish, at the same time as hustling four children to the table. Instead, he aimed for nutritional balance to be achieved not on a single plate but across the course of a week. In any case, it was a rare afternoon that didn't see his mother-in-law descending the drive on her quad bike, a tiffin tin on her knees. Cooking for her grandchildren distracted her, she told Oscar, and they were all, at present, in need of distraction. In London Natalie had been admitted to hospital after a heavy bleed, where doctors were also monitoring an 'increasing discordance of foetal weight', translated by Dan as concern that while the singleton baby was on track, the two sharing a placenta were growing at different rates. At twenty weeks, they still had a way to go.

But this evening the sound of wheels turned out not to be Natalie's mother and instead Levi Mendoza and the vet, delivering back his eldest son. Oscar's relief wavered but did not entirely falter when Cecil climbed out and Oscar saw the state of him, covered in grime, and wearing only a man's checked flannel shirt, which hung below his knees like a dressing gown. No limbs appeared broken, at least. Oscar looked to Levi for explanation.

'*Ijiko* done some adventuring,' Levi told his friend, getting out to stretch, 'but he all good now. Just a graze on his shoulder there, and that my fault. No scolding him for being late, you hear me?'

Oscar crouched down and took Cecil by both hands.

'You all right, *kerido*?'

Cecil nodded. Oscar seemed about to ask another question when five-year-old Posy dashed from the house. She was heavily adorned in a gold tinsel wig and many plastic necklaces, and Charlotte noticed the same red cotton friendship bracelet that she had seen on Cecil's wrist. Apart from these, Posy wore nothing else. She waggled a stubby wooden sword at her eldest brother.

'I had two chops already and we ain't waited for you, you know. I am Princess Mary Conch Pearl. I ain't getting stains on my princess dress so I tooked it off.' As if to demonstrate how responsible this had been she carefully wiped her hand, greased with lamb fat, across the firm round of her belly. Then she disappeared again around the back of the house.

Cecil did not need a second invitation. He threw off the work shirt, which Charlotte had found in the truck and earlier wrapped him in, dropping it in a heap to run after his sister. As well as the graze, now cleaned and dressed beneath a neat square of white gauze on his shoulder, Charlotte noticed a bruise was coming up across his lower back. Nothing too terrible. All in all he had got away with murder.

'Wash yourself up!' Oscar hollered after the two naked children but it was too late, and although he had been loud, he had lacked conviction and was ignored. He turned back to Levi. 'Will you have a beer? Come round, I got Maisie in a playpen outside. You too, Dr Vet Charlotte. Beer?'

Charlotte glanced at Levi, trying to gauge his reaction. In the crisis there had been a camaraderie between them. Or, a something. Now the peril was over she felt less sure of how to be. But in answer he lifted an ironical eyebrow and swept out an arm, inviting her to walk ahead of him, a maître d' escorting her to her table. They followed Oscar through a row of climbing gourds and round towards the family's garden. Low and close behind her, Levi murmured, 'A beer. Or a couple of vodka shots, if it's that sort of an evening.'

Of all the day's evidence, this one allusion confirmed her mounting suspicion that Levi was being recklessly, outrageously flirtatious. It could only be a reference to the first night they'd spent together – a blur of alcohol and high feeling and beautiful, unprecedented risk. A blur, but not blurred enough. Charlotte was assailed by vivid and highly specific recollections. She began to walk faster, widening the distance between them, pushing out through a line of tall cucumber plants into the open backyard, where were ranged the safe diversion of Lindo children. She would stay ten minutes to be polite to Oscar, and escape home as soon as possible. It was an empty gratification to think of Levi flirting. Her body responded to his voice without the slightest concern for her rational mind, but it cheapened all she'd thought she knew of him, to see him disrespect an absent woman. *Zimbul*, she reminded herself. *Zimbul, Zimbul.*

Oscar gestured for them to take a seat on a bench, and indicated that they should help themselves to the chops piled up on a huge banana leaf, laid out on a stool beside a brightly painted oil drum. Another recent innovation – to only use disposable plates, as if every meal were a picnic. To prevent Levi sitting next to her, Charlotte went instead to a basket chair that hung from the mango tree. The bowl of this seat was deeper than she expected and she unbalanced backwards into it, her legs swept out from under her. Levi sat down in the middle of the bench, his arms stretched out along its back. He watched, amused, as she righted herself.

'Want me to push you?' asked Jacob, who was three. He had come up beside her dragging a long stick, and sipping from a beaker. Charlotte declined, but suggested instead he climb in so they could swing together. Oscar opened two beers, and before he could open a third, Charlotte asked quickly if she might have some fizzycan. Beside her, Jacob snuggled closer, and began to stroke her arm, and hum softly.

Oscar reached into the playpen and picked up the baby, placidly sucking on a toothbrush.

'I'm putting Maisie into bed. Ten minutes.' Then as an afterthought he bellowed, 'Grill still hot, don't touch it!' in the vague direction of the other invisible children, and disappeared into the house. Jacob sat up and wriggled free to crouch before the banana leaf.

'Bring me a lamb chop, *ijiko*?' Levi asked him. 'If they ain't too hot.'

'This one? This one?'

'The best one, obviously.'

'Best one is for me,' Jacob told him, with an appropriate note of commiseration. 'You have this one. It's good.' He picked it up and threw it, unexpectedly, and it landed in the grass at Levi's feet. Jacob looked worried, but Levi thanked him, and retrieved it without further comment.

'Will Annie be able to get back without her bike?' Charlotte asked Levi, who had given the meat a perfunctory swipe with a nearby tea towel, and was now tearing into it, with white teeth. 'Shouldn't we have left it for her?'

'She gave it to Cecil, she'd not use it even if we left it. Code of honour. Annie can get back, when she's ready.'

'She's so stubborn,' said Charlotte, with no real sense of whether she was criticising or praising. Then she smiled at Jacob, who still stood between them. The family had a pregnant sow, due any day now. The last time she had been here, Jacob and Posy had been her assistants.

'How's Duchess?' she asked.

'Fat,' said Jacob dismissively. He turned back to Levi. 'Will you fly me?'

Levi lay down on his back, and Jacob wiped his hands on the front of his shorts and positioned himself on Levi's raised knees.

'Stubborn, maybe, but also just knows her own mind. Like Marianne, actually. Like you, too. I admire that in you.' He lifted Jacob, who squealed.

'I thought you said I wasn't *sure on the things that make me happy*.'

This, she had not intended to say. The precise phrase had arisen quite without warning, in just the tones in which he'd thrown it at her on the beach, all that time ago. His behaviour towards her these last hours had stirred up her memory, and was making a mess.

Strings of solar-powered bulbs had begun to come on, looped between the cane frames of gourds, and around the Lindos' small porch. Levi set Jacob gently on to his feet, and then folded his arms behind his head, looking up towards the bright, glossy mango leaves.

'It seems you begun to know, these days. In any case. It ain't my place to do down the choices that make you happy, just because I ain't one of them.'

Charlotte opened her mouth to refute this. It felt all but unbearable that he could be so wrong, but she could not find any phrase that didn't reveal more than she dared. Instead she said, 'Thank you for today. I know you have better things to do than rappelling off the side of your truck.'

Relaxing on the ground with a cold beer, Levi did not look like a man with anywhere else to be. But something between them needed urgent destruction. With artificial ease Charlotte then forced herself to add, 'Probably you and Zimbul had plans this evening.'

Levi raised his head and looked up at her in genuine confusion.

'Ain't nothing going on with Zimbul this evening or any evening. Not for some time.'

He sat up, and faced her. Jacob frowned between them, and began to pat Levi on the forehead to regain his attention. Then Oscar returned, looking weary. He scooped up his little boy like a rugby ball, kissed his soft cheek, and set him down again.

'Inside, you. Go. Bed.'

Without protest Jacob went and, with all the children finally inside the cottage, Oscar sat down heavily on the bench. He looked grey with fatigue, Charlotte noticed, remembering how recently he had been hospitalised with a substantial internal bleed. She stood awkwardly from the swinging chair.

'Thank you for having me. I should leave you in peace now, I'll head back.'

For a moment Oscar hung his head between his knees, closing his eyes and pinching the bridge of his nose. Charlotte's gaze locked with Levi's and she watched, heart pounding, as he got to his feet and walked slowly towards her, his eyes never leaving her face. Then Oscar coughed and got up, smiling, and the two men shook hands.

'You both have a good evening. Thank you for bringing home my scamp. Now. I'm going to crack open one more and head into the barn to fix up the far stall.'

Levi had been following Charlotte back through the vegetable garden, but stopped and turned.

'What's up with the far stall?'

'Finally came down completely, it's been no good some time. I got to rebuild it tonight, before farrowing.'

'Tomorrow or next day, latest,' Charlotte affirmed. 'I'll come any time if Duchess needs a hand.'

For just a moment, Levi's fingertips brushed her wrist, and Charlotte felt a current pass through her. Then he cleared his throat.

'Come, *haver*. I'll stay and help you.'

'Ah, it ain't so bad, Natty's the one doing the hard work. Hooked up to a load of monitors, poked and prodded. I'm just getting on with home. Usual stuff. They might be doing something inside her with lasers, they said. Lasers. Like, like *Star Wars*.'

'Get on, Jedi,' said Levi firmly, 'I'm helping you. Let's get this done.'

And an agonised Charlotte watched, alight with longing, as he did the right thing, walking away from her down the yard, towards the barn.

54

By the time night fell Marianne had searched the island, increasingly frantic for a sign of her daughter. Charlotte always reported her Annie sightings, seeming to sense that Marianne was never consulted and rarely told, but Charlotte had not yet come back and next door, too, was silent. Annie had been gone more than twenty-four hours. It was true that in the past she had disappeared for longer. But she'd never before run away in anger.

The next day was Santa Esterica, which made tonight one of Marianne's busiest working nights. All men with daughters or sisters would be evicted from the kitchen to fend for themselves, and so in addition to her usual orders she had a quantity of buns to deliver all the way out to Conch, where the Davenport brothers had planned a salt harvest and a barbecue, and as many again for another group of banished men, who would be digging at the taro fields. Instead of any of this baking, she'd searched.

She had been to Betsey's and to the Rockhopper, had hiked out to Mac's Pantry, and from there had taken a donkey up to the waterfall, a place she knew the children had long ago made one of their camps. There had been no one at the Breaks, and at Out the Way beach a family who had been there since sunrise reported that they'd not seen another soul all day. The old cemetery was silent but for the gossipy chitter of high, invisible noddies. Not even old Grand Mary was there, muttering long monologues over her own future burial plot, mad as a brush. The vast sycamore fig that reached its heavy branches over the graves held nothing but its own strange hum of energy. It was daylight then, but still Marianne scanned her torch through the eastern branches, hoping the beam would catch the fierce, sharp little face of her daughter.

When darkness began to fall Marianne came home, tethering the donkey to a ring near Kidda's stall, just in case, though in case of what she could not say. Annie had gone, and Marianne did not know where to find her.

As well as the baking she had her own Santa Esterica meal to begin. Strewn across the table were fresh cashews and walnuts for masapan; a coconut to grate for curry; jars of light and dark sugars, long vanilla pods, and a fat scroll of cinnamon. She had planned to make prettyfish stuffed with rice and fresh mintberry, followed by a mango tart with whipped coconut ice cream. But these were plans from before yesterday's catastrophe, and she could not face the disappointment of preparing an elaborate feast for nobody. Instead she took a hard-backed chair and sat gazing out at the dark yard, breathing in the sweet scent of the climbing spiderflowers, which at dusk had begun to unfurl their modest blossoms. Kidda and the ducks and the chickens were asleep, but the donkey stamped and shifted. Marianne took out a bowl of chopped bananas and some water, and patted the jennet's warm flank, watching it eat and drink with surprising delicacy. Then she returned, quietly, to her chair.

When she heard steps she assumed it would be Charlotte, for Annie's approach was always preceded by the creak and clank of an old bicycle, followed by a crash as the bike was tossed unceremoniously into a shrub. But when she looked out it was Annie who stood in the yard, just beyond the open door. This time Marianne suppressed the instinct to reach out her arms. She would keep her ache of longing shut up inside her heart, where it could not frighten off her daughter. Annie's face was in shadow. Marianne held her breath, and waited.

At the sight of her mother Annie gave a little cry and stumbled forwards, falling to her knees and laying her head in Marianne's lap. It seemed she had been holding a bright bunch of marigolds, for these flowers scattered on the floor where she had released them. Marianne looked down at the tangled hair, the dirty hands that clutched at her skirts in tight desperate fists, as if fearing she might otherwise be prised away. She could not remember the last time her daughter had consented to her touch. Moving with painstaking slowness, she placed a tentative hand on Annie's bowed head.

'I'm sorry, Mama,' Annie whispered, barely audible. 'I'm so sorry.'

'Shhh. None of that, my baby girl. It's OK, I'm here.'

Annie looked up, her eyes pink-rimmed and swollen.

'I made a bad mistake today, Mama.'

'Did you try and fix it?'

Annie nodded, biting down so hard on her lower lip that it paled with pressure. Then she buried her face again. Marianne paused. She did not know how much Annie wanted to talk; how much Annie would want to listen. Eventually she said, 'I make mistakes most days, *mi alma*.'

'You don't,' said Annie fiercely. 'You're perfect. I got the best mama in the whole wide world.' She tightened her grip on Marianne's skirts and began to cry in earnest. 'In the universe.'

'No,' said Marianne softly. Tenderly she lifted Annie's chin, cupping the tear-stained face in her two hands. Here she was, this magic girl.'I ain't anything like the best, *mi vida*. I'm just the luckiest.'

55

A velvet darkness had fallen by the time Levi finally turned the truck down the Lindos' winding drive, his headlights visible long before he turned on to the main road. Charlotte stood up and as he drew closer she extended her arm, thumb up, like a hitch-hiker. In the jungle behind her came the click and creak of geckos, the call and response of an elaborate courting ritual. At the corner, a heavy tree had dropped ripe rose apples into the road, and a sharp scent filled the air as the wheels crushed the fallen fruits. Levi stopped the truck.

He jumped down and came towards her, leaving the door standing open. He had showered on the farm, for he now wore a pair of loose denim shorts she didn't recognise, and a faded black vest that must also have been Oscar's, slightly too small, on which were printed the peeling words 'My Other Car's a Porsche'. His hair was wet, pushed back from his face. A little way off, he paused.

'Evening, ma'am. You lost?'

There had been no slow-dawning awareness. Instead, the realisation that nothing any longer stood between them and with it one solar-bright truth: every moment spent without him was a moment wasted. Levi stayed very still, without seeming even to breathe. Charlotte shook her head.

'The thing is,' she said quietly, 'the thing is, you are my love,' and when she heard his slow exhalation she said it again, into the soft cushion of the surrounding night. 'You are my love, Levi. You make everything brighter, you've taught me how to be, how to live. I just need . . . '

She could not find the words, she realised, because it was pure feeling. What did she need? She needed to be close to him. She needed his lightness and strength, his deliberate reaching out for joy. Levi was safety, and pleasure. She needed his skin, his breath, his laughter, his hands. She needed a life with Levi.

'I want . . . ' she murmured, trailing off again. He had moved towards her and his face was close above hers, so close she could feel the shallow flutter of his breath.

'What do you want?'

'I want *you*,' she whispered, consumed, urgent, and Levi laughed, softly, her favourite sound.

'That ain't a problem, Dolittle,' he said, before he kissed her. 'That a done deal. I been yours a long time.'

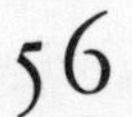

56

The morning of Santa Esterica dawned bright and clear. All across Tuga de Oro women were rising with the sun, pulling apart their curtains and reflecting, with love or with trepidation or some muddled intermingling of the two, upon all that lay ahead. This was not a public festival. It was not one that filled the streets with flags and music, not a drawing-together of the island community. Instead it was a constellation of quiet, miniature celebrations, a turning inward for private rituals of tenderness and affirmation. Santa Esterica was the transmission of love and lore from generation to generation, and it took place not in the Rockhopper nor in Harbour Street nor in the orchards beneath a clear white full moon but in kitchens and gardens, in homes, where women had cleaned and cooked and decorated, only and entirely for one another. Which was not to say it was a festival without fireworks. After all, in some households, four generations of women might pass the day enclosed together in a small, hot kitchen.

On the moshav, Hattie Fairclough was kneading dough for *folares*, while on the table beside her ranged a family of chipped teacups, in each of which two white hen's eggs soaked in food colouring. Grape purple, azure blue, rose pink. Her own mother and grandmother had used natural island dyes, but Hattie preferred the expediency of gel colours, which the moshav ordered every few years from a catering catalogue. Around these bright eggs she would twist and plait a traditional brioche sweetened with Tugan vanilla, one for each of her daughters, Linda and Zimbul. Linda had recently had her first baby and was tired and teary, and Zimbul was irritable with Hattie's attempts to comfort her after a break-up, resistant to her mother's tentatively proffered wisdom. The Mendoza boy had been in love with the vet since she'd landed, anyone might see that – anyone except Zimbul who'd had her head turned but not, Hattie knew, sustained any real injury to her soul. She'd lost face, was all. In any case her Zimbul had work to do, and might one day be a senior councillor like Ruth dos Santos had been all those years ago, powerful and respected, a true community leader. There was no need to rush to the yoke. Look at Linda, exhausted by the baby, and yet still keeping house for her new husband with a zeal that suggested she believed she could one day reach the finish line of cooking and cleaning. That it never ended Linda would learn, and no one else could teach her.

But today it was Santa Esterica and Hattie felt full of light. She threw open her kitchen windows, and the welcome breeze rustled the starfruit leaves and lifted the curtains, soft white netting on which Hattie's great-aunt had embroidered a pattern of tiny flying fish in gold thread, still winking like sequins. She put on the radio, just in time to hear the final verses of 'You Can't Lose Me', Faith Hill's celebration of enduring maternal love. Taxi had a country singer's instinct to go simultaneously for the guts and the jugular. It would be a day of relentlessly sentimental tearjerkers. No, thought Hattie, flouring the table again, her girls could not lose her, because she was with them, and within them. Hattie could see beyond their struggles. They were brave young women, and they would be, she knew, brave old women too, and these would be their stories. Heartbreak and childbirth, sorrow and recovery, bruised pride, and redemption.

Mothering did not stop when they grew, rather it morphed and regenerated, becoming more diffuse and yet somehow more expansive, for it now enfolded a network of those who one's daughter loved, in whom a fragment of one's daughter's heart had lodged. Her heart, after all, was a piece of your heart. Hattie loved her son-in-law because it was another way of loving Linda; she loved that perfect new baby to distraction. She would have loved Levi Mendoza if he had loved her girl; instead she released him to irrelevance. The heart expands without limit. Today her daughters would come back to her and she would be permitted to nourish them and tend to them, and she sang as she plaited sweet dough. The eggs were ready to be nested in the pastry, bright as gems, more precious than gems because here were memories; here was a gift of devotion. She moved to check the t'beet and wept a little, happily, breathing in the rising scent of cardamom, ginger and cinnamon, and now humming along with 'Mama Said' by the Shirelles.

In the old Cole house, Katie Salmon lay in bed, looking dreamily around the room. Ahead lay a day of arthritis patients, three of whom would promptly and dutifully visit her at the clinic and the fourth, she knew, would have to be hunted down and cornered somewhere on his own farm, where she would no doubt catch him hauling feed, or some other activity she'd cautioned against. As an act of gentle public service she was running a six p.m. men's Pilates class in the Old Kal, marketed as 'Muscle Conditioning for Farmers'. This event had been conceived after Moz Gabbai had mentioned that on Santa Esterica it was helpful to delay the men's gathering at the Rockhopper as long as possible, as a gift to the women to whom they would then stagger home.

But all that was much later. For now, it was still early. The sun was rising and pale morning light streamed in across her old rose-patterned sheets, washed to an impossible softness. Above her hung a picture she'd bought at a long-ago student poster fair, a black and white photograph of two elephants whose entwined trunks formed a heart. It was astonishing how fast this room, this house, this island, had come to feel like home. Accustomed to a dawn run, or swim, or cycle, or all three, her body woke her early but for now she stayed where she was, feeling a rare, delicious contentment in the stillness. Across the floor lay a trail of yesterday's clothes cast off in a hurry, entirely unlike this morning's languor.

She had come to Tuga as the fiancée of a Tugan, but had found a world that so far exceeded her hopes that the loss of him had been, in the end, no very great one. What Katie truly loved was the sun and the cliffs and the beaches. She loved the hikes and the climbs and the rough ocean currents; the sheer physicality of existence here which was, in only the best ways, akin to her own hard childhood. A life of exertion, and participation.

And unexpectedly, gloriously, she loved someone who shared her commitment to these earnest, simple joys. Katie looked over with something akin to exaltation at the sleeping form beside her. Then she wriggled deeper beneath the covers to press her length against the warm, muscled back. Waking, Elsie turned over and reached out reflexively for Katie, pulling her closer.

'If we leave soon I could take you to the Lakes before work,' Elsie murmured, and then sat up and rubbed her eyes and yawned, beginning to mobilise for the day. She too was a woman of constant motion. 'Go-by-Donkey? Papasiegas?'

But Katie, who had never before realised anything could match the pleasure of an early-morning swim, simply shook her head. She rose to her knees, and in tender silence pushed a willing Elsie gently back down on to the soft pillow. If they had all the time in the world, still, this was how she'd spend it.

The nasturtiums and scarlet runner beans were in exuberant flower, twining up the tall cane wigwam that Walter had built for Rebecca at the bottom of the garden. Inside this verdant den were Maia and Rebecca, each close to tears of frustration.

'It's not waste, *mi vida*, I bought this tub extra, for baking.'

Rebecca snatched up the jar of Ovaltine that lay between them and held it possessively, as if to guard it from destructive forces, as if Maia might tip it wantonly into a biscuit dough right here, in the garden. This mistrust was provoking. When had Maia's behaviour become something to fear?

'It ain't *for* baking,' Rebecca said, sounding anxious.

'That's the point, it's meant to be a treat. I promise you they're delicious, I made them with—' but here Maia stopped herself. She tried never to speak the names of the children she had cared for in London. 'I practised when I was away, so that I could make Ovaltine cookies with you, *mi vida*.'

But Rebecca shook her head, her lower lip projecting, and Maia was filled with guilt to find herself so irritated. All the time she'd been away, irritation with Rebecca had seemed for evermore to be impossible. When they were finally reunited on Tuga the rest of their lives would stretch ahead a paradise; day after day of sunny gratitude and mindfulness, bright-lit with new perspective. Instead the day was derailing, most likely due to Maia's own excessive expectations. Today was meant to be her own reward, too. She had kept this additional jar a secret, living in her imagination the joy that such an indulgence might bring to the daughter she ached to be near; determined to bring to her little Tugan girl just a moment of the blithe privilege that London children took for granted. It hurt her to see Rebecca guard such modest resources so jealously. It was just a stupid jar of powdered cocoa, Maia knew now. She would have had to add about twenty to the online order for her employers even to notice. Soon she and Rebecca would have to leave for Conch to visit her own mother, and they would have missed their only chance to celebrate at home, just the two of them.

'I don't want to,' Rebecca said again. She was smoothing the front of her new dungarees, too big for her, too warm for the weather, hand-me-downs sent back with Maia. 'I don't even want to drink it. It's mine and I just want to keep it.'

What could Maia say? One cannot have one's Ovaltine and drink it, but Rebecca had surely learned that already.

At Martha House, Grand Mary stood alone in her kitchen. From the fridge she drew a plate on which lay an unseasoned, lightly grilled tuna steak, a mound of plain rice, and a slow-baked sweet potato. She broke a piece of the tuna into smaller flakes and mashed it in a mixing bowl, adding a tablespoon of white rice and a scoop of the sweet potato flesh. It took a long time to combine, pressing the fork with arthritic fingers, but once finished and transferred in a mound to a willow-patterned saucer it looked rather lovely. This feast she would take upstairs as an offering to Virginia, who at this moment was asleep, curled on a sheepskin on Mary's own bed, and looking for all the world like a sleek, silvery fur hat. Meddling Island Council would be closed-minded and petty about the cat if they got wind, fussing about illegal mammals and the threat posed to the useless, unappealing endemic birds. And so no one knew of her existence, and Virginia lived a private life, an indoor life, a life of monastic dignity, not unlike Mary's own. This made her all the more deserving of a banquet, on Santa Esterica.

Returning to the fridge, Mary then hefted on to the table a huge serving bowl of chopped fresh fruit in a light mango syrup. She no longer had the dexterity to peel her own pomelos, though the scent of her old pomelo trees filled the air of her extensive garden. As usual the girl had prepared enough to last the week. At dusk Mary would take this vast fruit salad out into the garden, where the far smaller Dusty and Goldie had been put away for the night. For herself, she would bring a bowl of vanilla ice cream, and she and Martha could enjoy their puddings together.

Marianne and Annie did not bother to cook, in the end. The fish went into the freezer. Instead they ate scrambled eggs on toast for supper and now sat together on the patched sofa, Annie's head upon her mother's shoulder, their fingers interlaced. Marianne had been reading aloud from *Harry Potter*, just as she had when the children were small, but now she'd set down the book, for each was content to watch the flames in silence. On the little table in front of them stood a ring of slumping candles, encircling a jam jar of frothy orange marigolds. Most stems were bent and broken, but nonetheless. Their golden petals caught the light.

The ward lights were never truly dimmed. Not even in the middle of the night, as it was now. Natalie Lindo stirred, woken from an unsettled sleep by the usual discomfort, a long tightening across her belly that she would soon see as a leap and lurch upon the blinking screen beside her. She was trussed up with straps, restrained like some huge farm animal. Whatever they did to her she was acquiescent. But still, her body would not behave.

Santa Esterica was almost over. It had been her first away from her daughters; her first away from her own mother who she missed tonight with an ache of longing that hurt as much as any false contraction. The nurses had made her remove her red cotton bracelet when she was first admitted, together with her wedding ring. But when she looked over she saw that Ruth dos Santos was still there beside her, awake and placidly knitting. The click of Ruth's needles and her soft voice singing 'Durme, Durme' could make Natalie pretend, with her eyes closed, that it was indeed her own mother who kept this loving vigil. From around the world the island had reached out its arms to her, and had sent comfort.

'She's a good mum,' the nurse had said approvingly, going on to add that a National Express coach from Slough must surely take an hour and a half each morning and perhaps longer still, on the way home. Natalie would manage fine when all these babies came, with such a devoted mother.

When she sensed Natalie's open eyes upon her Ruth stood and came to her side. This frightened homesick girl was of her island and, on Santa Esterica and all other days in this strange exile, she would be an island mother, and would love her as she could.

'What can I bring you, *kerida*?' she asked softly, and stroked Natalie's cheek. 'What do you need?'

57

It was a quirk of the Foreign and Commonwealth Office telecommunications network that Tuga's only phone box had a London number, and so for anyone in the UK, it was only a local call. Despite this Lucinda was bellowing, in the manner of someone presented with an ear trumpet.

'Charlotte? Where are you?'

'I'm here, I can hear you. I'm in the phone box. You rang me in the phone box. How are you?'

A few days earlier Charlotte had managed a call to arrange a gift to be delivered to chambers. It had taken some time to persuade the customer service department that she was unable to perform this transaction on their website, which had repeatedly failed to load. Her confidence was therefore low.

'Did you get the candle?' she asked now. 'It's frangipani and vanilla, I thought it sounded like it might smell Tugan.'

'Diesel and goat manure would have been equally authentic in my recollections, if less popular among the clientele of Liberty. Thank you, darling, I did. Very thoughtful.'

'It's the festival of Santa Esterica today, it's a celebration for mothers and daughters. You don't have to – *do* anything. So I just thought, maybe we could light candles at the same time. Traditionally you and I should be cooking one another a banquet.'

'Darling, neither of us can boil an egg.'

'I know. Perhaps we should do something else together. I don't know: read something, watch something.'

'In case you hadn't noticed, your recent life choices have rendered our doing anything together somewhat of a challenge,' said Lucinda drily. The strange clarity of the line had the paradoxical effect of making her mother sound present, and feel very far away.

'I know,' said Charlotte, but could think of nothing else to say, and fell into silence. The waves crashed against the harbour wall.

'Well, as it happens, I've just sent you a poem I thought you might appreciate,' said Lucinda eventually, having apparently relented. 'You'd never find it digging about on that awful internet connection so I've had Evangeline type it up and pop it in an email.'

'I'll go to the clinic right now, and I'll light my candle and read your poem. Will you do the same?'

'I'm in court tomorrow, I don't have all the time in the world to be performing Wiccan spells. Evangeline is leaving shortly and I must finish off some bits. Having recently returned from a round-the-world voyage I have something of a backlog.'

'Of course. Don't worry. Thank you. For the poem.'

There was another pause, and then a heavy sigh.

'Yes, all right. I won't be home but I shall light it where I am, at eight o'clock. By chance my chambers window does face south.' Then Lucinda added in a new, softer voice, 'Well, we are in the same time zone, that is something, I suppose. You have chosen a different latitude, but our longitudes are not so very different.'

'What's the poem?'

'What? Oh, nothing, just something I came across. A sixteenth-century Marrano poet, João Pinto Delgado.'

'Of course. I come across sixteenth-century Marrano poets all the time. Casual.'

'You don't need to affect to be even more of a philistine than you actually are. Anyway. Have a look. Of local interest, perhaps. It's called *The Poem of Queen Esther*. Your saint, you know. Santa Esterica. Saint Esther. Anyway, I'm going to run, darling. Under the cosh for tomorrow, and all that.'

And she was gone, her departure quick and sudden as ever, catching Charlotte by surprise.

There was, in fact, frangipani on the air. There had been no panes of glass in the phone box for many years, and only the cast-iron slats of the door segmented an ink-black sea and navy sky into tall rectangles, and through one of these apertures Charlotte looked out. The brightest star tonight would not be a star at all but Mars, glowing butterscotch among the sequins. She would have got short shrift from Lucinda, had she tried to interest her in astronomy.

But somewhere, beyond the vast dark ocean, her mother had been thinking of her. *Golden poison frog*, she thought and smiled. Then she turned on her torch and began the familiar walk south, through her town, through her jungle, to Levi and home.

Epilogue

In London, Lucinda set down her phone on the high, wheeled bedside table. She was not in chambers.

'You didn't tell her,' said Evangeline, who had whisked the blue paper curtains around the cubicle on their clattering rings to create an illusion of wider privacy, but made no pretence that she herself had not been listening.

'Oh, not all that business again. There was absolutely no need,' said Lucinda, waving her hand dismissively, as if shooing away a fly. She unhooked the small beige controller on its sprung cord and pressed buttons, to sit the bed up at a better angle.

'Light it there, quick, on that filthy windowsill before the officious little nurse comes back. Which way does this window face?'

'South,' said Evangeline, smoothly, and without hesitation. 'I saw the sun go down earlier.' Ms Compton-Neville's surgery was tomorrow morning, after all, and it was best not to upset her over minor compass points. Lucinda nodded with satisfaction.

'There you go, then. All shall be well, and all shall be well, and all manner of things shall be well. Or that mournful oncologist will be proven correct and they won't, and if that is the case then Charlotte will learn of it soon enough. Probably we shall set off a smoke alarm. That'll liven them all up.'

'You're nil by mouth from midnight, remember. Shall I get you anything else before I go? A cup of tea?'

But Lucinda did not reply, or appear to be listening. She was gazing down at her hand, and more particularly at a huge cocktail ring that she had worn ever since coming home, huge and round as a penny, winking in the yellow candlelight. Evangeline had recently collected it from Tiffany's, where jewellers had replaced a tiny diamond missing from the encircling pavé.

'Hmm? What? No. I'm fine. I might rest for just a moment. She's happy, you know. My daughter sounds happy.'

Lucinda lay back and closed her eyes, and the smile remained on her lips for some time.

About the Author

Francesca Segal is an award-winning writer and journalist. She is the author of the critically acclaimed novels *The Innocents* (2012) and *The Awkward Age* (2017), and a memoir of NICU motherhood, *Mother Ship* (2019). Her writing has won the 2012 Costa First Novel Award, a Betty Trask Award, and been longlisted for the Women's Prize.

Island Calling is the second novel in the Tuga Trilogy, following *Welcome to Glorious Tuga* (2024). Francesca says: 'Writing the Tuga novels was a deliberate reaching out for joy. The world can feel very bleak, and bringing this island to life became my own magical portal to wide beaches, crystal seas, endless sunshine and, most vitally, to a warm, eccentric community of good people mostly just trying to do their best. Tuga de Oro was a refuge for its first settlers, and I hope will offer refuge for readers, too.'